THE PONDEROSA
EMPIRE

STEPHEN CALDER

BANTAM BOOKS

NEW YORK · TORONTO · LONDON · SYDNEY · AUCKLAND

THE PONDEROSA EMPIRE

A Bantam Domain Book / November 1992

ISBN 0-553-29042-8

Published simultaneously in the United States and Canada

Bantam Books are published by Bantam Books, a division of Bantam
Doubleday Dell Publishing Group, Inc. Its trademark, consisting of the
words "Bantam Books" and the portrayal of a rooster, is Registered in
U.S. Patent and Trademark Office and in other countries. Marca Reg-
istrada. Bantam Books, 666 Fifth Avenue, New York, New York 10103.

PRINTED IN THE UNITED STATES OF AMERICA

RAD   0 9 8 7 6 5 4 3 2 1

**THEY SETTLED A RUGGED LAND—
AND FOUNDED A FRONTIER DYNASTY!
THE CARTWRIGHTS ... IN THE BEGINNING:**

BEN CARTWRIGHT—The rugged patriarch of the Cartwright clan, he is about to realize a lifelong dream of creating a shipping empire. That is, until he runs afoul of vicious Wild Bill Dunnigan, the corrupt businessman whose own deadly schemes of expansion and revenge could cost Ben his precious ranch—and his two boys, Adam and Hoss. . . .

ADAM CARTWRIGHT—Ben's "little man," the restless thirteen-year-old is determined to prove to his father that he can help run the Ponderosa. But then Adam finds himself directly in the path of a mad bull—and only one brave man stands between him and certain death. . . .

JEAN-PIERRE DeMARIGNY—Ben's loyal foreman, he sacrifices his own life for young Adam Cartwright's. But before he dies, he entrusts Ben with a promise that will take the owner of the Ponderosa to far-off New Orleans—where he will meet the woman destined to change his life forever. . . .

MARIE DuBEY DeMARIGNY—Jean-Pierre's beautiful young widow, she wins the heart of virile Ben Cartwright. Together, they set out on the perilous journey back to the Sierra Nevada—where they must stop an evil plot to seize the budding Cartwright ranch. . . .

WILD BILL DUNNIGAN—Wealthy, treacherous, and deadly, he has grandiose plans to create a corrupt political empire that could make him the most powerful and feared man in the West. But Dunnigan's just been bested by rancher Ben Cartwright. Now, driven by greed and vengeance, Dunnigan devises a chilling scheme to destroy the Cartwright family. . . .

Other books in the Bonanza™ series

Book 1—THE PIONEER SPIRIT

THE PONDEROSA
EMPIRE

CHAPTER 1

"If this is such a gol'dang good idea, how's come we're hiding it from the grown-ups?"

"Hush your mouth, will you, and do what I say."

"But I don't think—"

"Shush!"

The stocky little fellow hushed but stubbornly refused to relinquish the dissenting scowl that bunched in the middle of a broad, moon face.

"Now here's what we're gonna do," the taller, dark-haired, lean boy persisted. "You open the barn door an' hold it just barely ajar, you see. You wait right there at the door while I go in and open the stalls. Don't let the door swing all the way open, though. We got to keep them all together. When I've got them all out of the stalls an' in the alley, I'll whistle. That's when you pull the barn door open an' scoot hard as you can across the yard and get that pasture gate open. Stand behind it, mind, so they don't see you. If they see you there, they might spook, so you hide real good. Then quick as the last one is in, you push that gate shut again. Quick, mind."

"Adam?"

"What?"

"I can't work that ol' latch."

"Just you get the gate closed. I'll take care o' the latch."

"Adam?"

"What?"

"What if they ... you know."

The lean boy shook his head impatiently. "They won't, dang it. They're tame as puppy dogs."

"But Pa said that bulls—"

"Did I tell you to hush?"

"Y-Yes."

"Then hush."

"Ok-k-k-kay."

"And quit whining."

"I am not."

"Well all right, then. You ready, Hoss boy?"

"Y-Yes. I s'pose."

"C'mon."

The two boys, the difference in their sizes not nearly so dramatic as the six-year difference in their ages, left the shelter of the parked wagon they'd been hiding behind—standing behind, Adam would have insisted, not hiding—and dashed across the beaten gravel of the Ponderosa ranch yard.

Adam reached the barn first and lifted the heavy bar. He tugged the door open, paused a moment to make sure Hoss was poised ready to shove the door closed again if the need should arise, then slipped inside.

The interior of the barn was shadowed and comforting. It was filled with the warm, not unpleasant scents of fresh hay and stinging ammonia, of dried sweat and humid, salty, bovine breath. Spikes and sharp spear points of sunlight lanced through gaps in the age-warped siding, the shafts of golden light piercing clouds of dust motes that danced and gamboled on the gently swirling air.

Adam loved this barn. He had played inside it for countless hours as a child.

But this business today was not play. And at thirteen he no longer considered himself to be a child.

"Easy now. Easy," he crooned as he stepped briskly—quick, lest he lose his nerve—to the nearest stall.

The great bull inside was so large, its back swelled massive and dark above the topmost gate rail.

There were eight stalls in the home-place barn. Six of them were occupied by these magnificent beef bulls the boys' father had brought in to upgrade the quality of the ranch's herd of cattle. They were marvelous creatures, huge and proud and virile. They were, Pa claimed, the future of the Ponderosa, what with the need for oxen as draft stock declining and the need for good beef on the increase. That part of it was all rather confusing, Adam thought. Something about stagecoaches and freighting companies and shipping lines reducing the need for oxen while an increasing population wanted more and more for good beef. All of that had something to do with these bulls being on the Ponderosa now.

The important thing, the way Adam saw it, was that these bulls were really and truly necessary to the Ponderosa.

And right now Pa wasn't here to see to the health and safety of these all-important animals.

That darned old Jean-Pierre had been left in charge. Adam believed—*knew*—that he should have been put in charge, not Jean-Pierre. What did a Frenchy like Jean-Pierre know about bulls? Nothing, that's what.

Adam had been around—maybe not bulls, exactly, he freely admitted that much—oxen and horses and mules and other such living stuff his whole life long, practically, and he knew a *lot* more about livestock than dang Jean-Pierre.

These bulls had had a hard ol' trip to get here to the Ponderosa. Pa bought them out of Virginia 'way back in the States and had them shipped all the way around Cape Horn and then up the Sacramento River and the American and finally by wagon—the bulls were so valuable, they hadn't been allowed to walk on their own even when they were that close; instead they'd been crated and laboriously carried—over the Sierras and down again to Lake Tahoe and the Ponderosa.

And now they were here and Jean-Pierre had them cooped up in these dark and musty old barn stalls, when anybody with half a lick of sense would know that what they needed to recuperate from all that mauling and hauling was to be put out onto pasture where they could get fresh grass and sunshine instead of standing inside the barn here needing to be hand fed.

Never mind that Adam was the one generally assigned the laborious chore of hauling the hay and the water needed for that hand feeding. That had nothing to do with it. Adam really and truly believed the bulls needed to be out there in the pasture. And he really and truly believed that Pa would have wanted them out there too, if only Pa had been here instead of being off to San Francisco on business.

And so the hell—the heck with what ol' Jean-Pierre said, him and his claims that the bulls needed time to settle down and get comfortable here for a spell before they were turned out. Adam knew better and he was going to do something about it.

He pulled that gate open and then the next and the next, and right on down the line until all the gates were standing open and the great, hulking animals began snuffling and snorting and blowing strings of snot as, nervously, they commenced to low and paw and investigate the relative freedoms of the alleyway.

Now that the bulls were free in the alley, Adam felt a tight-clenched knot form low in his belly. The bulls were all so powerful. And so big. And their horns were so wicked and pointy-looking. If they should take a notion to turn on him . . .

But they wouldn't. He wouldn't let them.

"Hyah!" he bellowed, slapping his palm against his thigh as sharp as he could manage. Too late, he thought about needing a popping whip or something. The buggy whip would've done, or the lunge whip that was used for training horses with. But there was no time to be running off and fetching things. Not now that the bulls were already out. "Hyah!"

He remembered the instruction he'd given to Hoss and jammed two fingers into his mouth. The sound of his whistle brought the bulls' heads up, and their ears flicked and turned as if to pinpoint the source of the noise.

A moment later the big door swung open. There was no sign of short, stocky little old Hoss now. Of course, there wasn't supposed to be. Hoss was supposed to already be across the yard opening the gate to the pasture—it was really intended to be a horse trap, a fenced area of not more than a few hundred acres where saddle horses could be kept loose on grass but close to the house for when they might be wanted—and now it was up to Adam to drive the bulls through the open yard and into the pasture.

If the bulls took a notion to turn and go off into the mountains . . . Adam closed his thoughts to that idea. They wouldn't do that. They simply wouldn't. He wouldn't permit that to happen.

But if they did . . .

From the top rail of a stall the bulls had looked wonderful and strong and handsome. From ground level now, with nothing between him and them to keep them from doing whatever they wanted . . . that knot in his belly pulled tighter and began to twist. Adam felt sweat prickle his forehead with tiny points of icy moisture, and for half an instant he was just the least bit woozy.

He didn't let that stop him, though. He couldn't. There was no turning back now. No way to get the bulls back into their stalls even if he wanted to, because now they had their heads up, their great nostrils flaring and fluttering as if they were reaching out on explorations of discovery by way of airborne scents, and now they, all of them, were tentatively, hesitantly, taking short little stiff-legged steps out into the afternoon sunshine.

"Oh, Lordy," Adam moaned. And started forward. "Hyah. Hyup, bull, hyah!"

He slapped his thigh and bent to scoop up a handful of loose soil and small gravel that he threw at the broad backside of the nearest bull. That one snorted and bolted forward a step, jostling the off hindquarter of the dark-bodied creature immediately ahead and drawing a stamp of protest from that offended bovine.

"Hyah!" Adam shouted, his voice small and feeble against the combined power of six mighty bulls. "Hyah, dang you, hyup."

He couldn't see Hoss, but that was all right. The pasture gate was standing open. Hoss was supposed to be behind it, and if Adam couldn't see him there, then neither could the bulls. That was perfect because Adam sure didn't want these bulls spooking on him now that they were outside with nothing but a skinny thirteen-year-old between them and freedom.

Lordy, why had he ever gone and started this anyway? Maybe he should've listened to Hoss just this once.

"Hyah, bulls, hyah."

The critters had their heads and their interest up now. Adam could see in their stance that they'd become interested in what was going on. He could see that they were looking off toward the grass that lay beyond that gate straight in front of them, not seventy, maybe sixty yards smack ahead of the one that was in the lead.

Something caught in Adam's throat as that lead bull snorted and pawed and then broke into a shuffling trot right straight for the open gate.

Perfect. Wonderful. This was going to be just fine after all. Just the way he'd planned it. And if Jean-Pierre wanted the bulls back inside that musty barn, he could just put them in there himself, darn him. But he wouldn't. Jean-Pierre would see now how right he was. Even Jean-Pierre would be able to recognize the improvement once these bulls had them some grass and sunshine and could roll and clean off their dry, dusty hides and get to gleaming and become fat again like they properly ought. Give it just a day or two and Jean-Pierre would see that he was right. And he wouldn't have any choice but to tell Pa that when Pa got home too.

Adam's chest filled and swelled up just a mite as the lead bull trotted docilely into the pasture. And then another. Another. Another one after that.

"Hyah, bulls, hyah."

The fifth bull went inside. Or started to. Then it stopped, smack in the middle of the opening. It flared its nostrils and tossed its head.

The last bull stopped too. It had to throw its head in the air to keep from running into the back end of the fifth bull, which was already contrary and peevish from the shenanigans a few moments earlier.

"Hyah, dang it." Adam bent down, picked up some gravel and sprayed the ground underneath the bulls, peppering their hocks with stinging bits of sharp rock.

The bull at the gate snorted and lashed out with its hoofs, catching the last bull in the chest with a crashing thump. The trailing bull whirled to escape the pique of its companion.

"No!"

Adam jumped in front of the creature. He waved his arms and shouted. He didn't dare let the animal turn away from that gate. "Hyah, bull. Git back there." He jumped up and down in an attempt to make himself seem larger, and he waved his arms madly as he tried to frighten the bull back toward the pasture. "Hyah!"

"Adam." There was a hint of panic in little Hoss's voice. "They're all coming back, Adam, what'll I do?"

Adam had no time to mess with his baby brother at the moment. He was face-to-face with a big old dang bull, and it just wasn't doing what it was supposed to. He swallowed, unable to dislodge whatever the obstruction was that had of a sudden risen inside his throat, and waved his arms again.

"They're trying to get out, Adam, what'll I do?"

Adam jumped up and down. Then his eyes widened. The bull saw him now, all right. Its head dropped and its nostrils flared wide. Strings of slobber glistened in the slanting sunlight. A patch of dust, pale as a lady's face powder, stood out on the left side of the bull's jaw. The patch of pale dust was shaped like a rabbit's head, ears and all.

The bull had short, sharp, curving horns that were black except at the tips, where they were yellowed white like old ivory. The horns looked sharp. And close. Oh, Lordy, they were close. The bull was coming. Adam wasn't even sure that it was charging. It all seemed too casual for that. Just that the bull had seen him now and was coming at him. And its head was down and those horns were sticking out straight forward, and . . .

"Adam. No, Adam, no!" Hoss was screaming. There was terror in his voice. Adam had no time to listen to his little brother. Not right now. "Adam!"

Adam was backing up as fast as he could go. He didn't dare turn his back on the bull. He couldn't turn his back on the bull. He couldn't take his eyes off it. The bull was so close. So close. So . . .

The boss at the base of the bull's horns butted him hard in the stomach, driving the breath from him.

He could feel the heat of the bull's breath and the wet of its slobber drive through the cloth of his trousers' legs.

He was so scared he couldn't see or feel or think except for the tiny, closely defined area of focus linking the flat of his belly and the top of the bull's head.

He had hold—he had no recollection of reaching out or of wanting to grab for them, but he had a tight grip on them anyway—of the bull's horns, one curving horn in each of his hands. He was pushing, trying to push the bull away.

That was silly, as he conceded when he realized that he was no longer standing on the ground.

Somehow he was up in the air. Up over the bull's head. The ground spun dizzily beneath him. Then the world turned upside down.

He landed on his back with a thud, what little breath was left to him being driven out.

The bull was looming over him like some evil, malevolent monster. It was rooting and pushing at him. Pressing down onto him with the top of its head. The tips of its horns scraped the ground on either side of Adam's ribs. He could hear the crunch and grind of it as the horn tips rubbed through the grit.

He had lost his grasp on the horns sometime in all that. He didn't know when. He balled his hands into fists and beat on the back of the bull's thick, powerful neck as the creature wallowed and snorted and shoved at him. The bull's flesh felt no more yielding than a saddle seat when he beat on it. He pounded until his hands were sore, but the bull never acted like it so much as knew he was pummeling it.

He kicked out with his feet and tried to squirm out from under the horrifying presence that was crushing him.

He couldn't get his breath back. He felt his strength ebb and his vision dim. The bull was killing him. He knew that it was. It had him down and it was killing him and there wasn't anything he could do now to stop it.

Oh, Lordy! If only he hadn't tried to move these damn old bulls anyway. If only Pa hadn't gone to San Francisco. If only that dang Jean-Pierre listened to him. If only . . .

There was a roaring in Adam's ears that was like the sound you heard when you listened at one of Pa's conch seashells, except this was a thousand times louder.

There was the roaring, and a thick red fog that swept across his eyes and blotted out everything. Even the ugly sight of the back of the damn ol' bull's thick neck. Adam couldn't see anything now but that red mist, and couldn't hear anything but the roaring that was in his ears.

Damn old bull hadn't gored him, but it was killing him anyway just from pushing at him so hard. He hadn't known something could do that.

Oh, he wished things had been different.

Adam realized that he could no longer feel the press of the bull against his belly. He felt detached from everything and really quite comfortable. He supposed this was what it felt like to die. It didn't hurt nearly so much as he would have expected. But even so, he wished it wasn't happening to him. Why did it have to happen anyway?

Things might have taken a different path, mightn't they? Like that day a couple months ago when the wagons came. If only . . .

CHAPTER 2

B en Cartwright straightened, coming upright from bended knee and reaching down again to brush the dirt and bits of loose gravel off his trousers.

Everything here was as tidy as he could make it. The fence was tight again after a winter of abuse and would keep out browsing deer or grazing cattle, either one.

The carved stone was straight, and the lilac bush he'd planted behind it looked like it might be established well enough this season to thrive and for the first time come into flower. Both the headstone and the bush had been brought across the mountains from San Francisco.

The stone read: Inger Borgstrom Cartwright, Beloved Wife and Mother, May 1822–September 1848, Slumber Sweetly.

Ben would have preferred to be more specific with the dates, but he simply hadn't known what the exact date was when she died in his arms that September day nearly seven years earlier.

Seven years. It seemed so much longer. And yet in another way it seemed there had hardly been time enough to blink an eye or catch his breath.

He looked first at the headstone with a cascade of freshly gathered early wildflowers at its foot, then up toward the magnificent Sierra Nevada mountains looming so close above.

Inger hadn't lived to share with him the great beauty of those mountains. She had died here at the base of the foothills, but he knew she would have loved the high country every bit as much as he did.

They had shared so much in the short time they'd had together. Their tastes and hopes and joys had been so very much alike. And Inger would have been proud of what he and his sons had built here.

Elizabeth would have been proud of that too. Ben could not honestly decide if Elizabeth would have shared the joy he found in this mountain splendor. Elizabeth had been a child of city and sea. Probably she would have, though. Certainly she would have been willing to share whatever life he chose, whether that proved to be in Boston or here.

He was a lucky man, Ben Cartwright told himself now. Thinking about the two women whose love had enriched his days brought him much more joy than sadness, for many reasons.

Ben smiled as he looked down from the knoll where he himself had placed Inger's grave that heart-wrenching day so long ago. He was looking at the two primary reasons why memories of his dear Elizabeth and of Inger were still so strong and yet even in their absence so joyous. Down there ambling along the banks of the Truckee River were the sons those two wonderful women had given him.

Adam was thirteen now, dark and lean and quick in both body and mind. Elizabeth Stoddard Cartwright had been Adam's mother.

At his side now—always at big brother's side, it seemed—was cheerful, sturdy, laughing Hoss. Eric Haas Cartwright, really, but Adam long ago corrupted his baby brother's name into something more to his liking. At this point Ben supposed seven-year-old Hoss would be indignant if anyone were to begin calling him Eric. After all, whatever his infallible guide and mentor Adam wanted was law so far as Hoss was concerned.

Oh, they were wonderful boys, Ben thought with pride and pleasure.

While their father watched from the knoll, the two youngsters stopped, bent, straightened again. Ben could see that they were in close consultation about something. He wished he were able to eavesdrop on their conversation.

Hoss threw something into the creek. Adam shook his head and then patiently spoke with his brother for a time, finally demonstrating, and then Ben knew what they were talking about. Adam was teaching Hoss to skip pebbles off the water.

From this distance it appeared that Hoss's enthusiasm exceeded his ability. What he lacked in dexterity Hoss tended to make up by way of determination. In this particular matter, though, Ben suspected a certain amount of technique would be required. Unless, that is, Adam knew of some magic that would allow his brother to shortcut the normal learning processes. Ben was convinced that if such a method were physically possible, then Adam would surely invent it.

In the meantime, though, Hoss would just have to keep trying.

The blocky little boy, built square and solid, so that he almost looked chubby, although there wasn't an ounce of fat on him, laboriously peppered the surface of the Truckee until finally he was rewarded with a splash that might—if the observer were in a charitable frame of mind—be considered a skip.

Adam grinned broadly and said something to Hoss and patted him on the back, and little Hoss squirmed and preened in the glow of his big brother's approval.

Together the boys started off again in the direction of the lush glade where Ben had left them with their fishing lines and willow poles and picnic makings.

The boys always insisted on coming along whenever

Ben came down from the mountain to tend to Inger's grave, but they rarely joined him on the knoll itself. Ben suspected Adam kept his distance because the memories of Inger were so painful to him. Adam had no real memory of his own mother, but he had adored Inger and admitted that it was she who was in his mind when he thought about his mother. Hoss, of course, stayed away because Adam did. He had no memory of his mother, nor even of the succession of sympathetic and warm-hearted pioneer women who had taken care of Adam and Hoss in those earliest days.

The wagon train Ben and Inger and the boys came westward with had to go on or risk becoming snowbound that fall, even though one of their number lay dying of a festered wound. Ben sent the boys on ahead with helpful friends, but insisted on remaining behind with Inger despite the danger to himself. They had had long, peaceful days to share their love, the time made all the more precious because they both knew that Inger was dying. They had talked and held hands and made the most of what time they were given. Later Ben nearly died too as he tried to cross the Sierras alone in winter. It was only the intercession of a band of Pah-Ute Indians that saved him then.

He spent that winter learning from the Pah-Utes. And becoming ever more captivated by the majesty of the great mountains.

When spring released him from the bondage of its grip, he had hurried west to California to find and reclaim his boys. And then came right back here to these mountains he had come to love so very much.

The land he took up then would be his home for however many days he had left to him, he swore. And if he was lucky, his sons would love it as much as he and continue on this land long after Ben Cartwright's time was past.

Ah, but that was a serious matter to think about. And today, despite the nature of their visit here at the Truckee Meadows, today was a far from serious day. Today, like the other days when Ben came down from the mountains to Inger's grave, was a break from the dull and normal routine of ranch life, and gave the boys a chance to get away from home for a day on horseback with their father. Ben was always glad for the company. And for any other excuse to spend time with his sons.

He stood on the knoll a moment longer, enjoying the bright sunshine of a fine spring day, then let himself out through the gate he'd installed two years earlier and started down toward his two fine boys.

By the time he reached the meadow and started across it toward the grove where the boys were fishing, he could hear the intrusion of a persistent noise from the emigrant trail downstream. If wagons loaded with movers and gold seekers were arriving at Truckee Meadows this early in the season, then Missouri and the plains must have had an exceptionally mild winter just past, he realized.

Surely no one could be this far west so quickly. Why, he wasn't ready for them. He hadn't brought the oxen down off the foothills. Hadn't prepared the vast quantities of dried meat that would be needed, nor yet sent his own wagons across into California to bring back flour and salt and coffee.

Surely no one could have made it this far yet.

Yet there someone was. Ben could see the lead pair of a mule-drawn light wagon burst out of shadow into sunlight on the open, grassy sward.

The mules pulled steadily in a smooth, easy-swinging trot, one team after another, until there were four lightly loaded rigs in view, each carrying five or six passengers, and none of them seeming burdened by much in the way of supplies or equipment.

Adam and Hoss heard the jangle of the harness and came up the creek bank to see. Ben increased his pace to join his sons. The boys saw him and hurried to meet him halfway, positioning themselves one on either side and close to their father. They stood together there to greet these months-early newcomers from the east.

*   *   *

"Bless you, Mr. Cartwright, you're everything they told us you would be."

"Frankly, Mr. Hamer, I'm not sure how I should take that. Not until I know everything you were told."

The leader of the party threw his head back and roared. "That's a good one, Mr. Cartwright. Not till you know all we were told, ha ha."

"Seriously, Mr. Cartwright," the man's missus put in, "we appreciate all you are doing for us. Why, I declare, any gentleman who invites twenty-three perfect strangers to dinner without warning must be a saint."

"Why, thank you, Clarissa, for implying that I am perfect," Hamer teased.

"Charles!"

"You are the one who said that we strangers were perfect, Clarissa, not I."

"Mr. Cartwright, I ask you. Whatever shall I do with him?"

Ben chuckled and accepted the reins of his horse from Adam. With this interruption in their down-valley outing, the boys had been dispatched to bring the mounts in from grazing. Ben noticed that Adam had gone to the trouble of saddling and tightening the cinches on all the horses, not merely his own. Ben was pleased with the display of thoughtfulness.

"Son," he said now, "why don't you and Hoss ride ahead and tell Mr. Malloy we'll be having company tonight. It wouldn't do for us to show up with this many extra and not give him a bit of notice."

Adam sat up straighter on his saddle and he tried his best to appear serious and responsible and mature . . . but the telltale upturning curves of a poorly hidden grin kept flickering in and out of view at the corners of his mouth. Being sent off like this up the lonely mountain road from the Meadows to home—alone save for the responsibility of his baby brother—why, this was heady stuff indeed. "Yes, Pa. Should I take the rifle, Pa?"

"Yes, I think probably you should, son."

Adam stifled an incipient yelp and walked—swaggered was closer to the truth of it—to the side of his father's horse to take down the short-barreled mountain rifle that was hung from the pommel of the saddle there. His chest puffed out to mighty dimensions as he lifted down his father's "possibles" bag with powder, ball, and caps and slung the leather bag over his own skinny shoulder. Not for a moment would he have considered hanging the heavy bag from the horn of his saddle.

Chunky little Hoss scaled the side of his horse—Jean-Pierre DeMarigny, the Ponderosa's foreman, had tied on some knotted thongs that the boy could use like a rope ladder when he wanted to climb the heights into his saddle—and was ready and waiting by the time Adam mounted, his dignity impeded only a little by the rifle.

"Count on me, Pa. I won't let you down," Adam declared.

"We," Hoss corrected with a show of mild indignation. For after all, he was a part of this mission too.

"Right. The two of us won't let you down, Pa."

"I know you won't." Ben restrained an impulse to remind Adam to take care of Hoss—Lord knew, no such reminder was needed—and bit back another, even stronger inclination to tell the boys to be careful on the road.

The children set off up the well-marked and perfectly visible wagon road that would take them to the Ponderosa Ranch headquarters, Adam leading the way at an easy lope.

Ben noticed with a mix of pride and pleasure that the boys, even little Hoss, rode as if they were part of the horses, as if somehow they had become perfectly natural, perfectly balanced outgrowths that rose from the backs of the equines so that man and horse were blended into one creature.

Ben himself, coming to riding as an everyday means of transportation relatively late in life after a youth spent on the decks of ships at sea, knew that he would never experience such a mastery of horsemanship as his young sons already found to be as normal as breathing.

"Are you sure they will be all right?" Mrs. Hamer asked in a nervous tone of voice.

"Ma'am?"

"Should you have let them go alone like that, Mr. Cartwright? I mean, if the older boy fears he may need a firearm . . ." Her eyes were wide and worried.

Ben smiled. "There isn't anything or anyone that would harm them, Mrs. Hamer, I assure you. Not within fifty miles, I wager. Carrying the rifle makes Adam feel that much more grown-up. He's at that age, you see, when he's wanting to leave childhood behind, but isn't quite yet ready. You will understand that when the time comes."

Mrs. Hamer blushed a little and quite involuntarily touched the slightly bulging front of her dress. "You are a very perceptive gentleman, Mr. Cartwright."

"No, just an experienced one." He took Mrs. Hamer's hand and helped her back onto the box of her husband's wagon. "Best we should be getting along now if we want to get to the Ponderosa in time for supper." Ben mounted, and the wagons rolled slowly forward while Ben rode close beside the box of Hamer's lead rig.

"Ponderosa," one of the men in the party said. "I thought that was the name of a tree."

"So it is, sir. It is a tree that I particularly admire, graceful and yet sturdy and true. That is why I chose to name my home for it."

"They tell us you're the only whites this side of the Sierras, Mr. Cartwright," another said.

"Oh, there was a time when you might have been able to say that, but a few folks have chosen to settle on this side of the mountains since I came. There is a small settlement to the south, and right here at the Truckee Meadows there is seasonal occupation when traders come across the passes with wares to sell to the emigrants and the gold-seekers."

"Like you, Mr. Cartwright. I'm surprised you don't keep them away."

Ben laughed. "To tell you the truth, sir, I don't think of them as competitors. More like unofficial partners who take some of the load off me and my sons."

"But I thought that was your business, Mr. Cartwright, trading with the travelers on the California road."

"It was, more or less. At least to begin with. This was where I happened to be, and that was the business that was available to me. Mostly, though, I chose to stop here because this is where my wife is buried—on that knoll up there, actually—and this is where I found a peace and a beauty the likes of which I've seen in no other place. The business aspects, such as they were, came afterward.

"For some years, you see, travelers abandoned livestock on these meadows. They turned loose any stock too weak to attempt the passes to the west. And because of this, the Indians came here each fall to claim the recovered oxen and mules and whatnot for their winter meat. Those same Indians saved my life when I found myself alone in the mountains after my wife died. We've become friends, those Indians and I. They know they're always welcome at the Ponderosa now, and my sons and I are welcome in their shelters." He smiled. "But it was the trade you asked about, wasn't it? Sorry.

"That first year I went over to California early and brought back some food that I might sell to the emigrés. And there were some oxen in the thickets too, animals abandoned earlier and long since fully recovered from the fatigue of travel. An ox hauling a heavy wagon from the States will be footsore and thin by the time it reaches the Meadows here, you see, but given a few weeks to recuperate, it will rebound completely to good health. Well, I soon realized that I could trade fresh oxen for tired ones. Two worn-out animals for one fresh one. Then in a few weeks, when another train came through, I would have two fresh oxen to give in exchange for four tired ones. Give four, take in eight. Give eight, take in sixteen. You can see that in no time at all I had oxen to spare. Oxen to sell and oxen to slaughter for jerky, both to sell and to give to my friends the Indians. And there were other creatures too. Dairy-bred cattle too emaciated to go any farther but still living and able to recover; calves whose dams had lost their milk; colts whose mothers died along the trail; any number of such things.

"Before long I was in the business of raising livestock as well as of trading with folks on the road. At this point I am quite frankly concentrating on livestock for the future. Not just oxen, but horses, both saddle and draft stock, and beef cattle, even a few head of dairy cattle. I have more than enough grazing land here on the Ponderosa. And timber too, if there should ever be a means to transport timber from this side of the Sierras over to the gold-mining country. In any event, I believe my sons have a good prospect on this land I've taken up for their future."

"They say you own half of California, though, Mr. Cartwright. How is that?"

Ben laughed. "It's a bold claim, sir, and I wish a true one. If you want the full truth, though, and I'm not ashamed to give it, I have no idea how much of California—or any other state or territory—I might own. The thing is, I've always believed in the honesty of my fellow man, and I am pleased to be able to tell you that I've rarely been disappointed. No one has ever left here without food enough to carry him across the mountains. That would be cruel and greedy of me, and I don't want to think either of those things about myself. I've always been willing to give a man whatever he needs, and if he is able to repay me later, that will be fine. It is something we can think about at that later date. Fortunately, a good many of the people who've taken advantage of this find themselves in excellent circumstances once they are established in California. Some of them have repaid me with shares in their ventures. Mines, banks, mercantiles, what-have-you." He grinned and added, "Would you believe, sir, that I own a one-sixteenth share of a barber-cum-bathhouse-cum-funerary parlor in a place called Doolin's Gulch? I have a letter somewhere that so informs me, although I can't claim to have seen any cash dividends from this joint venture quite yet."

The gentlemen and two ladies in the Hamer party laughed.

"You, uh, you still have that policy of allowing no one to leave without sufficient supplies to reach California, do you?"

"Yes, Mr. Hamer, I do."

"And, um, what guarantees of repayment do you require, sir?"

Ben could see easily enough where this conversation was leading. "Don't worry yourself about it, Mr. Hamer. You and your people will be just fine now."

Mrs. Hamer and the other lady, a Mrs. Cumberland, seemed unnaturally bright of eye now, Ben noticed, as if they might be on the verge of tears. It occurred to him that perhaps these travelers, who were on the plains many months in advance of what was normal, were in poorer shape than he'd realized.

Because their mules seemed to be in excellent condition, he hadn't thought to question the state of the humans in this small group. Now he reconsidered that oversight and realized that the wagons were virtually empty save for a few items of luggage. There was little evidence of edible supplies in any of the four Hamer wagons.

"You know," he said, "I'll bet these mules could handle a spritelier gait than this, at least until we start to climb. We're hours away from my ranch, but I can't see any need for us to dawdle and make the time longer than it has to be. What do you say we quicken the pace just a little, eh?"

Charles Hamer snapped a whip above the backs of his leaders. On the seat beside him his wife once again touched her belly.

Ben hoped that darn cook Malloy put plenty on the

table this evening. Humph. First, he supposed, he should hope that that darn Malloy was sober enough tonight to cook something for these poor folks. One of the few drawbacks of being so far off from everything and everyone else was that it was difficult to find help worth hiring, Edgar Malloy being a particularly telling case in point. The man was a drunkard and sometimes a problem, although when sober he was as good a cook as could be wanted. Anyway, Ben did not have the heart to turn Malloy out. The fellow was bad enough here where alcohol was seldom to be found; Ben was afraid to think what might happen to him if Malloy carried his self-destructive habit with him to one of the gold camps where liquor would be readily available to him.

"You're in for a treat tonight, folks," Ben promised the emigrants. "Just wait until you see my home place." Of a sudden he found himself as eager to arrive there as Hamer and his party obviously already were. "Just wait."

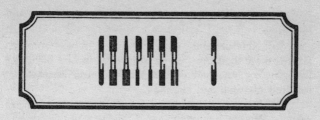

CHAPTER 3

The compliments and exclamations offered by the men and ladies of the Hamer party were offered from a sense of politeness on the part of the visitors more than they were earned by the aesthetic style and industry of the ranch owner. As a creator of architectural beauty, Ben Cartwright acknowledged, he made a pretty fair sea captain. Which is to say that his efforts had to be regarded as crude, albeit effective.

The Ponderosa headquarters/Cartwright home was . . . sturdy. And perhaps a bit on the homely side. Built of native logs laid up with more enthusiasm than skill, the ranch house was a low, rambling lump of a thing that had begun as a cabin perhaps a dozen feet square and which had been added onto over the years, a bit here and a room there, each segment constructed of logs and roofed with poles and sod until, now, the assemblage resembled a long, shaggy wood rick more than a house.

Chimneys sprouted here and there. Doors and windows had been cut through at whatever points seemed desirable at the time. Weeds had taken root on the sod roof and were growing now with mad abandon.

Ben had to admit that the compliments so politely given by his guests were not deserved. Why, the barn was actually larger and better built than the house was. The

23

same might almost be said of several of the many out-buildings.

Still, this ungainly mess was home. It was comfort-able. It more than satisfied the simple needs of a man with two growing boys and a great many business interests that required his time and attention.

"Welcome to the Ponderosa," he announced, as grandly—and as genuinely—as if this were a majestic and beauteous manor. "Welcome to my home."

"You can't know how happy we are to've found you, Mr. Cartwright," Hamer said. "How we've worried—" The man's voice caught in his throat and he reached for his wife's hand to find and squeeze it.

"Your party is here awfully early," Ben suggested. It was considered impolite in this country to ask questions, but a man couldn't help experiencing a little innocent cu-riosity now and then.

"Aye, that's the truth," Hamer agreed. The man shook his head. "We got a late start last year, you see. Thought we could beat the weather. Well, we couldn't. We were stopped just this side of Bridger's post. Found shelter with a man there who'd built a roadhouse."

"Pest house is more like it," one of the men muttered. Both ladies cast their eyes low and turned their heads away.

"It was indecent, the things that went on there, Mr. Cartwright," Hamer said. "I'll not say any more, but it was indecent. And expensive. My word, sir. For a bit of shelter, we paid out all we owned. Paid and paid and paid again. Used up all the foodstuffs we'd brought from the States and had to pay dear for anything more to eat, you see. We couldn't even hunt for ourselves because somehow—we'll never prove that he done the deed him-self, but we know, sir, we know—somehow all our supply of powder became damp and ruined. We were dependent upon that man, and he took all we had. Wagons, tools, ev-erything but what little you see here. Lucky for us, some men hunting out of the settlements at the Salt Lake talked to us. Told us about you. They said you would help us if we could just get this far. Except for that hope, Mr. Cartwright, we would've turned back. We would've had to. So we started out again quick as the snow began to melt. And now ... Bless you, sir. Bless you and yours."

Ben nodded to Jean-Pierre, who had come outside to greet the guests, and the gentle and considerate Acadian quickly took charge. There would be time enough for introductions later. Jean-Pierre helped the ladies down from the wagons and guided them and the men inside while Adam and Hoss bustled about to assist with the unharnessing and the disposition of both livestock and equipment.

"Inside, everyone. There's room enough for all. And my nose tells me that Mr. Malloy has our supper waiting. No, don't be shy. Right in there, please. Take a seat and help yourself, no need to wait on the rest of us. Go ahead, please, and eat hearty."

This was hardly the first time that travelers reached the Ponderosa in need, nor would it be the last. The way Ben saw it, helping his fellow man was a pleasure, and an opportunity to make new friends. This right here was the exact sort of thing, far more than any possibility of profit, that made running the Ponderosa so worthwhile. All the rest was merely incidental.

"Sit down now. There's room for all, and if we haven't enough food prepared, then we'll cook some more. That's right, help yourselves to all you can hold. No need to stint, folks, you're among friends now."

It pleased him no end to see how the travelers enjoyed the simple meal Edgar Malloy had laid out here. Ben's only remaining concern now was to discover how else he could help these people who were his guests.

Ben Cartwright propped his heels onto the smooth and almost level top of the section of tree stump that he used as an ottoman. He drew deep on his pipe and sighed. This was fine. He and all his guests had been sumptuously well fed, and now the ladies had retired for the evening while the menfolk sat with tobacco and toddies. Hamer and the other gentlemen had much to talk about now that they were safe at the Ponderosa, and Ben was enjoying listening to them.

". . . must remember to park with that wheel in water lest the wood dry out and let the tire slip . . ."

". . . stumble-footed thing really ought to be roasted, not harnessed, except then what would I do for a . . ."

". . . since we were three days this side o' the North Platte, but I never expected to . . ."

Wisps and tatters of unhurried conversation eddied about Ben's ears much like the ghostly tendrils of blue-white smoke from his pipe. He glanced across the warm, crowded room and caught Adam's eye. The boy was perched on a log bench, silent but interested. Hoss, eyes closed and mouth open, leaned serene and secure against his big brother's shoulder. The hour was simply too late for the little fellow to endure. But he hadn't been willing to abandon the festive occasion. Ben winked at Adam and was rewarded with a grin. Adam seemed to be enjoying the company too, after being so many months without visitors.

"What was that?" Ben asked, becoming belatedly aware that one of the men was speaking to him.

"I asked about your business here, Mr. Cartwright. Do you have to order your goods in all the way from the States, sir?"

"Less and less of it as time goes on," Ben told him. "You might be surprised at all that's produced in California now. Most of what we need here can be brought over from California. Why, San Francisco is really quite civilized. I suspect you'll be surprised when you see it."

"Log cabins and muddy lanes, that's what we were told to expect."

Ben chuckled. "Yes, sir, I dare say you will be surprised indeed."

"But there *is* gold, isn't there?"

"Not in San Francisco. There you will find commerce aplenty, but the only gold is that which is carried in men's pockets. The gold mining is all in the mountains these days. The easy pickings down below 've already been gleaned."

"But there is gold?" the man persisted. Nearly all who passed through the Ponderosa these days wanted to talk about the gold that was to be had free for the taking.

"There is," Ben agreed. "For those who have the luck to find it and the persistence to dig it and the skills to collect it and the mettle to defend it. The mining of gold is not easy, gentlemen. I hope you understand that. Nor is fortune so common as the tales back east may have led you to believe."

"But there is gold. And there have been fortunes made," a new voice put in. "Isn't that so, sir?"

"It is indeed," Ben told the man quite truthfully.

Hamer cleared his throat and helped himself to the pouch of Ben Cartwright's tobacco that had been set out for all to enjoy. "First things first," the leader of the party said. "We still have some hundreds of miles of mountains to cross before we can begin to think about gold or what it might buy us. Including, I must add, repayment to Mr. Cartwright here. In the meantime, sir, could you advise us about what we can expect between here and the mining camps? Will all the passes be free of snow by now? Is the road well-marked or might we accidentally stray? How much do you recommend we buy in the way of eatables to carry us until we've taken up mining claims of our own and can reasonably expect to be self-sufficient again? I have too many questions, I know, but—"

"No such thing," Ben insisted. "Any question is a good one when you don't already have its answer. Unfortunately, I don't have all the answers you need. About the likelihood of success in the mining camps in particular I would be a poor one to advise you. I've never engaged in mining myself, you see. And anything I might say about what I've heard, well, what you folks need is encouragement, not sad stories. Besides, some truly do make their fortunes in the camps. I would hate to discourage the very man who could be the next soul fated to be in bonanza."

"Bonanza?" someone asked. "What does that mean, Mr. Cartwright?"

"It's a term you'll hear often enough over there across the mountains, Mister . . . Krites, is it?"

"That's right." The gentleman seemed pleased that Ben recalled his name from among the many new introductions made during the day. But he still wanted an answer to his question. "You were saying . . . ?"

"Mm, right. Bonanza." Ben puffed on his pipe for a moment, the smoke from it wreathing his head and drifting on the still air inside the spacious cabin that was his home. "It's a word that means, oh, good fortune, so to speak. It applies to a mine that is producing and growing more productive all the time. It's something that is already good, you see, and is still in its ascendancy. Bonanza is the obverse of borrasca, which is something that's on the downhill slide. And may I say, gentlemen, that what I wish for you, one and all, is that your futures and your fortunes be in bonanza." He raised his glass with a smile and toasted the group of travelers. The gentlemen, most of whom were from Ohio, responded with a yip-yip and a toast of their own.

"Three cheers for Mr. Cartwright, fellows."

"Hurrah, boys, hurrah!"

Tumblers turned bottom upward, and for a few moments there was a good deal of coughing and mustache wiping going on. Then the jug went 'round again—a dark and fruity Portuguese brandy that had arrived at this distant point by some convoluted process of commerce that only the Lord above would ever be capable of unraveling—and the smiles subsided into simple contentment. This was the sort of evening that Ben loved.

A thought came into his head and sped immediately out of his mouth without pausing for him to weigh or consider it.

"You know," he said aloud, "I have to go over to San Francisco anyway. I still have to make my purchases for this coming season's trade. Your party certainly isn't typical in coming along so early. But if you were able to leave this soon, others will be setting out soon too from other points on the highway. From Laramie and Saint Joe and all manner of wintering-over points in between. I really should go as quickly as possible. Why don't I travel with you folks when you pull out of here? There is plenty of snow in the high country yet, but I know the best routes and the places to avoid. I could guide you through and point out the roads you want to reach the best camps, then head on down to San Francisco to take care of my own affairs. What d'you think, Mr. Hamer?"

"What do I think, Mr. Cartwright? I think that is one of the most generous things I've ever known. Why, I think every man and every woman in this venture will be indebted to you for your help. All this food, fresh livestock . . . and now this? There's no way we could ever repay this kindness, Mr. Cartwright."

"It wasn't repayment I was thinking of, Mr. Hamer. The point is, would you accept my company on your journey?"

"Mr. Cartwright, we would be honored. Truly honored. And just to make it official, sir, we do indeed accept your generous offer of assistance."

"Three cheers war'n't enough for Mr. Cartwright, boys," a voice called out. "We'll do it again an' this time do it right. Three cheers for Mr. Cartwright, boys. Three cheers and a tiger."

Again a roar went up through the smoky, low-roofed room, and again the jug of Portuguese made a round.

Ben chewed happily on the stem of his briar and once more winked at Adam, who seemed to be quite thoroughly enjoying himself.

CHAPTER 4

They were ready to travel, the four mule-drawn wagons of the Hamer party and Ben's blue roan saddle horse all standing idle in the ranch yard while the good-byes were being spoken. Jean-Pierre already had the few instructions Ben deemed necessary. Jean-Pierre and Edgar Malloy were standing in the doorway. Hoss had already said good-bye to every man and woman in the Hamer party and now was quite proudly holding his father's bridle ready for Ben to mount. The only one who refrained from showing any active interest in the departure was Adam, who was moping about with his hands in his pockets and a sulky expression dragging down the corners of his mouth.

Ben gave his older son a sympathetic look and, guessing at the reasons for Adam's displeasure, drew the boy off a few paces to where the others wouldn't overhear.

"You're growing up fast, Adam."

It would not be many years before Adam's height surpassed his father's, but that time had not yet arrived. He had to peer up now to give Ben a sour look. "You say that, Pa, but you don't do much to show you mean it."

"What I said, son, was that you're growing up. I didn't say you've grown up. You have a way to go still."

"I'm old enough to—"

30

"Hush now. We've gone through all this, Adam. My mind is made up. Jean-Pierre is our foreman, and I'm leaving him in charge. You mind him just like you were one of the hands." Ben smiled. "Fact of the matter is, until we take on the seasonal help, you and Hoss *are* the hired hands." Ben's smile was not returned by his son.

"All right, Adam," Ben persisted. "Be as grumpy as you want, but I'll not change my mind. Until I get back, Jean-Pierre is in charge here, and you're next in line. I expect you to do whatever Jean-Pierre tells you and to watch out for your brother. You know I've always counted on you for that. I expect you won't let me, or little Hoss, down now."

That brought a reluctant acknowledgment from Adam in the form of a shrug and a nod. For as long as he could remember, Adam had watched over Hoss. And for as long as either of them could remember, Hoss had idolized and imitated Adam.

"Is there anything you need while I'm in San Francisco?" Ben asked.

A hint of sparkle came into Adam's eyes as some desire occurred to him. But it was quickly quelled, and whatever he might have said lay stillborn on his tongue.

"Hoss wants some of that horehound candy from Mr. Eppiger's store. Can I bring you some too, son?" Ben could see the eagerness in Adam's expression. But of course the boy was much too old and entirely too mature to be asking for candy. He shook his head, the expression on his thin face once again mulishly stubborn and sullen.

"Well, no matter. I'll bring horehound enough for all and maybe some of those peppermint sticks you like. They are still your favorites, aren't they?"

Adam shrugged and looked away.

Ben sighed. There was no getting around it. Adam was at a somewhat difficult stage, half grown and never certain which half would prevail in his shifting moods. Today he wanted to be left in charge of the Ponderosa while his father was away. Tomorrow he and Hoss might well be stripped off and splashing in the stock pond, sailing wood-chip ships with oak-leaf sails and pretending they were merchantmen and buccaneers.

"I'm counting on you, Adam. Watch out for your brother and mind Jean-Pierre. I won't be gone long." Ben smiled and changed the subject. "I'll check with the shipping company while I'm in the city. Perhaps we'll have some word when to expect our new breeding stock. Why, just think. They may be somewhere at sea this very minute, close-hauled and coming around the Horn." He reached out and ruffled Adam's hair. "It's fall there now, you know. Soon winter down south. Isn't that something? We'd better hope they shipped our bulls in time to avoid the winter storms off the Cape, else they could be in for a battering." The reversal of the seasons that their father told them about was a subject that never failed to both mystify and intrigue the boys. Hoss accepted the idea as a matter of blind faith in Ben's word, while Adam tended to pick and worry at it. Several times Ben had overheard the boy questioning strangers about this incomprehensible phenomenon, Adam quite obviously wanting to verify his father's claims on the subject.

"Did I ever tell you about the winter gales off Cabo Virgenes? In July they were, but bitter cold and snowy." Ben whistled. "The worst I ever saw, I think."

"I thought the worst you ever saw was the time you were in that hurricane in the Abacos."

"When I get home I'll tell you about the winter storms off Virgenes. You can see what you think."

That prospect struck a more responsive chord, and Adam began to show some enthusiasm. Adam loved little more than listening to his father's sea stories. "When you get home," he said.

"I won't be away long."

"Yes, sir."

"Hoss is your responsibility, you know."

"Yes, sir. I'll take care of him."

"I know you will, son. I depend on you."

"Yes, sir."

Ben smiled at his son and squeezed his shoulder. He wanted to lean down and give the boy a kiss on the cheek. But of course he could not. Not with everyone watching. Adam would have been humiliated.

"I'll see you in a few weeks, son. A month at the most."

"We'll be all right, Pa."

"I know you will, son." Ben squeezed Adam's shoulder again, then turned away and walked back to Hoss and the blue roan. Hoss was not too old to accept a good-bye kiss from his papa. "Ready when you folks are, Mr. Hamer," Ben said as he swung onto his saddle.

Trace chains chimed and gravel crunched beneath iron tires as the wagons began to roll forward.

"God speed, m'sieu," Jean-Pierre called, lifting his hand and sketching a crucifix in the air by way of a wave good-bye.

Ben touched a finger to the side of his forehead, then bumped the flank of the roan with a spur rowel. A month, Ben thought. He should be back within a month or less, ready for the summer's trade.

Five days. Not bad. Not bad at all. And it would have been four except for that one slumped and slushy drift that even Ben could not find a way past, that one they'd had to dig through—swim through was more accurate, the mules brisket deep in a blue, rubbery slurry of ice and old snow. But now the last of the serious passes and the last of the dangers lay behind them, and after only five not particularly arduous days on the road. At this time of year that was more of an accomplishment than these people could know. But then helping them avoid the sort of lessons that must be earned the hard way was one of the reasons he had chosen to come along with them. With the worst of the trip comfortably behind now, Ben and the four wagons of the Hamer party rolled downhill past Little

Australia and onto the flat at the south end of Blue Nose Gulch.

"We're almost there," Ben assured the ladies. And, without especially seeming to, the menfolk as well. "You see the roof yonder? That's right, missus, there where you see that smoke rising. That smoke is from Alfred's stove. I can practically smell the bread baking, even from this far away." To emphasize the point, Ben stood in his stirrups and inhaled deeply of the clean and invigorating mountain air. There was no scent of baking bread he could detect, but he found the natural odors of fresh spring growth and sun-warmed mud and rising pine sap equally welcome.

"We will miss you, Mr. Cartwright."

"That's kind of you, but from here on the road is well-marked. You can't go wrong." From this point the gold-seekers in the Hamer party would turn north, remaining in the mountains to find whatever fate and fortune decreed for them. They would turn north while Ben would continue traveling west and down, out of the Sierras to the fertile river plains and on to San Francisco.

"We'll never forget you," Anthony Krites pledged.

"Just being neighborly," Ben responded. "I've done nothing for you that you wouldn't have done for me if our situations were reversed."

"You can be sure of this, Mr. Cartwright. If ever you need for anything, you shall have it if it's within my power to provide it. That I can promise you."

"That's kind of you, Mr. Krites. Thank you."

Krites, a large and competent man with broad shoulders and the light of a keen intelligence gleaming in his eyes, nodded abruptly as if to seal the promise, and then turned away, perhaps slightly embarrassed.

"There's Alfred, Mr. Hamer, by the shed there. You can turn off the road here if you like and head for the corral you can see past the shed."

Alfred Troyer stepped out into the sunlight and lifted a hand to shade his eyes. He was a squat fellow with graying hair and a spade beard. He was broad of body, broad of face, and broad of welcome. Back in the States he had been a baker. He still was, miners coming literally from miles and mountain ranges distant just to buy his breads and his delectable sweet pastries. Here, though, he had added a number of other lines of business to his activities, thanks in large measure to Ben Cartwright's help when Alfred first appeared in the Sierras. That had been some years ago, and now his family was with him and he was firmly established. Troyer's smile brightened and became all the more energetic when he saw who the horseman was that was leading the wagons in.

"Ben? Is that you, Ben? 'Tis, aye. I was telling my Jimmy just t'other day we'd be seeing you soon, Ben. Now here you are. And welcome. Step down, please. You too, folks. You're welcome here. Any friend of Ben Cartwright will find a place at my table, always."

The travelers gratefully brought their wagons to a halt and climbed down to the ground where they could stretch and stomp about and try to work out some of the aches and kinks of the long, bouncing journey.

Ben made the introductions. Before that was done, all the members of the Troyer family had poured outside to help welcome the guests. In addition to Alfred, there were his wife EmmaBeth, four sons, two half-grown daughters, and a shy cousin. A third girl was missing since the last time Ben passed this way. But then she—Ben thought the oldest girl's name was Rebecca—was of marrying age and by now might be well started on a family of her own.

"You'll be taking supper with us, won't you?" EmmaBeth asked. "Of course you will. Silly of me to've asked. Come along now and you can tell me what the latest fashions are in Saint Louie." Clucking like a hen gathering her flock of chicks, EmmaBeth Troyer collected Mrs. Hamer and Mrs. Cumberland and led them away toward the low-roofed log structure that housed the Troyer family and all their many enterprises. The men remained outside.

"My friends will be going north tomorrow, Alfred," Ben said.

"You'll be going with them?"

"No, I have to go down to the city."

Alfred grunted. He blinked and glanced absently about the horizon, took a moment to scratch himself, then grunted once more and motioned to his next-to-oldest boy, Kenneth. Kenneth nodded and, without need for specific instruction, trotted off into the shed to return a moment later with a pair of crockery jugs to pass around. Jimmy took it upon himself to lead Ben's horse away and tend to it.

Ben smiled a little. Charles Hamer and his people had no way to know it, but quite a lot had just taken place there. And each step of it dependent upon the one before.

The four wagons would be going north tomorrow. That meant they would be traveling on the short but crucial toll road Alfred and his sons had carved into the north wall of Blue Nose Gulch. Of course Alfred would be collecting a fee for the passage, which was a shortcut out of the deep gulch and eliminated some seven miles of exceptionally rugged travel. The size of the fees Alfred Troyer charged for the use of his road was variable. Had Ben been traveling as a part of the group, there would have been no payment asked. Since he was not, payment would be expected. But as the Hamer party was effectively under his tutelage, the amount would be considerably less than it might have been. And because a toll would be collected, EmmaBeth's fine supper—Ben never missed a chance to enjoy EmmaBeth Troyer's cooking—would be given as a matter of open-handed hospitality, as would this round of drinks for all the gentlemen. On the other hand, Alfred was a businessman of many interests and multiple talents. No doubt he would charge handsomely for the use of his wagon park and corrals and forage. A man may be hospitable to human travelers, but an animal's keep is something else again. All of this, Ben knew, Alfred would have worked out in those brief moments between determining Ben's role with these people and his signal to Kenneth.

Alfred saw to the passage of the jugs, then rubbed his hands together and gestured toward the house. "Come in now, gents. Let's see what my missus has put together for us tonight."

The boys shepherded the guests toward the house while Ben and Alfred hung back to trail along slightly behind the others.

"It's good to see you, Ben."

"Good to see you, Alfred. We've some catching up to do after the winter."

"Aye, so we do, Ben. So we do. After supper we'll see can we find a pipe and some privacy, eh?"

"I'd like that, old friend."

Alfred beamed, quite obviously accepting that as a compliment even though what he said was, "Old? Old, is it? Huh. I'll show you old, Ben Cartwright. Why, I'm still man enough to whip the likes of you."

"Are you willing to prove that, Mr. Troyer?"

"Aye, I'll take you on, Cartwright. I'll take you on and I'll whip you thoroughly."

Up ahead of them some of the gentlemen from the Hamer party had overheard and were beginning to glance back in alarm, word of the impending conflict spreading rapidly through the group so that steps faltered and heads turned.

"Weapons, Mr. Troyer?"

"Aye, of course."

"And what would your pleasure be, sir?"

"Knights, knaves, and elephants, I should think."

"White or black, Mr. Troyer?"

"I issued the challenge, Mr. Cartwright. You may choose your colors."

"Then I'll take the white, if you please."

"White it is, and I do please." Alfred grinned.

One of the men in the Hamer group, a young man in his early twenties named Damien, drifted close to Ben and leaned near to whisper, "Are you really gonna fight him, Mr. Cartwright? And what kinda weapons was it he said? I didn't understand all of that."

Ben chuckled. "It's a game of chess we're talking about, that's all. Alfred and I play every chance we get."

"Only a game. Whew! I thought—"

"Ha! But don't ever say 'only' a game when it's chess and Alfred Troyer you're talking about, Damien. With Alfred and me, chess is a serious subject indeed. Even if it isn't blood that flows while we're at it."

"Be that as it may, Mr. Cartwright, I'll not watch this fight if you don't mind. Though I have to admit I'd've been quick to watch the other kind. Uh, no offense intended."

"Nor any taken." Ben motioned for the young man to precede him into the log cabin. "Go ahead now. I promise this isn't a meal you'd want to be late for. Mrs. Troyer just may be the best cook in these mountains."

"May be!" Alfred protested from behind. "Now you've raised my dander, Ben. Now I'm out to get you. May be," he snorted. "Huh. Just wait until I get you to the chessboard. I'll give you 'may be' and then some."

"Loud talk for a fat old man," Ben accused. Broad as he was, though, there wasn't an ounce of fat apparent anywhere on Alfred Troyer's frame.

"You're digging yourself in all the deeper, Ben Cartwright," Alfred said happily. "Just wait. Just you wait, sir, and see how you suffer for all of this."

Ben grinned and went inside in the company of his smiling host.

"I concede." Ben leaned forward and poked the white king with a fingertip until the carved ivory figure toppled over on the playing board. The black pieces were made of ebony.

"So quick? Come on, Ben, you could get out of that. With your bishop there. See?"

Ben shook his head and reached for his pipe. "You

just want to run me around for another ten or fifteen moves, play cat to my mouse. No thanks, Alfred. I concede."

The stubby little baker/builder/businessman looked disappointed, but he accepted his friend's decision with a shrug and a hint of satisfied smile. "Fourteen, actually," he said.

"What's that?"

"Fourteen moves. If you covered with the bishop, it would have taken another fourteen moves for mate."

Ben chuckled and leaned down to the fireplace to light a broom straw and hold it over the bowl of the pipe. "I swear, Alfred," he said, sucking on the stem of his pipe between words, "I don't know why we play."

"Huh. Because we both like it, that's why."

"That must be it. But sometimes I think I should question my own sanity. You always win."

"If I always won, Ben, I wouldn't enjoy playing against you so much," Alfred countered.

"Seems like you always do anyway." Which was an exaggeration, but only a mild one. Ben managed to eke out a victory perhaps one game in five. One in four if he was on a roll.

Alfred winked at him, then began packing the chess pieces back into a leather-bound case custom fitted for their care and preservation. Alfred Troyer took his chess very seriously indeed.

The two men were alone in the dining hall, with only the crackling warmth of the fireplace for company and the light of one closely trimmed oil lamp to play by. Ben had no idea what the hour had gotten to, but everyone else had given up and gone off to bed long ago.

"Will you have a beer while you smoke that pipe, Ben?" Troyer offered. "This one isn't a bad batch if I do say so my own self."

"Are you having one?"

"If you do."

"Then it would be poor manners for me to refuse, wouldn't it?"

"Aye, a body could say that, yes." Alfred closed and latched the case of chessmen and carried it away into another room. He came back without the chess pieces but with a pair of dark brown, quart-sized bottles that had the corks wired tightly in place. When Alfred Troyer bottled beer, he didn't waste time messing with little bottles. He carefully pulled the corks and handed one of the bottles to his friend.

"To your good health, Ben."

"And to yours, Alfred." Ben swallowed, took a moment to savor the bright, rich flavor on his tongue, then grinned. "Ah, now that's a good one, all right."

"Beats that foamy water they ship up from Sacramento, don't it."

"Somewhat," Ben agreed.

"The boys and me been thinking about doing some brewing on a scale large enough that we'd be able to sell a little. What d'you think, Ben?"

"I think you'll be a success at it if that's what you decide to do. I don't generally care much for beer, but I like this. It really is very good."

"It'd cost some for the equipment," Alfred said. "Two thousand three hundred fifty dollars, we figure."

"Just kind of off the top of your heads, that is," Ben teased.

"Kind of," Alfred solemnly agreed.

"If you need a loan, Alfred, you've got it. I can get the money from my bank and bring it back with me. Or deposit it into your account in the city while I'm there, if you'd rather do it that way."

Troyer threw his head back and began a booming laugh that he as quickly cut short when he remembered that others in the house were sleeping. He ended with a subdued chuckle and a shake of his head. "We aren't needing to borrow from you this time, my friend. We have more than enough to buy with our own cash. Thanks to you."

"Thanks to your own hard work, then. I had nothing to do with it."

"We both know better," Alfred insisted.

"I did nothing."

"We both know better," the baker/businessman, perhaps now brewer, insisted.

Ben shrugged and took another swallow. As beers went, this one truly did stand out head and shoulders above the crowd, its flavors hearty and clean and very slightly effervescent.

"What I wish to offer," Alfred went on, "is a share, Ben. If you want—since always you complain and try to turn away—if you want, this time I will not insist you take your share of the business in cash. If you want, this time I will put your share into the brewery, eh?"

This was an old and sometimes almost embarrassing situation. Ever since Ben Cartwright gave Alfred Troyer a bit of help long ago, Alfred had insisted on assigning Ben a five percent participation in the Troyer affairs. That wasn't so bad now, but Ben had found it awfully uncomfortable in those first years when pennies were being set aside for Ben Cartwright when they should have been spent to provide a better living for EmmaBeth and the children. Then as now, though, every toll collected, every loaf of bread sold, every rick of hay or peck of grain gave Ben his mite. Alfred was as honest as he was proud, and never would have thought of trying to break off an obligation that Ben himself counted long since paid in full and then some.

"Why, I think the brewery is a fine idea, Alfred, and if you want to make me rich off the sweat of your brow, well, who am I to complain?"

"You do not take this serious, Ben, but you will. One day I think you will."

"I already do take it more seriously than you think,

Alfred. I take *you* seriously, you see. I have real faith in your abilities. And your boys'."

"Ach! The boys, yes. And yours, Ben. Forgive me, I have barely inquired of your sons."

A smile lighted Ben's expression like a lantern, and the two men talked for some time about family, about the small but good things of life. They talked and finished those first two beers, and Alfred opened another pair. The fire was burning low, the shadows closing in tighter around them, but neither man wanted to add wood to the fire. Ben yawned and began to think about bed. Daylight was not terribly far away, and he had miles to ride tomorrow.

"One thing I almost forgot, Ben. Do you remember George Foster?"

"George and Irma? Certainly I do. They were in the same party that brought you, weren't they, Alfred?"

"Aye. I've known them all that long, 'tis true."

"How are they?" Ben asked the question, but he was sure he already knew the answer. He hoped he was wrong this time.

"You know George. Star-crossed. That's how he explains it. My EmmaBeth, she has other words for George. But then she didn't near die in the desert with him that time. She only came out later. Me, I've a soft spot in my brain for George and Irma and the others in that poor, sad train. Thank the good Lord you rescued us then, Ben. Those few of us as was still alive. Thank Him an' thank you too."

"I didn't—"

"I know. We won't go into that again. What I started off to talk about here was George. He was asking after you, Ben. Wanted me to rush word to him when you came by. I, uh, suppose it's the same old thing. He'll be wanting a loan of you."

Ben sighed. "I suppose so."

It was odd, he mused, how two men with such seemingly identical opportunities as Alfred Troyer and George

Foster could find themselves on such wildly opposite courses now.

Since that time years ago, Alfred Troyer had prospered, and was continuing to expand and grow and plan and prosper all the more. If Alfred Troyer and his sons determined to build themselves a brewery, then a brewery there soon would be. And a fine one too. Ben had no doubt about that.

But should George Foster decide to build himself a brewery, it was not inconceivable that the Germans and the Dutch would all rise up and declare they would no longer wish to drink beer and the market for the sale of beer would instantly collapse.

George had a way about him. A talent. He possessed a rare but true ability to take a good situation and make the worst of it.

George and Alfred had come into these mountains together. By the time they finally departed Truckee Meadows, neither one of them owned much more than the clothes on their backs and the power contained within those same broad backs.

Alfred . . . well, all a man had to do was sit where Ben was now and look around him. That was proof enough of what Alfred had made of himself.

George Foster had climbed into these same mountains. Waded through the same placer streams. Burrowed into the same hillsides.

George squeezed a bare living out of a marginal placer claim, then managed to find a buyer for his claim just three days before a spring torrent scoured the stream down to bedrock and disclosed a pocket of corn nuggets worth thousands.

George and Irma scrimped and starved and worked themselves ragged so they could accumulate enough capital to, for once, do things right and buy a truly paying proposition. They bought a hardrock claim that held genuinely excellent prospects. The vein assayed better the farther they dug. Then the shoring gave way—George swore it couldn't have been his fault, that he had done everything just exactly right this time—and the drift was obliterated in a fall that George barely escaped with his life. Water below, and dangerously loose and rotten rock above, made it impossible to open the mine again. George wound up selling the claim for pennies on the dollar, to someone who had capital enough to go back in. The new owner was said to be reaping a fine harvest from his investment.

George launched a freight hauling venture—using mules and pack frames purchased on interest-free credit from Ben, as a matter of fact—only to be wiped out by an avalanche. He hadn't chosen to purchase insurance against such a loss.

And those were merely samples. George's and Irma's lives in the gold camps of the Sierras were one long litany of many such losses and failures and almost-but-not-quites.

So it would not be at all surprising if now George was wanting another loan from Ben. Not charity, of course. Not a handout. But a loan. George seemed always to be in need of a loan for one purpose or another.

"If you'd rather I didn't say anything to him ..." Alfred suggested.

"No, by all means do as he asked, old friend. I, uh, I'll be leaving first thing in the morning. But I'll be coming back through here in, what, three weeks. Something like that. That gives you plenty of time to send word to George. He can meet me here on my way back to the Ponderosa if he likes. And Alfred ..."

"Yes, Ben?"

"Tell George I'm looking forward to seeing him again after all this time. Would you do that, please?"

"You make a terrible businessman, Ben. You know that, don't you?"

"I never claimed to be a good one, Alfred." Ben smiled. "And anyway, tell me, how much is it you charge George and Irma for room and board when they come down? Hmm?"

"Bah! I charge them plenty. Same as anybody. You ask EmmaBeth. She will tell you."

"I believe that too, Alfred. Sure I do," Ben said with a knowing smile.

"That George." Alfred shook his head. "What can a man do?"

"His best, Alfred. I expect that's all any of us can do." Ben tipped the brown bottle back and drank off the last, sudsy swallows of good beer. He set the bottle carefully down onto the table that had held the chessboard and placed his now cooling pipe beside it. "It's late," he said. "And dawn comes earlier every year I get older."

"I have noticed this same thing, my friend."

"Good night, Alfred."

"Good night, Ben."

CHAPTER 5

B en had mixed feelings about saying his good-byes
come morning. He genuinely enjoyed the people he
was leaving behind, both the Troyer family, who
would be staying at the mouth of Blue Nose Gulch, and
the Hamers, who would be journeying onward on the
strength of faith and determination alone. He liked all of
them and would miss them.

On the other hand, he looked forward to seeing San
Francisco again. He had friends there too. And he had
business in the city as well.

Unfortunately, he could not linger here enjoying his
visit and also attend to his affairs.

He mumbled all the obligatory phrases, shook all the
hands that were extended, and as quickly as possible accepted the reins of his horse from Alfred's next-to-
youngest son, Phil. With a few final words he swung onto
his saddle and pointed the blue horse westward. It was still
a long way to San Francisco. A very long way.

Nightfall found him approaching the navigable limits
of the American—assuming, that was, that water conditions, moon phase, and pilot's luck were all running on a
high cycle. Ben truly hoped that all those necessary conditions were at their optimum levels right now, because the
slowest and most creaky of side-wheel steamers would be

46

able to carry him on in greater speed and comfort than this or any other horse could manage. And even if water travel lacked those advantages, what old seaman could ever choose horsebacking over the pleasures of being afloat once more?

He turned off the main road at the lane to Pittman's Landing and followed the glow of lamplight to the peeled log wharf that sometimes, but certainly not always, represented the head of navigation on the river. It was with pleasure that he found a flat bottomed, side-wheel waterbug tied to Pittman's rickety pilings. The craft was long and narrow, crudely made but clean and well enough tended. She carried a carved wooden plaque at the bow proclaiming her the *Queen O' Sheba*. The name seemed a trifle grandiose for so humble a craft, but the captain earned full marks for ambition. The scene was lighted by lanterns suspended from light cable strung around the quay. Despite the level of lighting, though, there were no people in evidence at the moment.

"Ahoy, *Sheba*," Ben called out as he dismounted and tied his horse to the wheel of a parked wagon.

"Ahoy yourself," a deep, rumbling voice responded from the shadows nearby.

"Are you the captain?" Ben asked as a burly man stepped out into the light. The fellow was barefoot and bearded and graying. His trousers were cut off and wildly fraying at calf height, and his jersey pullover looked like it might once have been issued to one of His Majesty's naval ratings. The gentleman's entire personal history seemed on display for anyone who possessed the ability to read what he saw there.

"Captain," the man agreed. "Also mate, deckhand, an' general roustabout." He cocked his head to the side and squinted. "You don't look like any o' Bill Dunnigan's bullyboy bill collectors, mister."

"I never heard of the gentleman."

"Then what is it you'd be wantin' o' me, matey?"

"Passage downriver," Ben told him.

"You got cash money fer a fare?" the aging tar demanded.

"A little," Ben confessed.

The riverboat captain grinned and muttered a few oaths. "Just my luck. Y'know? Find me a gennulman with coins in 'is pockets, an' wouldn't y' know. Here I be with no fireman. The jasper swore on a keg o' whiskey—much more sincere t' the likes o' him than any stack o' bibles—that he'd hire on fer the whole trip around, then first thing we tie up here an' 'e scarpers. By now I expect he's hip deep in gold dust, 'ey?" The captain winked and tipped his head the other way. "Mayhap the oath woulda taken better if the keg'd been full when he swore upon it, but him an' me had found other uses for the contents before that. What d'you think, mate?"

Ben laughed. "I think I need passage downriver, and that I can fire a broiler as well as the next man. Considerably better than some, if I do say so myself."

"Huh. Boats wobble. Even on a dinky little river like this they can wallow and tilt. How d'you know you won't be lookin' fer a rail t' lean over so you can pass yer dinner along t' the fishes?"

"If the deck of a windjammer in a high gale can't turn me green, friend, then I don't think that overgrown rowboat of yours passes for much of a threat."

"An' what would the likes o' you be knowin' about ships, 'ey? Or did ye take sea passage t' get here? Is that it?"

"Huh. I'll match you ship for ship, my friend, and storm for storm."

"Y' don't say."

"I do say," Ben insisted. "My whole early life was spent at sea sailing out of Boston, mostly to the Caribee."

"No."

"Aye."

"D' ye know the Spanish guns at Port Royal, then?"

Ben laughed. "You mean the ones a man can see on the bottom when the sun is angled just so and the water's

clear? The ones on the mole that the earthquake sub-
merged all those years back? Aye, I know them. You won't
trip me that easy."

"You've been there a'right, mate."

"So I said."

"An' so I believe." The man stepped forward and
held out a hand. "I'm Prince Royal. S' help me, it's true.
Just don't blame me for my old da's twisted humor. That
warn't his fault, y' see, for he, poor man, suffered all his
life under the name Truly Royal. After that I can't blame
him for what he done t' me."

Ben introduced himself and said, "I'll drop my bag
and bedroll here for now while I go find Pittman and ask
him to keep the horse till I get back."

"Take your time, Ben Cartwright. I still got a little
cargo t' finish off-loadin' before we can cast off. That
dang deckhand run off on me afore we was done un-
loading, an' you caught me takin' a breather when you
come up."

"Then give me a few minutes to get the horse tended
to, Captain Royal, and I'll bear a hand with your cargo.
Between us we'll get the job done."

"Dammee, Ben. A man as pays his way and lends his
muscle too? I'm thinkin' I could like you."

Ben chuckled. "Just don't cast off without me, Prince.
I'll be right back."

With Ben stoking the boiler and Prince Royal man-
ning the wheel, the *Queen O' Sheba* steamed downriver
until the moon set and there was no longer enough light to
steer by. Royal veered ashore then and they tied up for the
night, securing the shallow draft river runner with light
hawsers tied to trees. Once the boat was secure, Ben
banked the fire and made his way aft along the uncrowded
deck to join Royal. However much cargo the *Queen* may
have carried on the up haul, the deck was virtually empty
now. But then commerce in this country, Ben knew, ran

mostly in one direction: from the cities into the goldfields; there was very little freight traffic moving downstream on any of California's rivers these days.

"You're a good fireman, Ben. Know the job, you do. I, uh, don't suppose you'd be lookin' for work?" Royal ventured.

"No, but I'll take that for a compliment and thank you."

"You earned it, right enough. Sure 'bout that job, are you?"

"I'm sure."

"Oh well. Can't blame a man for tryin'."

Ben spread his bedroll on the planked deck and sat cross-legged, leaning back against the low railing and thoroughly enjoying listening to the soft, burbling rush of water moving against the hull and the feel of a vessel gently moving and shifting beneath him. It had been a very long time since he'd spent a night on the water, and the sensations, slight though they were under these tame conditions, brought back a flood tide of good memories. He pulled out his pipe and loaded it, then offered the tobacco pouch to Prince.

"Don't mind if I do, thanks." The captain of the *Queen* reciprocated by rummaging in his duffel until he found an unlabeled quart bottle. He pulled the cork, sniffed of the neck of the jug and, with a smile, passed the bottle to Ben.

The liquor proved to be uncommonly raw even by gold camp standards, as sharp on the tongue as broken glass and as subtle as a belaying pin. The first swallow took Ben's breath away. He gasped aloud and belched, then, eyes watering, took a second, much more palatable swallow of the awful stuff. "Whew! That puts the heat in a man's belly." He smiled and returned the bottle to Royal, who duplicated Ben's performance, gauged the amount remaining, and then reluctantly pushed the cork back into place.

"You may've noticed we'll be needing fuel pretty soon," Royal said.

"I noticed."

"There's a fella downstream a few miles. He sells cordwood that's fairly dry."

"You figure to load some aboard come morning, I take it," Ben said.

"Aye, but there's a wee problem."

"And what might that be, Prince?"

"I kinda hate t' bring it up, you bein' such a good hand an' all, but, well, we spoke earlier 'bout you payin' a fare for the travel?"

"You want it now?"

"In the morning'd be good. If, um, you wouldn't mind."

"I don't mind at all. How much do I owe, anyway? I don't believe we ever settled that question."

"No, but . . . well look-a here. How would five . . . no, four . . . how would four dollars sound to ya?"

"Isn't fifteen the normal fare?" Ben asked.

Royal shrugged and looked embarrassed. "I couldn't ask all that. Not with you doin' half the work. I mean, I wouldn't ask for that much, but I'll need two dollars for the wood tomorra an' I'd kinda like t' have another two laid by for a bottle when we tie up."

Ben smiled. "Royal, you're a prince among men, I'm sure, but a businessman you are not."

"Huh. Never claimed t' be one."

"And it's a good thing you didn't. Now listen to me. The regular fare is fifteen dollars, so it's fifteen you must charge. That is only fair, my friend."

"But your wage for—"

"A favor. Which I know you'd gladly do for me as well."

"But—"

"No, we'll not discuss it again. Now thank you for the nightcap, and hush up. I'm sleepy."

"You're full o' it too, Ben Cartwright."

"You aren't the first man to tell me that, Prince. I doubt you'll be the last." Ben stretched out on the deck with the starlit sky overhead and the friendly sounds of the river all around.

The wood lot was a rough and ready affair consisting essentially of a patch of muddy, beaten earth where lengths of split wood were piled in long, low windrows close by the riverbank. There was no wharf to tie to, just some pilings driven into the river bottom and a gangplank long enough to reach ashore.

Prince guided the *Queen* into a berth downstream from two of the sturdier looking pilings, and Ben tied the boat fore and aft. A thin, freckled man with red hair and wispy chin whiskers came down to the bank to muscle the gangway into place. Ben followed Royal down the bouncy, springing gangplank to shore.

" 'Lo, Prince."

"Hello yourself, Elroy."

"Do you got you some money this time, Prince? I can't load you on tick."

"I can pay, Elroy."

"In advance, Prince."

"I have it here," Ben put in.

"Who're you?"

"I'm the new deckhand. The captain asked me to hold his poke."

Elroy looked decidedly skeptical. He exhibited no reluctance, though, about accepting the two dollars Ben handed him for the firewood. He took the money with a satisfied grunt and placed it carefully—almost reverently, Ben thought—into a spring-mouth coin purse. "Help yourself, Prince. If you need me, I'll be up to the house." The house, Ben judged, must be the flimsy shanty he could see set high on the bank beyond the stacked wood. It looked little better than a brush arbor and hardly worthy of being called a house. Still, that really wasn't for Ben to decide, he realized.

"We have to load by ourselves, Elroy?"

"Sorry, Prince, but Angel's gone down to Sacramento for a couple days, and I hurt my back t'other day. Other than that, you know I'd lend a hand."

"I dunno, Elroy. Maybe you oughta knock somethin' off your price if you ain't gonna help with the loadin'. A quarter maybe."

"If you don't want the wood, Prince, all you got to do is say so. I'll give your two dollars back. Or this fella's two bucks, that is. So which is it?"

Royal scowled, but he had little choice and Elroy obviously knew it.

"Help yourselves," Elroy said, turning and quickly disappearing into the maze of wood piles. The wood was piled higher than it had appeared from afar. Ben couldn't even see the top of Elroy's head once the man went behind the nearest stack.

Ben looked at his hands. It had been years since he'd done this kind of hard, physical labor. Firing the boiler had been enough to make his palms sting and send twinges of hot, sharp pain shooting across his shoulders and down his back. Carrying aboard a full load of wood to fire the steam engine was going to be considerably worse. Still, it was a job that needed doing, and contemplating it wouldn't accomplish very much. He removed his shirt—it was already soot-stained and sweaty, but there was no point to compounding that by getting it snagged and torn too—and prepared to start carrying wood off the nearest stack.

"Wait a second there, Ben, an' let me look things over. You know how 'tis. Everybody wants t' take what's near, so that's usually the greenest. Might not burn s' good, 'ey? Give me a minute, mate, an' I'll see what we want t' load here."

Royal was walking up the bank as he spoke, his attention centered on Ben, who was walking behind him.

The riverboat captain was slow to see the two men who suddenly appeared in the gap Prince was approaching.

The men were very young, very ugly, very large. And each of them was carrying a hickory axe handle. The axe handles were almost as menacing as the dark and nasty expressions the two plug-uglies wore.

"We figured you'd stop here, Royal."

Prince blinked and took a step backward.

"You know what it is we want," one of them said.

"It's either that, Royal, or . . . you know." That one snickered and bounced the hard edge of the axe handle in his palm by way of demonstration.

"One leg and one arm, Royal," the first one said. "That buys you a week to reconsider and come up with the money."

"In full, Royal," the second added. "Every penny. Or the next time we get serious."

"But today it's only one leg and one arm." The first one grinned. "Tell you what, Royal. We ain't all bad. We'll even let you pick which arm an' leg you want busted."

Captain Royal looked a little pale. "Go back to the *Queen,* Ben."

"But—"

"I'd appreciate it if you'd come back in a little while an' help me aboard, 'ey? I, uh, might be feelin' a wee touch worser fer the wear by then. Y'know?"

"The man's giving you good advice, bub. Give us a half hour or so. Then you can come back and strap him back together, huh?"

Ben smiled. "What makes you think he's the one that will need strapping together?"

"Last chance to butt out, mister. Otherwise you get hurt right along with his royal highness here," one of the bullyboys said, lifting his axe handle in a menacing gesture.

Ben's response was to pluck a chunk of firewood off the nearest stack. The pale, brittle wood made for a poor cudgel, but it was the only object handy. And an axe handle can be a fearsome weapon if properly applied. Ben's guess was that these boys well knew how to apply that or many another sort of weapon.

"Please, Ben. Go back to the *Queen*. This isn't your fight, y'know."

Ben grinned. "Not my fight, Prince? Are we shipmates or are we not?"

"Aye, Ben, we're shipmates. So t' speak. And I'll be thankin' you." He winked. "When we've a bit more time, 'ey?"

"We tried to be nice," the bullyboy said. "Remember that, mister."

With that he moved forward.

Or started to. Ben had no intention of trying to spar with the young thug or of attempting to parry the hard, cutting strokes of an axe handle with only a clumsy hunk of stove wood as a defensive measure.

Instead Ben went immediately to the offense. He hefted his four pounds or so of split wood and threw it hard and fast, aiming at the hired bone-breaker's teeth.

The fellow ducked. Which was precisely what Ben counted on.

Before the man had time to recover, Ben slammed into him, striking him full tilt and knocking him to the ground. Ben wrenched the axe handle out of the fallen man's grasp, jerked it away before the one on the ground could grab him, and charged on toward the second thug.

With a roar, Prince Royal joined the fray, throwing himself atop the one Ben had disarmed. Ben figured he needn't worry about that first bullyboy any longer. Prince Royal wasn't any youngster, but he wasn't any newcomer to the rough and tumble either. Any man who could survive years in a ship's fo'c'sle could hold his own in a hand-to-hand tussle.

The second thug was startled, but he was no coward. He met Ben's charge with an assault of his own, throwing himself forward and swinging his axe handle in a wild, sweeping arc aimed at the crown of Ben Cartwright's head.

Ben blocked the blow with the hickory he'd taken from the other thug. The impact of wood on wood stung his hands. But that was nothing compared with what the hickory stave would have done to his scalp had the strike connected.

The man took half a step backward, obviously trying to gain room enough for another blow with the axe handle. If that was what he wanted . . .

Ben crowded forward, intent on denying the younger and larger and, frankly, quite probably the stronger man, the advantages he sought.

Again the man tried to strike a slashing blow with the hickory. Again Ben blocked it. And moved forward into the fellow.

The man tried to make room enough to swing again by moving backward. This time Ben, shoving hard upon him, pivoted on one foot, whipping his other around in a leg sweep that cut the thug's feet out from under him and dumped him unceremoniously onto his backside in the drying mud of the wood yard.

The man hit with a thump and a whoosh of forcibly expelled breath as the wind was driven from him. Quickly, before he had time to recover his wits, Ben snatched the axe handle away from the thug and gave it a backhanded throw. It spun madly through the sunlight to land with a splash in the brown waters of the river.

The fallen thug gasped for breath, then gathered himself ready to come off the ground in a rush. Ben raised the axe handle he had taken off the first man and prepared himself to meet the coming charge with exactly the sort of devastating blow this man had just been trying so hard to inflict upon him.

The impending rush, and Ben's response to it alike, was halted in an instant by the sharp crack of a gunshot.

The bullyboy and Ben both froze in place.

Ben looked quickly about and saw that Prince Royal had been stopped in mid-blow also. Prince had the first thug down on the ground with the fellow's face bloodied and surrender in his posture. Until now.

A quick scan of the surroundings showed a dapper, handsomely dressed man in his early thirties or there-abouts wearing, incongruously, a dark gray suit of finely tailored clothing, a pearl-gray beaver hat, and spotlessly clean white spats over high-top shoes with yellow laces. The newcomer might have appeared something of a fop and a dandy save for the chunky little pepperbox revolving pistol he held in one hand.

The pistol was of small caliber, as had been attested by the sharpness of its report. But small bullets are capable of large damage, and anyway, the pepperbox, with its seven or eight tiny barrels all ranged around a common axis had much more firepower where that first shot came from.

"You can drop the stick now, if you please," the gentleman suggested.

It occurred to Ben that he was the only one holding a weapon at the moment. Other than the gentleman, that is. He quickly dropped the axe handle.

"Don't be too quick to judge what you see here," Ben suggested. "These two set upon us, not the other way around."

The gentleman smiled. "Oh, I believe that, to be sure."

"Ben," Prince said softly.

"Mm?"

"He knows who these plug-uglies be, Ben, fer he's the one as sent 'em."

"Pardon me?"

"That gent wi' the wee gun, Ben? That's Wild Bill Dunnigan his own self, Ben. That's the man as wants to . . . how shall I be puttin' this . . ."

"Wants to collect that which is his right and proper due," Dunnigan finished for him.

"Aye," Prince agreed. "Just what I was fixin' t' say me own self."

Dunnigan glanced down at his erstwhile bill collectors. The look he gave them was not pleasant.

"Dammit, boss, if it hadn't been for this fella here, why—"

"Shut up. You too, Tip. Both of you crawl out of here like the whipped dogs you are. Get out of my sight."

The two thugs picked themselves up and limped off into the maze of wood stacks. Dunnigan himself—and his pistol—remained.

"No doubt you were already on your way to see me, Captain Royal," Dunnigan sneered.

William Dunnigan was a man who looked and dressed every inch the gentleman. Somehow Ben disbelieved the image the man tried so very hard to project.

"If ye'll believe that, Willie, then o' course I'd be pleased to attest to it," Royal said lightly.

"We both know better, don't we, Captain?" Dunnigan took a deep breath and ended it in a loudly theatrical sigh of disbelief. "So sad, Captain, but I must make an example of you. Sorry." He raised his pistol, the blunt snout of the little gun aimed more or less in the direction of Prince Royal now.

"Now just hold it a minute here," Ben protested. "May I ask what this is all about?"

"Commerce," Dunnigan said calmly. "Collection of a just debt."

"You would maim a man or kill him for the sake of a few dollars?" Ben asked.

Dunnigan gave him a cold, uncomprehending look. "Of course."

"How much does he owe?" Ben assumed the debt must be considerable. Several thousand dollars, probably. He guessed Prince must have borrowed from this usurious scoundrel in order to purchase the *Queen O' Sheba*.

"Seventy-two dollars," Dunnigan said. "Payable now, old man. Or else."

"Seventy-two?" Ben gasped. "And you would have his arm and leg broken for seventy-two dollars?"

"He owes me," Dunnigan insisted. "What does it matter how much? The point is, he owes me."

"I borrowed twenty," Prince affirmed. "The rest of it's 'is interest demands. Six back fer five. An' it rises each week. I owe 'im, though, Ben. No mistake 'bout that. I owe 'im. I just don't, um, happen t' be able t' pay. T'day, that is. T'morrow I'm sure t' get a good cargo. Enough t' set me right up again. You'll see."

"Tomorrow, old man, you'll be dead and . . . I was about to say buried. But who would pay to bury you, hmm? No one, that's who. They'll likely just dump your body into the water and let it rot there."

"Then be kind enough t' push it out inta the saltwater, 'ey, an' I'll hold ye no grudge."

"Both of you quit talking like that," Ben grumbled. "Seventy-two dollars?"

"That is what I said, yes."

"You'll leave him alone if that is paid?"

"Reluctantly," Dunnigan answered. "I would still need to find an example for the others to remember and tremble over. But naturally I would be forced to leave the old fool be if his debt were paid."

"Then put the gun away. I'll pay it for him."

"Ben! You can't."

"I probably shouldn't, but I can and I will. Although I must say, Prince, you charge an awful amount for a simple passage down to San Francisco on the bay."

"But I couldn't possibly—"

"We'll talk about this later. Mr. Dunnigan, I'll ask you to wait here while I go get your money."

"Be happy to do just that, mister. As long, that is, as the royal Prince here remains where I can see him."

"Prince?"

"Oh, I ain't goin' anywhere, Ben."

Ben made a face. "No, I suppose you aren't. Mr. Dunnigan, if you would excuse me now ..."

"Be my guest, sir."

Ben bent and twisted, trying to ease painful muscles. Then he turned and went back aboard the *Queen* to find his poke and take out the seventy-two dollars that stood between Prince Royal and death.

CHAPTER 6

"Oh, I did like that," Prince Royal said with a chuckle.

"What's that?"

"You payin' the man that extra ten cent so's he could buy his bullyboys each a beer. That was good, Ben. That was real good."

Ben winked at him and glanced at the firebox of the *Queen O' Sheba*'s boiler. They were under steam and moving swiftly downstream with the assistance of the river's current. "Mind if I ask you something, Prince?"

"Ben, after what you done t' help me, you can ask me anything you care to. Anything a'tall. An' I mean that."

"I know this is something of a personal question, Prince, but there seems to be more than enough commerce on this river to keep a man busy. How come your freight agent doesn't keep your decks loaded and your pockets full?"

"Oh, I don' have no agent, Ben."

"Most do, I should think."

"Aye. Mayhap they do. But me, I can't see the sense o' it, payin' a man a tenth o' small wage when there's scarce enough t' start with."

"The point, Prince, is that a freight agent can find and book cargoes that you wouldn't otherwise have. It isn't

61

that he takes ten percent of what's yours, it's that he gives you ninety percent of what you otherwise wouldn't ever get."

Royal blinked. "I never thought o' it that way."

"Wouldn't it be better for you if the *Queen* was booked full?"

" 'Course it would."

"A good agent could do that for you."

"Ye reckon?"

"I do, Prince. And I'll tell you what. When we get to San Francisco, why don't you go with me to see my factor there? I suspect he'll know a good agent. He can arrange an introduction with someone who needs another good boat and captain."

"You'd do that fer me?"

Ben laughed. "We're shipmates, aren't we?"

That brought a sparkle to Royal's eye. "Aye, mate, so we be. But what can I do fer you in repayment, Ben?"

"Get yourself situated with a good agent, Prince, and you'll be making a good income. You can pay me back the seventy-two dollars I loaned you back there."

"Seventy-two dollars an' ten cent," Prince said.

"No, not the ten cents. That was on me," Ben said with another laugh.

"Ah, Ben. It's a glad thing that I run inta you back there at the landin'."

"Excuse me a minute, Prince. I have to see to this fire or we won't have steam enough to get out of the way of that handsome stern-wheeler I see coming around the bend."

"Then step lively, mister, if you expect t' be named chief firetender o' the grand little *Queen* here."

"Aye, Captain, it's lively I am, sir." Ben winked and playfully knuckled his forehead before he trotted off to stoke the fire and check the pressure gauge. It really did feel good to be afloat once more, he was thinking. Even if it was just on a side-wheel riverboat.

*   *   *

It was fairly early on a Thursday afternoon when the *Queen O' Sheba* tied up at a wharf so old it still had lettering carved into its timbers welcoming newcomers to Yerba Buena. San Francisco hadn't gone under that name for years now.

"You're welcome t' stay aboard long as the *Queen*'s in port, Ben. Save yourself the price o' a room that way."

"I appreciate the offer, Prince, but I'll be fine. Truly."

"If you change yer mind . . ."

"Aye, I know the offer is open. I tell you what, give me a few hours to get settled, then I'll come back and pick you up. I still want you to meet my factor and get that introduction to a good shipping agent."

"Oh, Ben, I don't want—"

"I know, but it will be no bother, believe me. Besides, afterward we can have supper and share a bottle. How does that sound?"

"If ye're sure t'would be no trouble . . ."

"It will be a pleasure, Prince, not a problem."

"Then in that case, mate, I'll be changin' t' a clean shirt an' mayhap e'en haul out me shoes an' see do they still fit." He laughed. "If I c'n recollect what I done wi' 'em last spring when last I put 'em away."

"I'll be back in a few hours, Prince." Ben shouldered his gear and walked away from the busy wharf. He found a hansom cab and climbed in. "The Carlisle Arms, please."

The cab driver turned to stare down at him with a skeptical expression. "The fare is two bits, mister. I don't suppose you'd mind showing it to me in advance."

Ben's initial reaction was to bristle. Then he realized, coming off two and a half days of stoking the old *Queen*'s boiler, his appearance was not exactly that of the upper crust. In fact, he probably looked as disreputable by now as the old side-wheeler did. It was no wonder the cabby was questioning him. "I don't mind at all, my good fellow," Ben said.

Once that matter was attended, he sank back into the

soft upholstery and enjoyed the ride along the San Francisco waterfront. The city had grown remarkably since Ben first saw it, and was growing still.

One of the things that did not change was the beauty of the ships that called at this far harbor. Their sails, stark and bright against the blues of wave and sky, were a source of never-ending delight to Ben's eyes. At times the ships seemed so appealing they very near called him back to sea. But still . . .

"Carlisle Arms," the cabby said as the hansom rocked to a halt on its leather-strap suspension.

"Thanks." Ben crawled out of the cab and the doorman snapped to attention.

"Mr. Cartwright. A pleasure to see you again, sir."

The cabby blinked, obviously taken aback that so scruffy a visitor would be greeted here by name, for the Carlisle Arms was a small but exclusive hotel where discriminating gentlemen could find accommodations of exceptional comfort. It was the hotel where Ben always stayed when he was in town.

The doorman whistled, and a bellboy sprang smartly to life. Ben's bags were whisked out of sight, and a moment later the assistant day manager was on hand to extend a welcome. "Welcome, Mr. Cartwright. Your usual suite is being prepared for you, sir. Please come in."

The cab driver shook his head in bemusement, then clucked to his nag and clopped slowly away down the street.

"I'll need a bath first thing, Nathan, and I've some laundry to be done," Ben instructed as he allowed himself to be led inside. The effect of the transition from riverboat to elegant hostelry was really quite startling.

"Captain Prince Royal of the steam vessel *Queen O' Sheba,* I'd like you to meet Mr. Alton DeShong, late of Sipes Mill, Pennsylvania. Mr. DeShong has been my factor here . . . how long has it been, Alton? Ever since my first visit to the city. Anyway, Prince, you'll not find any man more honest than Mr. DeShong. You have my word on that. And if he has a recommendation, I advise you to take it."

Prince's needs were quickly explained, and DeShong's recommendations were as quickly passed along. "If you wish, Mr. Royal, I would take the liberty of performing the introductions and, um, smoothing the path for you, so to speak."

"You'd do that fer a shabby old tar such as meself?" Prince Royal seemed to have been having almost as much trouble as that cab driver did when it came to accepting the idea that his recently discharged passenger/fireman— and friend—was in truth a gentleman of considerable means.

DeShong looked at Ben and winked. "You should have seen the two of us when we started. Right, Ben?"

"I'm afraid so, Alton." They both chuckled. "Both of us poor as church mice, Prince. But ambitious and determined."

"The thing I liked so very much about Mr. Cartwright, Mr. Royal, is that he was honest and true as granite. Was and still is. This man's word is better than most men's paper. And that's the truth."

Ben smiled. "Look who's singing whose praises, Alton. Why, Prince, I've known Mr. DeShong to surrender thousands rather than take unethical advantage of a competitor. More than once too."

DeShong blushed. Praise, it seemed, embarrassed him. He was normally of a ruddy complexion, and the embarrassment made him all the darker red of hue.

Ben's factor was approaching middle years. He was a large man with a barrel chest and a bit of paunch, with dark hair and a massive handlebar mustache. He had bright brown eyes and a quick, boyish smile warm enough to melt the ice off a still pond.

"If you're interested, Mr. Royal, we could get together, say, tomorrow afternoon? I'm sure we can work something out to your satisfaction."

"Reckon I'm game if you are," Prince said.

"Then I'll look forward to it. Here? Immediately after lunch tomorrow?"

"Done," Prince said.

DeShong turned his attention to Ben. "I can still cancel those appointments if you need, Ben."

"I wouldn't think of it, Alton. In the morning will be plenty soon enough."

"There are some things I'll want you to consider, Ben. There's an investment opportunity in Oregon timber. The key to it is the shipping, of course. You can buy up all the stout bottoms you want, what with all the ships still being abandoned in San Francisco Bay. But finding captains and crews to haul lumber in from the north, that's the rub. No time to talk about that now, though. We'll go over it in the morning, Ben. Now if you gentlemen would excuse me?" DeShong shook hands with both men.

Oregon timber. Ben Cartwright didn't care a thing about investment opportunities in Oregon timber. Why, he had all the timber anyone could ever want back home on the Ponderosa. No way to transport all that good timber across the mountains, of course, but the fact remained.

As for an excuse to buy into shipping, though . . . that was intriguing to him. Oh, he hadn't the time to go to sea again himself, of course. Nor would be want to leave the boys, even if he could walk the decks of a ship again. But to own ships of his own? There would be a great deal of satisfaction in that. There truly would. This might be an investment Alton would find it easy to talk him into, Ben knew.

There was always the problem of reliable crew, of course. But Ben knew he could put his mind to that too. Between him and Alton, surely they would come up with something.

"If you're ready, Prince, we'll go find that supper I promised you."

"Aye, mate, lead on."

*   *   *

"Lookit them Kanaka boys, Ben. Lookit. Why, me 'n you, Ben, we can whup twict our weight in Kanakas, 'ey? C'mon, Ben. Let's whup 'em, me 'n you." Prince raised his voice and shouted. "C'mon, boys. Me 'n' Ben, we're gonna whup th' bunch o' ya."

Prince staggered and would have lost his balance except for Ben's steadying arm around his shoulders.

"Some other time," he said to the muscular Polynesian sailors, each of them half Prince's age and in twice his physical condition, who seemed amiable enough but willing to enjoy the pleasures of a scrap if that was what was wanted. "Bartender, give our friends there a round—make that three rounds—of whatever they wish. And put it on my bill, if you please."

That brought grins to the faces of the Kanaka sailors and some whistles and shouted catcalls from other tables where the drinkers wished they had been the objects of Prince's exuberant, if ill-advised, challenges.

"Come along, Prince," Ben said. "I think it's time we call it a night."

"Aw, Ben. D' we have to?"

"I think we do, Prince, yes."

"If you say so, Ben."

"I do, Prince. Steady now. I'm going to let go. Can you . . . no, I guess you can't. That's all right, Prince. Lean on me. I've got you. That's right. Now the other foot. You're doing fine."

Slowly, very slowly, the two made their way out into the cool, salt-laden air.

Ben checked to see that Prince was securely propped in the corner of the cab seat, then leaned out to speak to the driver. "Why are we slowing down?" They were still several blocks away from the wharf where the *Queen* was tied, and Ben did not relish the task of having to drag Prince all that distance. The closer the cab could get them, the better it would be.

"There's a crowd up ahead, sir, an' some sort of commotion in the street. Looks to me like there's a fire or somethin', sir. Can you see the glow from that side, sir? You might want t' look out the other side o' the coach. I think you can see it better from there."

Ben frowned and shifted position. The driver was right. There was a bright yellow glow against the night sky, and the street for the next block or two was full of scurrying figures, most of whom were carrying buckets or pails.

Half a block farther the cab came to a halt. "This is as far as I can take you, mister."

"All right, thanks." Ben paid the man—in his suit and fresh linen, there hadn't been any suggestion this time that he show his money in advance—and opened the door on Prince's side of the hansom. "Wake up, Prince. Wake up now, man. You have to walk. Give me some help, Prince. Stand up. That's better. Now a step. Good. And another."

"Hey. Is that Cap'n Royal?" someone shouted. "Zat you, Prince?" A man Ben had never seen before but who obviously knew Prince came rushing over. "If your damn boat has set mine afire, Prince, I'm gonna sue you for everything you own," the stranger said, his voice ragged with anger and fear. "If my *Pretty Harriet* catches fire from that rattrap of yours, Prince—"

"Whoa," Ben advised. "What's this about a fire?"

"That leaky damn tub of his is what's caused this mess, mister. Damn ol' thing wasn't tended to proper before Royal here took off to go drinking. Likely the boiler fire was left too hot an' some clinkers spilled out. Something like that anyway. The old tub caught fire, and now she's threatening to send the whole damn waterfront up in flames."

"Wha . . ." Prince, more than half supported by Ben's grasp, stirred and pushed himself upright over his own hind legs. "What's that you say about the *Queen*, Marvin?"

"You heard me. The damn thing's burning out o' control. And if she catches my boat afire too, Prince, I'm gonna sue you just as sure as God makes little apples. I'll sue you for everything you got."

By then, though, Prince was no longer listening. With a cry of alarm he pulled away from Ben and went lurching forward into the confusion of men and buckets.

"No!"

They rounded a pile of stacked bales, and Ben, trailing a few paces behind Prince, could also see what prompted that anguished cry.

"No!"

But the denial was in vain.

The men who had rushed to the fire had—quite sensibly, Ben could see at a glance—abandoned the stricken *Queen* to her fate and were trying to save what they could.

The *Queen O' Sheba* was engulfed in flame, her planks blazing almost to the waterline.

The firefighters had chopped loose her moorings and pushed her into the bay into an attempt to keep the fire away from the timbers of the wharf and from all the other boats tied up nearby.

Probably the efforts of the bucket brigades were first directed onto the *Queen* herself, but by now they were concentrating on wetting down the nearby craft.

A light onshore breeze kept pushing the burning hulk back toward the wharf, and men with poles tried to fend the *Queen* away. That worked with the burning boat, but did nothing to stop the hot, bright embers that rose from the fire and were whipped downwind to spread their danger for a hundred yards or more. It was along this path of potential disaster that the bucket brigades were now soaking everything they could reach.

"Jesus," Prince intoned, his voice hollow and weak now. "Look at 'er. She's . . . she's . . ."

"She's gone, Prince. I'm sorry." Ben tried to turn the man away from the sight, but Prince resisted.

"Everything I own. Everything I worked for. All o' it, Ben. Gone."

As if to emphasize the truth of what Prince was saying, the fiery hulk shifted, listing steeply to starboard. There was a loud hiss as overheated metal came in contact with the cold waters of San Francisco Bay, and a cloud of sparks was thrown into the air like a swarm of malevolent fireflies. The men with the buckets had to scurry and scramble to meet this new threat, their voices harsh with smoke and fear, and their words angry and abusive.

A man in a dark coat with bright brass buttons came over to shove an accusing finger under Prince Royal's nose. "What do you have to say for yourself?" he demanded. "You left your fire unbanked and went off drinking, didn't you? Well, didn't you?"

Ben wasn't sure who this official was, but he was quite sure of what would happen to Prince Royal if his peers along the waterfront thought they had all been threatened by some failure on Prince's part. True or not, an accusation like that could make a pariah of anyone.

"He did no such thing," Ben said quickly. "I was his fireman all the way down from Pittman's Landing. The fire in the *Queen*'s boiler wasn't just banked, it was pulled completely. I can swear to that, mister, because I pulled it myself. When I left the *Queen* this afternoon, her firebox was empty. Every last ember was drenched and the cinder box washed out with bay water."

The official gave Ben a questioning look, obviously disbelieving that any gentleman dressed like this one was would have been serving as a fireman board a decrepit little craft like the *Queen*.

"It's the truth, and I'll swear to it," Ben insisted. "As for what you're thinking, you can ask any of the fellows who helped us tie up this afternoon. Though I wasn't dressed quite like this at the time, they'll tell you that I was the passenger. The *Queen* was the first and the quickest boat I could take down the river, and I worked my way. It was either that or wait until the captain could find someone else to crew for him. Anyway, you can verify what I'm telling you, friend. Ask . . . I think there was a red-haired man who handled the stern and the after springline.

Red hair. Mole at the corner of his mouth just about here."
Ben pointed. "Bushy eyebrows. I don't know his name,
but—"

"That's enough. I believe you." The harbor official
looked almost disappointed.

Ben glanced at Prince. The man was in a state of
shock, standing limp and listless now, staring out to what
was left of his world as the flames, so relentless in their
consumption of the dry planks above the waterline, subsided and began now to die away.

Before long the *Queen* would break apart. The heavy
bits, the engine and boiler parts, would sink into the mud
at the bottom of the bay. The charred pieces of wood that
the fire could not claim would scatter and become part of
the flotsam that littered the filthy surface of the bay.

In another day or two even the excitement of the fire
would have passed out of mind, and only a very few
people—like Prince Royal—would so much as remember
there had ever been a *Queen O' Sheba*.

"Dunnigan," Prince whispered.

"What?"

"Bill Dunnigan. He's the one as set my *Queen* afire."

"Careful what you say, Prince. Dunnigan had no reason. You didn't owe him a cent."

"He's a mean S.O.B., Ben. He fired my boat. I know
'e did."

"Even if he did, Prince, it's nothing you'd ever
prove."

"I'll kill 'im, Ben. I swear that I will."

"No, you won't. What you will do is come with me
tonight. We'll go back to my hotel and get a good night's
sleep. Then in the morning . . ." Ben shrugged. In the morning the *Queen O' Sheba* would still be lost. In the morning
Prince Royal would still be destitute. There was nothing
Ben could say that would change any of that.

"Come along, Prince. It'll all look better come the
morning."

"It was Dunnigan as done fer me, Ben. I know it was."

"Hush, Prince. We'll talk about that in the morning."

The wind shifted and began carrying what little was left of the *Queen* farther out into the bay. As the flames died, all that could be distinguished of the boat was a hot, red glow and an occasional spurt of swirling yellow embers, but now even those were no threat as this offshore breeze carried them harmlessly out over the water.

The men with the buckets slowed and finally stopped their work, and the atmosphere of concern along the waterfront turned to one of celebration. No other boats were lost, and no cargoes had been damaged. The crowds that had been so industrious in the emergency disbursed, the men moving swiftly out of sight in favor of the waterfront saloons where they could toast their own prowess as firefighters and saviors of each other's properties.

Saviors, that is, of everyone's property but that of Prince Royal.

Ben led a silent and sobered old seaman away into the night.

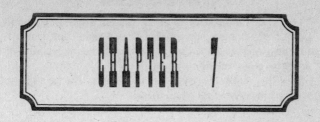

CHAPTER 7

"Dammit, Ben, I wisht you'd let me go on about m' business," Prince complained. They were in the waiting room outside Alton DeShong's office. Ben had insisted that Prince come with him to the meeting this morning, pointing out with depressing accuracy that Royal hadn't anything better to do with his time at the moment. "I got t' find a job, y'know. An' bein' pampered an' mollycoddled by you won't make that happen any the sooner."

"You promised."

"Aye, but ye tricked me inta the promise. You shouldn't ought t' hold a man t' a promise 'e was tricked inta."

"A promise is a promise, Prince, regardless of how the promise was obtained. Now humor me. Please."

Prince grumped and grumbled some, but he truly didn't have anywhere better to go. He sat with his arms folded and a stubborn expression on his unshaven face—his shaving gear, along with everything else he owned save the clothes on his back, were either on the floor of San Francisco Bay or were floating soggy and filthy on its waters—but sit and wait he did.

DeShong's assistant, a young man named Sterling, came into the room. "Please go in, Mr. Cartwright. And would you like some coffee? Perhaps some sweet rolls?"

"That sounds nice, Sterling. Thank you." Ben wasn't particularly hungry himself, but Prince hadn't felt like eating anything at breakfast. Ben was hoping he could be tempted with something now.

"You know the way, Mr. Cartwright. I'll be right in with a tray. And will your friend—"

"He'll be with me and Mr. DeShong, Sterling."

"Yes, sir. As you wish, sir." The young man smiled and bowed and backed away. Ben winked at Prince and beckoned him to follow.

Alton DeShong's office was like the man, comfortable and pleasant. Ben always felt very much at home here.

"Nice to see you again, Mr. Royal," DeShong said. There was nothing in his welcome to hint at any surprise that Prince would be sitting in on the conversation this morning.

Once the amenities had been dispensed with and the coffee and sugar buns distributed, the talk turned to business. DeShong brought Ben up to date on the things he'd undertaken on Ben's behalf since the previous fall, when the two last saw each other. The only surprise involved was the report on some breeding stock Ben had ordered from a farm in Virginia.

"They are already here? Why, that's a wonderful, Alton. I hadn't expected them to arrive for another month or more."

"The ship they were on made an excellent passage. Better yet, all six arrived here alive and in fine health. Frankly, I was afraid you might lose one or two en route. But they are all just fine."

"I'll take them back with me when I go home then, Alton. This should work out nicely."

"Oh, they've already left here. I didn't expect to see you quite so soon, and I knew you would want them in time for the summer breeding, so I hired John and Henry Marcellus—you know them, don't you?—to deliver them to the Ponderosa. John and Henry built cages to fit on their wagons and loaded everything, bulls and wagons and all, aboard the *Edwin Lee Sherman*. They left here day before yesterday. The *Sherman* will take them as far upriver as she'll float. The Marcellus brothers will drive the wagons across from there. I dare say your bulls will see the Ponderosa long before you do, Ben."

"We seen the *Edwin Lee* on our way down, Ben," Prince injected. "Remember?"

"Yes, of course. I wish I'd known my bulls were aboard her. I'm anxious to see them."

"They're fine stock, Ben, I can assure you. I looked at them myself. Not that I know anything about beef cattle, but these were impressive. Huge things, even after all the travel. If they breed true to type, you should have some fine beef stock in the future."

"Well, that's good, Alton."

"I wish I'd known you would be here so early, though."

"No harm done. My foreman Jean-Pierre will take care of them."

"Good." DeShong passed on to other business. After forty-five minutes or so, the flow of his talk slowed. "That pretty much brings you up to date on the state of your affairs here, Ben." He opened a folio and extracted a thin sheaf of loose-leaf ledger sheets. "As usual, there were a number of disbursements received from your, um, different interests." Which meant that a number of Ben's "partners" in the gold camps had sent money to him. "Here is an accounting. I spread the deposits among a number of banks, as always. It is all posted there. Let's see. There are the usual board meetings, none of them critical. Here's a list." DeShong passed over another sheet of paper.

Ben held appointments on a good many corporate boards of directors, but nearly all of those were cosmetic appointments, courtesies extended to him out of friendship by men whose business ventures he had assisted in the past. He rarely attended any of the board meetings, although he would have been welcomed at all of them.

"Let me see now. I believe that pretty well covers the past. Would you care to talk about the future now?"

"I would indeed, Alton. In fact, that's why I wanted Prince to join us this morning. I've been thinking about what you suggested last night."

"The Oregon timber?"

"That's right."

"You probably already know the gist of the deal. There is a man named Olsen who recently bought the machinery for a lumber mill. I know about it because I happen to have acted as his factor when he made the purchase. Found the saw blades at a failed company in the Sandwich Islands and took a flier on them, so I already had nearly everything he needed in my own warehouse. This Olsen seems like a good man. He was in the lumbering trade in Maine before he came here. He's been through the gold madness and found out the truth about it. Now he's ready to make a fresh start in the real world. He has the equipment, as I say. Now what he needs is a market. And of course I thought of you. You can contract with Olsen to buy the output of his mill and take delivery of the lumber at Astoria. The difference in market price between Astoria and San Francisco is ... well, frankly, Ben, it is remarkable. I think you will be well pleased. As for venture capital, I recommend that you start with two vessels. Ships are always cheap here. I have my eye on two rather nicely found schooners, each about a hundred fifty feet."

Ben glanced at Royal. The old seaman's interest in the conversation had quickened now that the gentlemen were talking about something he understood and loved quite as much as Ben did himself. Saltwater, it seems, is hard to remove from a man's blood. Once there, it tends to become a part of him.

"Of course you would know much more than I do about that," DeShong said.

Which was only partially true. About the ships themselves, yes, Ben would know much more. But about their values in the local market and their potential earning power in the coastal lumber trade, that Alton DeShong would understand infinitely better than Ben Cartwright ever could.

"If you are interested, Ben, I can talk with the broker and arrange a tour of inspection."

"I'm interested, Alton. How about you, Prince?"

"Par'n me?"

"I asked, are you interested?"

"Why, Ben, I got nothin' t' say 'bout such as that."

"Oh, but you do, Prince. At least I hope you will. I intend to offer you a berth as captain of my flagship if I do go into the lumber business with Alton and this Olsen fellow."

"But Ben . . . !" Royal gasped.

"No buts about it, Prince. It came to me last night. You are a seaman. And a man I trust. You would rather be afloat than grubbing in the bottom of some mountain stream. And you have no ship of your own at the moment. So what do you think? I'm offering you a partnership deal, Prince. You help me as captain, and I'll pay you in a percentage of the business. If we show a decent profit, why, there's no reason you can't be master of your own ship again in a few years."

Royal was so flabbergasted that for a moment he couldn't speak. Alton DeShong was under no such handicap. "I thought Captain Royal already had his own, um, vessel," Alton said.

"Until last night that was true." Ben explained about the fate of the *Queen.*

"I'm sorry to hear that."

"Aye, we all are. All but the one as set the fire," Prince snarled. He was not so astounded by Ben's offer that he forgot his anger over the loss of the *Queen.*

DeShong's eyebrows went up, so again Ben explained. "It is all entirely supposition, of course. This man Dunnigan had no reason to harm Prince. And there was no suspicion attached to him last night."

"Wasn't no reason for my *Queen* t' burn neither, was there?"

"No," Ben agreed, "I really did pull that fire and clean out the cinder box myself. When we left the boat yesterday afternoon, there wasn't a lighted lamp nor a live coal anywhere aboard her. I have no answer to how the fire could have started."

"I do," Prince grumbled.

"You'll never prove it either."

"If you gents don't mind," DeShong put in, "I have certain, um, irregular sources of information along the waterfront. You might say that such sources are a large part of my success in locating items that are needed by my clients. If you like, I could make some inquiries. If there are rumors, I might hear them where one of you might not."

"It wouldn't hurt to ask," Ben said. "Not that I expect there is anything to hear. But just in case."

"Aye," Prince said. "You won't hear nothin', but that'll be 'cause that S.O.B. Dunnigan plays things close to 'is vest. You won't hear nothin'. But 't won't hurt none t' ask."

"Very well." DeShong smiled. "And in the meantime, shall I pursue the question of those schooners?"

"By all means, please do," Ben said. "If you are in agreement with that, Prince."

"Agreement, mate? Aye, ye could say that in spades. Agreement an' more, bless you, Ben Cartwright. I almost feel a man ag'in, an' me poor *Queen*'s ashes scarcely cold."

"I'll talk with the ship broker and get back with you in another day or two," DeShong suggested.

"You know where to find us."

"Find you maybe," Royal said. "Me, I'm for asking an advance against salary, mate, so's I can refit an' find my own digs till I'm afloat once more." He winked. "You can put it on me tab, partner. Atop the seventy-two Colonial dollars I a'ready be owin' ye."

Ben grinned. "Fair enough." He stood and extended

his hand to Alton. "For a change, my friend, you've come up with something that I am genuinely looking forward to. Thanks."

"My pleasure, Ben. Just give me a few days."

"Not too many, please. Now that I know those bulls are on their way home, I'm anxious to get back and get a look at them."

"Quick as I can manage it, Ben, however long that proves to be."

"I can't ask fairer than that, can I?"

Ben and Royal said their good-byes and left the office. Prince Royal's step seemed considerably livelier going out than it had coming in.

CHAPTER 8

The big door creaked and groaned in protest as it swung open on the massive, handmade iron hinges Ben Cartwright had laboriously—and inexpertly—forged years before. Little Hoss looked up with a broad and innocent grin. Adam responded more cautiously.

It was the foreman, Jean-Pierre DeMarigny, who stopped in the doorway long enough to knock the hot dottle from his pipe before coming inside the barn to where the boys were standing in awestruck watch over one of the stalls.

Jean-Pierre joined the youngsters, hooking his forearms over the top rail and looking down into the straw-filled compartment. "He is pretty t'ing, no?"

"He's awful purty," Hoss agreed with enthusiasm. "An' Adam saved him, you know, Jean-Pierre. It was Adam." It was not possible to judge if Hoss was more enthralled by his admiration for his big brother Adam or by the small, trembling calf they all found so attractive.

"Oui, so you say."

"Isn't he just the purtiest little ol' calf you ever seen, Jean-Pierre? Isn't he?"

"Oui, Hoss, I t'ink maybe so."

"See, Adam? See?" Hoss practically squirmed with pleasure as he settled back onto the floor and peered into the stall at the brown and tan spotted calf that lay vulnerable and big-eyed in the nest of straw the boys had made for it. It seemed quite tiny there on the floor by itself, and quite sad. It's eyes, huge and brown and innocent, were as moist as if it were about to burst into tears. "Gol' darn, it's purty," Hoss said.

"We finished the chores, if that's what you wanted us for," Adam said.

"No, dat is not what I wan'," Jean-Pierre told him.

"You're mad 'cause I carried the calf in, aren't you? Well, he'd have died if I'd left him out there. The mama cow wouldn't take him, Jean-Pierre. He'd have died certain sure if I hadn't rescued him an' brought him in."

"He would," Hoss put in. "His mama wasn't nowhere 'round."

"So you tol' me, yes." Jean-Pierre chewed on the stem of his pipe for a moment, drawing air through it even though it was not loaded. "Hoss, I have for you an errand, yes?"

The little boy reluctantly but without protest abandoned his vigil over the calf. He stood and looked up at the foreman.

"I wan' you to go find Mr. Malloy, please. Tell him to make four cups chocolait tonight. An' Hoss. You tell Mr. Malloy from me I want you be da one to shave dat chocolait into da mugs 'cause you do it better'n anybody, no?"

Hoss's broad little face practically split in two from the force of his grin. The combination of hot chocolate and this compliment from Jean-Pierre together were almost too good to be bearable.

With a bob of his head and a partially contained squeal of delight, the chunky little boy left calf and brother behind and went racing away to find the cook and get that chocolate to cooking. After all, what choice did he have? It was an order from the foreman, and he simply had to obey it.

Adam, however, frowned. "You don't like chocolate. Neither does Mr. Malloy."

"But I do like the chocolait, Adam. An' if there is some left over, I t'ink it will not go to waste."

"Maybe. But why'd you want Hoss to go an' help make it? Mr. Malloy doesn't like having us underfoot in his kitchen."

"No, is true, Adam. I want Hoss away so you an' me, we can talk a little." Jean-Pierre absently fingered the empty bowl of his pipe, as if he were tamping tobacco. Jean-Pierre sighed. "You are one smart boy, Adam. You know dat. You papa know dat. I know dat. You see right 'way I wan' Hoss to not hear."

"Shouldn't you do the toasting before you put the butter on?" Adam growled. It was a comment he had heard his pa make before. It seemed appropriate to repeat it here and now.

"Just what I say, Adam. You one smart boy. But you must learn to t'ink, Adam. T'ink."

"I don't know what you're talking about, Jean-Pierre."

"Dis calf now. Ver' pretty calf. Ver' sad. Today you see him lay small in da grass wit' da eyes so big. See how he shiver an' shake. Even now, see. But dis afternoon, Adam, you see him, you not t'ink dat his mama have hide him dere an' will be come back for him. No, you see him dere, you grab him up, bring him home, save him, yes?"

Adam frowned.

"Adam, we got no milk cow here. We got no tame mama cow to put dis young one on. He too little to eat, an' by now his mama knows he is gone. Where you found him, Adam, she come back to dere long 'fore now an' see her calf, he gone away. Da mama cow, she won' be back dere no more, Adam. So dis pretty calf, he gonna die. Either starve to deat' or somebody got to kill him quick, keep him from die slow an' sad. You try to help, Adam, but you don't t'ink. Now somebody got to do a bad, sad t'ing or else let dat little fella die slow. Better you should learn to t'ink, Adam."

"No," Adam said. "That isn't true what you're saying, Jean-Pierre. What do you know about cows anyhow? You're just a damn Frenchman. You don't know nothing about cows."

"I am some damn Frenchman, eh? To you, yes. I say Acadian. You say Frenchman. It don' matter. We bot' agree I am different from you. More different from you I sometime t'ink dan from you papa. But that is no matter, Adam. Da point here is dat I know enough to know dat today you make a mistake. Because you don' t'ink. An' now dis little calf, he gonna die for you mistake. I am sorry, Adam, but dat is true. An' da reason I tell you dis, Adam, is not to make you sad, no. It is dat I want you should learn to t'ink before you do t'ings. You smart boy, Adam. Good boy. My fr'en Ben, he is ver' proud of you an' Hoss. He should be. You both good boys. But Adam, you mus' learn to t'ink more. T'ink ahead, no?"

"This calf is gonna be all right, damn you. You'll see."

"You listen, Adam, but sometimes you don' hear. I hope you will learn to hear, Adam. Hope you will learn to t'ink." Jean-Pierre pulled out his leather tobacco pouch and began slowly and methodically to fill the bowl of his pipe. "If dere is one t'ing I can teach to you, my young fr'en, it will be for you to t'ink. T'ink t'ings t'rough. T'ink about da consequences 'fore you do somet'ing, yes? Remember dat, Adam. T'ink ahead. If you don' learn not'ing else from me, learn dat, Adam. T'ink. Always t'ink. You do dat an' everyt'ing else will be hokay." Jean-Pierre placed the stem of his pipe between his teeth and gave the youngster a warm and quite obviously genuine smile. "I don' mean to be hard on you, Adam. I only wan' you to learn. Hokay? Hokay." He ruffled Adam's hair. Then, even though they were inside the barn where smoking was forbidden in theory if not quite always in fact, he lighted his pipe and smoked on it in silence while the two, man and boy, stood over the trembling newborn calf. After a while they went inside, and Jean-Pierre drank hot chocolate along with the boys.

At daybreak when Adam and Hoss went to the barn to start the day's chores, the calf was gone and the stall was empty of the straw they had put there.

CHAPTER 9

It was eight days before Ben and his partners were ready to sign papers and commit themselves to the purchase of two nicely found if not quite perfect broad-beamed coastal schooners, and to contract with Karl-Gustav Olsen for the purchase—Astoria delivery—of all the lumber his soon-to-be functioning mill could produce.

The partners were slated to gather in the early afternoon in the offices of Ben's attorney, David Kendall Jr. The partnership would include Ben's Ponderosa Enterprises Inc. as majority shareholder, with Captain Prince Royal owning a twenty percent position, Alton DeShong ten percent, and David Kendall Jr., who simply liked the sound of the venture's prospects and asked permission to buy in, nineteen percent. Because Captain Royal's initial contribution was to be in the form of labor rather than cash investment, it was agreed that profit dividends accruing to him would be returned to the corporation until such time as it met the value of the smaller ship; at that time Royal would have the option either of taking out stock shares or an uncontested ownership of the sailing vessel *Egan's Pride*.

Ben and Royal arrived at Kendall's offices a few minutes early. Prince was nervous and sweaty, dressed in a hastily tailored suit of blue broadcloth. During the entire drive he had moaned and mumbled his concern that the whole thing would surely fall apart before the papers could be signed because nothing in his whole life had ever gone so wonderfully well before and now surely this would fail at the last second too. At this point Ben was not sure if he were more amused with Prince's concerns or annoyed by them.

"Calm down, Prince. It's all cut and dried, you know. All the details have been worked out." Ben opened the office door and motioned for Prince to go inside.

"Somethin' will happen, Ben. I tell ye somethin' surely will."

"Nothing bad is going to happen, Prince. Go on now. Inside." Ben closed the door and smiled at the youngster he found in the anteroom with a book open in his lap. "Why hello, Davey."

The little boy brightened when he saw who had come in. "Hello, sir. Is Hoss with you, sir, is he?"

"Sorry, Davey. Hoss had to stay at home this trip." Davey—David Thornton Kendall III—was about ten years old, just between the ages of Ben's two boys. Adam thought himself a bit too old to pay attention to thin, bespectacled Davey Kendall, but Davey and Hoss hit it off famously on the rare occasions when they were together. Hoss was younger, but even so, considerably larger than Davey. At times he almost seemed the older of the two, leading the shy and hesitant Davey into boyish adventures that Davey never would have dared on his own. "Next time, perhaps."

"Yes, sir," Davey said with a sigh.

"Is your papa in, son?"

"Yes, sir. Mr. Haggarty had to go out on an errand, Mr. Cartwright. Daddy said if you came, you were to go right in. Mr. DeShong is already in with him, but the other gentlemen haven't arrived yet."

"Thank you, Davey." Ben tapped on the door to Kendall's private office and was quickly admitted.

As the child said, everyone was in attendance except the ship's broker, who held power of attorney for the absentee owners of the *Egan's Pride* and the *Coriapolis*.

"Ben, Prince, welcome. Come in. Sit down there. No, this chair should be more comfortable, Captain Royal, please." Kendall, a smiling, balding man in his middle years, rubbed his hands briskly together. His enthusiasm was obvious, his energy contagious. He had been Ben's attorney for several years now, and Ben trusted him implicitly. "Can I offer you anything, gentlemen? My secretary had to step out for a moment, but Davey could bring you anything you . . . no? If you change your minds, let me know."

"We're fine, David, thanks."

Kendall pulled out a bulbous, turnip-sized pocket watch and inspected its face. "I don't know what could be keeping Mr. Burdette."

"We aren't in any great rush, David. Don't worry about it." Ben looked at DeShong. "You're quiet today, Alton."

The big man smiled. "That's because I'm missing my after-dinner nap. I hope you appreciate the sacrifice."

"Oh, the prices we must pay, eh?"

DeShong laughed. "Something like that, yes."

"Are you sure I can't get you something?" Kendall tried again.

"We're comfortable, David. Really."

"If you say so. But I cannot imagine what is keeping Mr. Burdette. I told him distinctly that we would be meeting here on the hour. I'm sure I told him that."

"It's all right, David. Truly."

"While we have a moment," DeShong said, "there is something that might interest you, Captain. And you, Ben."

"Yes?"

"You recall that I told you last week or so that I would look into Captain Royal's loss?"

"Yes, of course."

"Yes, well," DeShong coughed into his fist, "there is a rumor. It might have no credence whatsoever. You do understand that, I hope."

"Speak up, man," Prince cried. "What've ye heard 'bout my *Queen*?"

"Yes, well, um, the thing is . . ." He coughed again and squirmed a little. "You should understand that this is only rumor, and—"

"Alton. Please. We understand that," Ben said.

"There is a man on the waterfront with money in his pocket and a sly look in his eye when the subject of the *Queen O' Sheba* is raised. A man named Fisk. But he won't say who hired him. If indeed he did the deed. He only hints at it, and that just to make himself seem the big, important man, you see. He doesn't actually come out and say—"

"Fisk? I know o' a man named Fisk. Thin fella with no teeth on one side o' his mouth an' a drooping eyelid on that same side."

"That, um, would be the one, yes."

"He's the one burnt my dear *Queen*?"

"Now I didn't say that, Captain Royal. I most definitely did not say that. I only suggest the *possibility* that someone may have, um, conspired with him about, uh, about your recent loss."

Ben would have expected Prince to become enraged by the information. Instead he became quite suddenly and quite thoroughly calm.

"You say you don't know who hired Fisk?" Ben asked. "If, that is, anyone did."

"No. There are the usual suspicions, of course. About the, um, gentleman Captain Royal mentioned last week. But there is no proof. Nor is there ever likely to be any. I, um, took the liberty of mentioning the situation to David. To, um, extract his opinion, as it were."

"Well, David?"

Kendall shrugged. "What can I say, Ben? There is no proof of wrongdoing. No prosecutor would so much as consider filing criminal charges, and as a practicing attorney I would have to advise against civil charges if anyone were to ask. There would be no chance of recovery. None. In fact, a civil suit would open one up to charges of false arrest, harassment, libel, malicious calumny ... who knows what. My advice is to drop the whole thing. Unless something changes, and changes drastically, I say you both should just forget the past. You have no grounds for legal recourse."

Ben glanced at Prince Royal, who, oddly, shrugged and said, "That's fine wi' me." It was hardly the behavior Ben had expected from the old seaman.

"If it helps, you might want to know that the gentleman in question is unlikely to concern himself with such small matters in the future," Kendall mentioned casually.

"How is that, David?"

"Oh, he is moving up in the world. He has big plans, that one."

"Really?"

"Yes, indeed. He has taken options on the purchase of four entire city blocks along the waterfront. He has plans to raze most of what is there and build a mecca for newly arriving emigrés. Hotel, saloons, house of ill repute, mining supplies, transportation services. It really should be quite something. The amazement is that he could have gotten all those purchase options without anyone realizing how large a project would be involved. But he managed it somehow. Managed it very quietly and very well. I hear it took everything he had or hopes to have just to get those options. But somehow he did it. Now all he needs is the development capital, and he will become a genuine power in northern California. At the very least he will become one of the wealthiest men in this part of the country, and I hear he has designs on even more than that. I hear he intends to use that power base as his entrée into politics. Who knows, he could become governor. United States senator. If he succeeds, there will be no limits to what he might accomplish."

Ben scowled. "A man like that—"

"Can write his own ticket," Kendall finished for him. Although not necessarily the way Ben would have liked to hear it. "All he needs is money enough and power enough. And now that he has secured those land options, I see no reason why all the rest shouldn't follow."

"I do," Alton DeShong quietly put in.

"What's that?"

"You know the man better than I do, Ben," DeShong said. "You said you and the captain had an encounter with him on the river. Is this the sort of man we could look to for the betterment of our community and our state?"

"Hardly," Ben said, shuddering. "Bill Dunnigan seemed to me a thoroughly reprehensible sort. He set his thugs on an unarmed man and fully intended for them to break one arm and one leg on their victim. They said as much themselves. They boasted of it. And Dunnigan's only disappointment was in their failure. Why, he was loathe to take payment for Prince's debt because it denied him the example he wanted to make for others to fear. He said that too. No, gentlemen, this is not a man we should hope to see in any position of authority. I only regret there isn't anything we can do to prevent his success."

DeShong yawned and scratched the side of his nose. "It could be, Ben, that there is something one of us could do about that. There is something *you* could do about it, in fact. If you wanted to."

"Me? I don't understand, Alton."

DeShong sniffed and leaned forward. Before he could explain, though, there was a tapping on the door. Burdette, the ship's broker, and a small coterie of prissy assistants had arrived with the papers on the *Coriapolis* and *Egan's Pride*. The afternoon's business was about to begin.

"Ben. I'm delighted to see you today. Please come in. We've reserved a seat for you here. Why, I simply can't tell you, Ben, how happy I was to hear that you would be sitting in with us today. Gentlemen! Do you all know Mr.

Cartwright? Ben is, ha ha, our invisible board member. The one who is never able to put in an appearance. Why, if I remember correctly, Ben, this will only be the third meeting you've been able to attend. A singular occasion indeed. Paul, get the gentleman something to drink, please."

"Yes, suh. And what would be yo' pleasure, Mr. Cartwright?" the huge Negro asked.

"Coffee please, Paul."

"Very good, sir." The man bowed—a man his size could be polite without seeming obsequious—and left his usual position at the back of the high-wheeled wicker chair that carried his employer, mentor and, indeed, friend, Marcus Simeon. He returned a moment later with a small tray that he set beside Ben's assigned chair at the impressively long conference table. Ben noted that in addition to the coffee, Paul had been thoughtful enough to also bring a plate of crisp, buttery Scottish shortbreads.

"I think everyone is here, gentlemen, if we would care to start now," Simeon said. Even though the man in the wheelchair did not raise his voice or attempt to project it in any way, he was heard and heeded by every man in the room. Without further prompting, the handsomely dressed gentlemen began drifting to their seats.

The long table was fully occupied along both sides, the only vacant spots open being at the two ends. When the other gentlemen were seated, Paul wheeled Marcus Simeon's chair to its place at the head of the huge table.

"I declare this meeting of the board of directors of the Golden State Marine Bank and Trust open," Simeon said formally. "Mr. Secretary, you may call the roll, please."

That was dispensed with, and the directors of the most influential house of finance in California began attending to the routine of business. Ben remained mostly silent, asking nothing, voting with Marcus whenever a question was placed on the table. He knew some of the other men here, but none as well as he knew Marcus Simeon, who was the founder and still the driving force behind Golden State Marine.

After an hour or so they broke for refreshments and cigars. It was immediately after that that the major request of the session was brought under discussion.

"Paul, please tell Mr. Dunnigan we are ready to receive his proposition now," Simeon said.

Paul left. When he returned, he introduced William Cole Dunnigan to the Golden State Marine board of directors.

"You already know something about why I am here, gentlemen, but let me tell you the rest. In particular, allow me to explain to you how this magnificent development will benefit each and every one of you. . . ."

Ben crossed his arms and, along with the other members of the board, settled back to give his full attention to Bill Dunnigan's application for a development loan in the amount of $117,000.

"Thank you, Mr. Dunnigan," Marcus said. "Your plan seems very complete and well thought out, if I may say so. Gentlemen? Any questions?"

There were a few. A man whose name, Ben thought, was Windemere wanted assurances once again that all the purchase options were securely in hand.

"I have them here for you to examine, gents," Dunnigan told them. "Each of them sworn and duly recorded in the Hall of Records. You can compare them yourselves with the plat map here to see that none are missing. There are no gaps in my holdings, gents. All I need more is the cash to meet the obligations. That and, of course, seed money for the construction. As I already told you, the overall development will proceed by stages. I estimate a positive cash flow and the commencement of service debt reduction beginning no later than February. The final development phases will be paid out of profits generated by these early projects. But your question, of course, had to do with the purchase options. I have them here, sir. Please examine them yourself." Dunnigan smiled and passed a folder thick with documents along the table to Windemere. Even from where he sat, Ben could see that the papers were larded heavily with wax and official seals.

"Is there anything else? No?" Simeon tapped a polished oak anvil with his gavel to capture the attention of all. "Are we ready for the question, gentlemen?"

"One moment please, Marcus."

"Yes, Ben?"

"I have no questions for Mr. Dunnigan, but I do have a comment to make. If this would be the appropriate time to do so."

"Of course, Ben. You have the floor."

Ben stood and cleared his throat. He sent a long, level look in the direction of William Dunnigan, who waited expectantly at the far end of the long table.

"It has always been my belief, gentlemen, that business has a purpose over and above that of profit. As businessmen, as men, we are obligated to follow conscience as well as opportunity. The project Mr. Dunnigan proposes today would without question generate immense profits for Mr. Dunnigan and, inevitably, some measure of profit as well for each man in this room. All you need do to capture a share of that profit is to vote Mr. Dunnigan the funds he seeks. But, gentlemen, I am here today to ask you to reject that request."

"Here now!" Dunnigan blurted. "You can't do that."

"Quiet please," Marcus said. "Mr. Cartwright has the floor."

"But—"

"Quiet." Simeon looked at Ben. "In all fairness, Ben, I hope you intend to explain yourself."

"He can't," Dunnigan snapped. "Why, this man doesn't know anything about me. He's never met me before this very meeting, and he—"

"You are wrong, sir," Ben said coldly. "Think about it. On a riverbank. A friend and I had just finished thrashing the pair of bullyboys you set upon him, and you came out to finish things with your pistol. You would have killed my friend, perhaps me as well, except that I paid your pound of flesh. Seventy-two dollars, Mr. Dunnigan. Do you remember me now?"

"But—But—"

"I know. I look a trifle different now that I'm not stripped to the waist and covered in soot and ashes. But I can assure you, sir, I am the same man you threatened then. And the same man who can now attest to your character." Ben turned his attention from Dunnigan to Simeon.

"Marcus, we've been friends for six years now, close as I can recall. I've trusted in your judgment and I believe you have trusted in mine as well. Marcus, I say to you now, do not put your faith or your capital in this man's hands. If you care about righteousness and civic duty—as I know you do, Marcus—you owe it to yourself and to your community to reject his request and to see that he fails. The harm he has already done to San Francisco and to California can never be reversed. But this board can help ensure that this harm will not be compounded on an even larger scale in the future. I am asking you to vote with me in opposition to a loan for Mr. Dunnigan, Marcus."

"Ahem. This is highly irregular, Ben. We don't normally consider things on the basis of personal involvement or sheer emotion. Mr. Dunnigan's proposal seems sound from a purely business viewpoint. It would, as you say yourself, generate handsome profits for each of us here today."

"I don't deny a word that you are saying, Marcus."

"Would you reconsider your position, Ben?"

"I would not, Marcus. In fact, I would take it a step further. I've enjoyed the honor of serving as your 'invisible' board member for these past several years, but if Golden State Marine in the wisdom of its board of directors finds that it should assist Mr. Dunnigan in the pursuit of his aims, then, Marcus, I must submit my resignation from this body and dissociate myself from Golden State Marine."

"You feel that strongly about it, Ben?"

"I do, Marcus."

Simeon rapped the anvil with his gavel another time or two and said loudly, "Gentlemen, I have known Ben Cartwright for as long as I have been in this country. I trust him without reservation. If he feels this strongly on the subject, then I have to go along with him. Do I hear a motion that Golden State Marine reject the application of Mr. William Dunnigan to— Murl, you so move? Thank you . . . Jason, your second? Good . . . gentlemen, I call the question, all in favor signify by . . ."

Bill Dunnigan, stunned and reeling from the shock of sudden reversal, gathered his papers into an untidy pile and crammed them back into his briefcase. Shaking his head, he stumbled out of the room.

"If you're wondering will he get his money elsewhere," Marcus Simeon whispered to Ben, "don't. Before dinner tonight, the word will have spread. No legitimate financier in California will touch him. Or in Owyhee or Oregon or anywhere else either. I can see to that."

"Thank you, Marcus. I owe you."

"One thing, Ben. You've not made a friend of William Dunnigan here today. I trust you know that and will take due care."

"I know it, old friend, but I doubt anyone has to worry about Dunnigan again. That one's fangs have been pulled, thanks to you and all these gentlemen."

Marcus smiled. "With excitement like this, Ben, we really should insist that you attend all our meetings. It would be good for us. Keeps the heart racing and the blood circulating, you know."

Ben laughed, and feeling considerably relieved, reached for one of the rich and crumbly shortbreads that Paul had brought for him earlier.

CHAPTER 10

Jean-Pierre found Adam out by the corral. Hoss was in the kitchen with Mr. Malloy, taking inventory of the tantalizing smells in anticipation of supper. Jean-Pierre was pleased for once to find Adam without his stocky shadow in attendance.

"Don' turn away from me, Adam. Stay one minute, *s'il vous plait*?"

Reluctantly, Adam returned to leaning on the corral rails. He had been watching one of the mares who was big with foal. Ben brought them in two years earlier, crossbred horses heavy with Belgian draft blood in them; they were huge and powerful and gentle creatures.

"You wonder if she have da baby soon, yes?" Jean-Pierre asked.

Adam nodded.

"Come. We take a look. No, I am serious now. Come wid me." He crawled between the rails to enter the enclosure, and after a moment's hesitation, Adam joined him.

Jean-Pierre approached the docile mare, who dropped her head in invitation for him to scratch her poll and the sensitive hollows behind her ears. Jean-Pierre complied, the mare's eyes drooping half closed. Then he patted her on the neck and motioned for Adam to follow as he made his way along the horse's massive, distended flank, the man's hand trailing lightly across the mare's coat the entire time so she could know where he was and not become frightened. "Good girl," he crooned softly as he knelt beside her hind leg and crooked a finger to Adam.

"See here," he said, reaching under the mare's belly and hefting her bag. "Da milk, it begins to come down, no? But she not ready to have da foal. Not yet. You see here?" He tugged on one of the small, fingertip-sized nipples so Adam could more easily see it. "Da end o' dis *tette*, it is clean. You see? Clean, dry. When she ready to have da baby, she get yellow stuff here, like wax. Den you know she gonna have da foal quick. You watch da *tette*, Adam, den you know."

"Is that true?"

"Is dat true? Hah. I tell you. Is true. You watch. You will see."

For a moment Adam looked pleased with this new bit of knowledge. Then he frowned again. That had been his expression for most of the past day and a half.

Jean-Pierre stood and gave the mare a pat, then went back to lean on the rails again, although this time from the inside. The horse stood there a moment more and then, no more attention coming her way from the humans, ambled away in the direction of the water trough.

"I t'ink, Adam, it would be good for you to not sulk no more," Jean-Pierre ventured.

That suggestion only intensified the darkness of Adam's expression.

"You don' agree wid me 'bout da bulls. Hokay. But you papa, he leave me in charge, Adam, not you. I do what I t'ink is best. Maybe I am wrong. Maybe you are. But it is for me to decide. Right or wrong, I do here what I t'ink is da best for dem bulls, for you papa, for you an' Hoss, last of all for me an' M'sieu Malloy. I ask you to understan' dis. When you papa get home—won' be long now—he will know better'n you or me either one what is da very best t'ing, yes?"

Adam refused to be mollified. He sent a withering

glare at Jean-Pierre and snapped, "You don't know anything about cows. You don't know anything at all, hardly. Pa should've left me in charge here, not you. I know what's best for them bulls, and it ain't being locked up in stalls. They been closed up long enough already. They need to be out on the grass."

"So you say. I hear you, Adam. I don' agree, dat's all. I do what I t'ink best."

"T'ink," Adam mimicked with a sneer. "T'ink, t'ing, dat, dem, you don't even speak good English."

"Better English I speak dan you speak French, what'chu t'ink."

"All right. All right. But that doesn't matter. You don't know anything, that's the point. You don't know a damn thing about cows or bulls or any of that. Why, you're from a damned ol' city. Pa's told me about New Orleans. So have you. It's a big ol' city. How could you get to know anything about cows in some city? Huh?"

Jean-Pierre shrugged and pulled out his pipe. He squinted at the sky and used a magnifying glass to light the tobacco. Only when it was comfortably started did he respond. "Men learn t'ings . . . t-things . . . many places. So do boys." He looked pointedly at the pregnant mare but did not refer to her, or to what Adam had just learned about horses from a city person, out loud. "I t'ink . . . th-think . . . what you need to learn, Adam, is dat . . . that . . . dere . . . hell wid it, I talk funny to you, you listen anyhow . . . I t'ink what you need to learn, Adam, is dat men don' have to get dey noses out o' joint ever' time dey don' agree 'bout somet'ing. I t'ink we do one t'ing, you t'ink da odder. Fine. When you papa get home, we ask him. You an' me. Whatever he say, dat da best t'ing to do because dey his bulls, yes? Oui. *Certainema'*. Meantime, Adam, I still lak you. Even if you don' lak me. I don' agree wid you, but I lak you. You see what I say?"

Adam did not answer. Jean-Pierre chose to accept that as agreement.

CHAPTER 11

Ben tipped his head back a little and sniffed. Then he smiled. The smell of Alfred Troyer's baking was unmistakable. It fair made a man's mouth water. Really, it was too late for dinner and too early for supper, and with so many hours of daylight remaining, it would be silly to think about stopping now. Even so, Ben determined to buy a loaf or two and take them along with him. A loaf of fresh bread should go a long way toward making tonight's camp a pleasant one.

He reined his horse off the road and toward the house. The first person who came out to greet him, though, was George Foster. Ben had completely forgotten about George and Irma and their desire to see him on the return trip. If he'd gotten across the pass before remembering his promise, he would have felt guilty for months to come, so he was all the more glad now that he'd decided to stop.

"Hello, George."

"Hello, Ben. Long time."

"So it has been." Ben drew rein and dismounted. He had been constantly in the saddle since an early nooning, and it felt good now to be able to stretch his legs and move about. Alfred and young Phil came outside. Ben could see glimpses of the ladies indoors.

"Howdy, Ben. Good trip?"

"Better than good, as a matter of fact." Briefly he told Alfred about the venture into shipping, not thinking to mention the lumber that had been the impetus for the whole plan. But then lumber was not important to him; ships and shipping were. "I can't wait to tell the boys," he concluded, his excitement showing. "Perhaps later on this summer I can take them with me to the city and we can all make a passage to Astoria and back. I can't think of much of anything I'd rather be able to do than that."

"If you'll be away so much this year, Ben, you'll be needing more help around your place, won't you?" Foster asked.

"Oh, I suppose I might, George. Did you have someone in mind?"

"Well, um, you know things haven't been so good for Irma and me. I don't know why it is, but things surely seem to work out against us one way an' another. Hard luck, I suppose."

Ben refrained from repeating the old saw about luck managing to attach itself to the fellow who works the hardest. That would have been cruel. Besides, George really was an unfortunate soul. He truly seemed to display a talent for taking the most and making the least of it.

"I hadn't much thought about taking on another hand, George. I already have Jean-Pierre for my foreman. You know him, don't you?"

"I do," George admitted without enthusiasm.

"Jean-Pierre is a good man. So are you, of course. It's just—"

"I understand. You've forgotten what it's like to be one of the little people, Ben, you and your partnerships and boats and everything. Alfred was telling me that you and him are going partners in a brewery now. I can see how you wouldn't have time for Irma and me. Not that I'm complaining, Ben. I got no right for that. You've helped us before. More than you ought. You got no obligation to the likes of us. Not anymore, you don't."

"Now dang it, George, you know perfectly well—"

"I'm sorry I brought it up, Ben. I won't bother you again."

"George, come back here. Now you know that isn't at all what I meant. I was only trying to say that I hadn't really thought about taking on any more help this year. Although now that you mention it, if I want to have any time to travel with my sons, I suppose I will need someone else. Jean-Pierre will have all he can handle with the beeves. That means I really should hire someone to run the store. That would work, wouldn't it? I could get someone to stay down at the Meadows and not have to be running back and forth between the store and the ranch. The accommodations aren't much there. Just a wide dugout near the river and some rock-walled sheds. But a man could fix it up nice if he wanted. Or a woman could."

"You saying you might hire me an' Irma, Ben?"

Ben scratched the side of his neck, wasted a little more time dragging out his tobacco pouch and filling his pipe. Alfred took the opportunity to slip away, obviously not wanting to overhear any more of this conversation than he already had. Young Phil acted like he was so curious, he would have liked to hang around and eavesdrop, but his father put an end to that. After another minute or so, Irma came outside to stand beside her man.

The pair of Fosters really weren't much to look at. Irma was plain and mousy, her lank hair drawn back into a bun so tight it pulled at the corners of her eyes. Her skin had a weathered, lifeless look to it that gave her an appearance a good ten years older than what Ben knew she had to be. Her dress was ratty and often patched. That wouldn't have been so bad except that she didn't bother to keep either her clothes or herself particularly clean. There was something about Irma that Ben had never much cared for. He did not know what it was, and he tried to pretend that it didn't exist, if only because it was not his place to judge George or Irma, either one.

For his part, George Foster was small and dark, with a drooping mustache and a cast in his left eye. He had only a few yellowed stubs of teeth, and his clothes were no cleaner or in better repair than Irma's.

George and Irma Foster were the sort of folks that charity was invented to protect.

"Twenty ... uh, twenty-five a month, George. And keep."

"Bless you, Ben Cartwright," Irma said before George had a chance to comment. "We'll take it. An' we'll be thanking you."

"Twenty-five, Ben? You know how prices are these days."

"You won't be in the mining camps where the prices are high, George, and you'll be running the only store for a hundred miles in any direction. Anything you want to buy you can have at cost. I don't think you'll have any problems getting along on twenty-five a month." Both of them knew, but neither of them mentioned, that the normal monthly salary down on the flatlands of California was twenty dollars a month, not twenty-five.

"In that case, Ben, we'll get our things together and come along to your place."

"I won't wait, George. I have some new bulls I'm anxious to see. I tell you what you can do—I bought the year's supplies for the store while I was in the city, and all of that is on its way about two days behind me. Chuck Crane's freight outfit is hauling it across for me. I'll give you a note to Chuck and ask him to carry you and Irma and your baggage. That way you'll be there to unload everything at the store, and you'll know what you have and where it is."

"That sounds real nice, Ben. Real nice."

"We do appreciate what you're doing for us, Ben, we truly do."

"I'm sure it's going to work out well for all of us,"

Ben said. "Now if you'd care to help me pick out some of Alfred's good bread to carry along for supper, I'll be on my way again. I've been away from home too long as it is, and I'm anxious to see my boys again as well as those new bulls."

CHAPTER 12

The bull. That awful bull. It was killing him. Pushing on him. Pressing the air from him and the life right along with it.

The danged old bull. He should have . . . never mind that.

Adam could hear Hoss screaming and crying. Adam wondered how hard little Hoss would cry when they buried him.

Oh, Pa was gonna be awful mad when he got home and found what he had done, Adam thought. But Pa wouldn't be able to punish him because there wouldn't be an Adam then. That was a terrible thought. But a true one. Funny how detached he felt right now, like he wasn't hardly a part of everything that was going on.

And he couldn't hardly see anything—he wasn't sure if that was because he really couldn't or if he just didn't want to right now.

But he could hear just fine. Mostly there were the two things that he could hear. Hoss screaming, and the dull, coarse, gritty sound the bull's horns made when they scraped through the gravel so close on either side of his own chest. Both those things were awful loud. Everything else seemed kind of unimportant at the moment. The sounds of a slamming door. Those of running footsteps. Those didn't seem much interesting to him. Not right now.

Oh, Lordy!

He could feel the weight of the dang old bull pushing at him. Pushing. Driving the life out of him. He was getting sick to his stomach. He was gonna throw up. He knew he was. Oh, Lordy, Lordy, this ugly awful miserable dang bull was *killing* him and—

Something thumped—a hard, resonant, *thunk* sort of sound like whacking a pumpkin that wasn't hollow . . . if that made sense, which he supposed it didn't—close underneath his chin.

Adam could hear . . . he wasn't sure what it was he was hearing now.

He opened his eyes and tried to concentrate on looking around. He could see the back of the bull's neck and the boss of its horns, but that wasn't all he could see now. This time when he looked he could see—he blinked—a boot? He thought it was. But what would a boot be doing on the back of a bull's head anyhow?

Kicking, that's what. The boot whipped back and then forward again, kicking at the ol' bull that was busy killing Adam.

The boot kicked the bull once, twice, four or five times.

Still the pressure was crushing down. Sending clouds of mist and misery like a shroud over Adam's eyes. Half blinding him. Slowly driving the life force from him.

The boot kicked again, and now there was a hand. Two hands. Grime in the creases of the thumbs. One fingernail discolored like as if it'd been hit by a hammer or something. Dark hairs short and curling at the wrists.

Hoss was still screaming.

So was Jean-Pierre.

Adam was sure he could hear Jean-Pierre's voice now.

Lordy, he never should of let those damn bulls out of

the stalls. He should of listened to Jean-Pierre. Why didn't he listen? Why didn't he?

Jean-Pierre—it was him who'd come running—was grunting and kicking and shoving at the damn ol' bull that had Adam pinned to the ground.

The rocklike boss continued to push hard against Adam's chest—something, cartilage or maybe a rib, cracked and loudly let go; Adam screamed for the first time since the bull began savaging him—and Jean-Pierre pushed and shoved at the horns, trying to drag the bull off Adam, trying to drag Adam out from underneath the bull.

The pain of the rib going had the odd effect of stimulating Adam into a clearer state of consciousness than he'd been in. The shock of it was cold and jarring and brought him wide awake. And terrified to a degree he hadn't had time to get in before now.

He screamed. And screamed again. Now that he'd started, he couldn't make himself stop screaming.

Jean-Pierre grunted and puffed. He kicked frantically at the side of the bull's face. Pulled and wrestled at its horns. Finally he bent and took a good, two-handed grip on one horn. With a mighty effort he lifted, pulling the bull's head up enough to ease at least momentarily the brutal weight that was pressing down onto Adam, enough at least momentarily to let Adam breathe.

The inrush of fresh oxygen-filled air sent lances and wavelets of pain stabbing sharp and cutting through Adam's chest. He did not mind that particular pain. The breath was more welcome than the pain was not.

"Run, Adam, go!"

Adam couldn't move. He felt paralyzed, as powerless as if the bull's weight still pressed him down against the earth.

"Go, boy, now!"

Adam was confused. Terrified. He began to cry. He lay there on the hard ground and began to blubber like a child.

Jean-Pierre shoved against the angry, snorting bull

with all his strength. Let go of the horn with one hand and used it to snatch at Adam's waistband. Plucked Adam out from under the muzzle of the furious bull and tossed the boy aside like a limp, corn-husk doll, like a scarecrow dressed in Adam-clothing.

"Run, Adam!"

Adam hit the ground. Rolled tumbling to the side, his chest afire with fresh pain.

He could hear Hoss screaming. Could hear his own racking sobs.

"Run!"

Adam could not run. He lay on the ground, immobilized with terror, while the bull, perhaps angered by the loss of its plaything, turned its fury on the man who had interfered.

With a loud, wet, fluttering snort, the bull tossed its head, throwing Jean-Pierre's grip off as easily as if the man's best efforts had been those of a bluebottle fly lighting on its ear.

Jean-Pierre lost his grip on the bull and stepped back.

"Adam . . . !" he cried out.

Too late.

Adam saw now what Jean-Pierre was trying to tell him.

The bull. The damn bull was still looking at him. At Adam. And Adam lay paralyzed on the ground not ten feet in front of the bull.

It was too late to run now.

The bull was coming again. This time it would kill him. Certain sure this time he would die, for the bull was coming at him with head down, horns extended. This time—

Jean-Pierre jumped in front of the bull to draw its attention away from Adam and onto himself.

He shouted and kicked the bull flush in the snout. The bull shook its head, not hurt, but perhaps puzzled.

Jean-Pierre shouted something in French, something

Adam did not understand, and kicked the bull again lest it have time to turn its attentions on to Adam.

The bull lifted its head, strings of slobber hanging out of its great mouth, and bellowed.

Then, pawing at the earth, it dropped its muzzle, lowering its viciously curved horns.

With all the force and fury of a railroad locomotive gone amok, the bull's powerful muscles corded, bunched, and drove furiously forward. It leaped, charging, swinging those massive horns in a sweeping, scythelike arc.

Adam screamed again and yet again, the noise of his screams and those of his brother's not nearly enough to drown out the dull, ugly, wet-meat thump of horn driving deep into living flesh.

CHAPTER 13

There was an ugly, empty, sinking sensation in Ben's gut as he pulled the blue horse to a halt and dismounted.

It took no great powers of deduction to see that something was terribly, terribly wrong here. His only questions were, what had happened, and were the boys all right?

A bull, dark and huge and bloating, lay dead in the ranch yard. Magpies scolded and fluttered at Ben's arrival, rising into the air only briefly and then settling down again onto the carrion that besmirched the Ponderosa doorstep.

Worse, no smoke rose from the cabin chimney, even though it was the middle of the day and dinner should have been on the stove.

Ben could neither see nor hear any sign of human activity.

He hastily tossed his rein ends around the hitch rail in front of the house and rushed inside.

"Pa! Oh, Pa." Hoss was there—the child was alive; at least there was that—and burst into racking sobs at the first sight of his father. The stocky little boy ran the length of the main room and threw himself into his pa's arms. "It was awful, Pa, it was just awfffful." He was crying so hard, Ben could scarcely make out the words.

109

"Hoss? Are you all right, son? Can you tell me what happened, Hoss?"

"I'll tell you, Pa. It'd be my place to tell you, not his."

Ben looked up. Adam was there. Standing at the bedroom end of the room. He seemed . . . different. Dark and solemn and . . . brooding, Ben thought. Something truly terrible must have happened here. But the boys . . . The boys were alive. Adam and Hoss both were here. He could see them, hold them, know that they were well. Ben breathed a little easier.

"Tell me, son."

"It was my fault, Pa. Jean-Pierre is hurt. He . . . he says he's dying. He's been waiting for you, Pa. He wants to talk to you before he dies. And, Pa . . . if he dies? It'll be all my fault. I . . . I . . ." Adam's face twisted. Ben could see that the lad wanted to join his baby brother in the relief of tears. But at thirteen, Adam could no longer do that. Instead he held his emotions in check as best he could.

Then Adam began to speak again. In a calm, chilling monotone he told his father of all that had taken place those days earlier. And Ben understood the guilt the boy felt now.

"You did . . . son, I can't tell you that you did the right thing. I won't make this worse by lying to you. What you did was wrong. But you didn't kill Jean-Pierre. Why, Jean-Pierre isn't even dead, Adam. And if we have anything to say about it, he won't die. Now take me in to see him, please." Ben held out his hand. Adam took it and led his father into the main bedroom where Jean-Pierre had been placed in the most comfortable bed in the house.

" 'Allo, Ben."

"Hello, old friend."

"Old but getting no older, non?"

"No," Ben insisted. "We'll fight this, Jean-Pierre. The two of us together."

"Bah! You t'ink dis hole in my ches' makes my nose not work? I can smell da stink of da poison. What you call? Gangrene, yes?"

It was true. Ben lifted the crude bandage that had been applied to the wide, deep horn puncture in Jean-Pierre's chest. He could see it for himself then. The rim of the nearly circular wound was discolored purple and yellow, and the smell of it was far worse than the sight. The stench that rose from the putrefying wound nearly gagged him. It was all he could do to keep from showing his distress to Jean-Pierre.

"We can cauterize it, Jean-Pierre," Ben tried lamely. "We can—"

"Ben."

"Yes?"

"You have never lie to me before. Don' start now."

Reluctantly, Ben nodded.

"Dis hole, you canno' clean it wid da fire. Not if you burn all da way t'rough me. Da poison is in my blood, Ben. I know. I have plenty time to t'ink about it. Is all right. We don' get no priest here, but I have time to pray for myself. Plenty time to pray. Now you are here. We will talk a little, yes? Den I die. Is not so bad to die, Ben. Somet'ing we all do by an' by, yes? So don' you worry. I t'ink dis over, Ben, make my peace. I got no regret."

"But Jean-Pierre, I—"

"No, Ben, please. Is all right. Truly. Only one t'ing. I ask of you a favor."

"Anything, Jean-Pierre." Ben was having a little trouble controlling his voice. Jean-Pierre looked so haggard and so very small in the large bed. He was dying and both men knew it, and there was nothing either of them could do about it. "You saved Adam's life, Jean-Pierre. I swear I will do anything you ask of me now."

"I ask much, Ben. You would hand me dat bag dere? Oui, dat t'ing made of blue velvet." He smiled. "Hoss, he a good boy, Ben. He bring dis to me from my room."

Jean-Pierre had difficulty plucking open the silken drawstring that held the soft bag closed. He managed it eventually and tipped the bag up so that its contents spilled into his palm. There was only one item. It was a ring.

"Like you, Ben, I 'ave a son."

"I didn't know that, Jean-Pierre."

"Oui, Ben, a son. Dere 'ave been reasons why I don' talk of him, but I love him ver' much, you see. I wan' him to 'ave dis ring. It is da . . . I canno' remember da word, Ben."

"Crest? Seal?" Ben guessed.

"Seal, yes. Family ring. Belong my great-gran'fadder an' his great-gran'fadder, maybe dat long back. You know? Ver' old, Ben. Many, many generation. Now I wan' my son to 'ave it an' give it someday to his son, to my gran'son, yes?" Jean-Pierre's eyes filled with tears for a moment. Or perhaps that brightness was only a reflection of the fever that raged inside him.

"What I ask, Ben, is dat you give dis ring to my son. An' dat you tell my Marie, Ben, you tell her dat I am sorry. I was wrong. You tell her dat Jean-Pierre say he make da mistake an' for dat he is sorry. You tell her dat I love her. You will tell her for me, Ben? Will you?"

"I will, Jean-Pierre. I will tell Marie, and I will give your ring, his ring, to your son."

"Marie Courlan' DeMarigny, Ben. Of N'Orlean. Mrs. Jean-Pierre DeMarigny, Ben. An' . . . oh, God." Jean-Pierre began to weep now. "Ben, I do no know under what name my son was christened. I am ashame' to tell you dis, but it is true."

"That doesn't matter, Jean-Pierre. I'll find him. I will give him the ring."

"You tell to him dat I love him too, Ben. You will do dis for me?"

"Yes, Jean-Pierre. I promise you that I will."

Jean-Pierre smiled. "T'ank you, Ben. T'ank you for dis favor."

"Thank you, Jean-Pierre, for my son's life."

Jean-Pierre sighed and closed his eyes. He seemed to shrink, drawing deep inside himself and actually appearing to become smaller in the big bed. He lapsed into a gentle sleep then, the worries of clinging to life and to pain long enough to speak with Ben all put behind him now, so that finally he was able to embrace the comfort of oblivion.

He died without regaining consciousness, drifting quietly away sometime during the night.

Hoss was inconsolable, but Adam only become even more silent and withdrawn than he had been since Ben returned home. Edgar Malloy merely used the event as an excuse to drink himself into a stupor, as he apparently had been doing much of the time since the incident, although according to the boys, it was Malloy who shot the bull and dragged Jean-Pierre inside to treat his wounds.

Ben decided to bury Jean-Pierre not down at Truckee Meadows near Ben's own beloved Inger, but up on a high ridge overlooking the magnificence of Lake Tahoe, a sight which Jean-Pierre had loved almost as much as Ben himself did.

Ben stopped for a moment to wipe the sweat from his forehead. "Slow down, son, we don't have to get it all done at once."

"I'm all right, Pa. Why don't you go back up to the house? I can finish this."

"That's nice of you, I'm sure, Adam, but there's no reason why we both can't tend to it."

Adam's eyes said more than his silence. There *was* a reason as far as Adam was concerned. Guilt drove him, and work was his punishment, or so it seemed. Ben was beginning to worry about Adam.

This chore, for instance, was something any normal thirteen-year-old would naturally want to shirk. Disposing of the too-long dead bull was as vile and disgusting a job as any Ben could think of. The animal had been dead much too long to be dragged away in one piece, and at this point being close to the carcass was enough to test one's stomach and one's nerve. Yet Adam attacked the nasty chore as if his salvation were at stake.

"Come on, son, let's walk up and see if Mr. Malloy has anything put by for a snack."

That was the wrong thing to suggest. Ben could practically see Adam's gorge rise at the thought of food. But the boy did not give in. Nor did he put down the sharp-tipped spade he was using like it was a flensing knife. He just kept working.

Thinking about Malloy, Ben glanced toward the house. The man was sobering up finally. Ben wasn't sure if that was because the boss was back or if it only meant Malloy had run out of the liquor he persisted in somehow acquiring. Ben wasn't sure but what Edgar Malloy would be able to find whiskey at a Temperance Society social.

Smoke spiraled lazily out of the chimney. That was a good sign. Malloy nearly always forgot to feed the fire when he was in his cups.

"Adam."

"Sir?"

"Up the hill there where the old road crosses the ridge. What do you see up there, son?"

"Could be smoke, Pa. More likely dust. I'd say somebody's coming."

"It could be smoke, though."

"Yes, sir."

"Do me a favor, son?"

"Yes, sir."

"You can ride bareback better than I can, and I don't think we want to waste any time messing with saddle and bridle. Why don't you jump on a pony and run up there real quick. If it's a fire, signal and the rest of us will come running."

"Yes, sir."

Ben was sure as sure could be that it was dust they were seeing. But the ruse of checking for a fire would be enough to make Adam take a break. Ben was really becoming concerned for the boy's well-being.

Adam trotted off to the corral. He took a bit of twine and tied it onto the halter of his favorite brown gelding, fastening the ends of the six-or-so-foot length of twine at either side of the horse's jaw to fashion a makeshift hackamore. With a lithe bound, Adam was seated comfortably on the horse's back. Ben pulled the gate open, and Adam jumped the brown into a run.

As expected, Adam's signal from the distant ridge showed that all was well. The boy pointed to indicate that someone was coming, then he trotted out of sight among the trees. Ben grunted and went back to the work of disposing of the bull that killed Jean-Pierre DeMarigny, and that all too easily might have killed Adam as well.

Twenty minutes later Adam rode into view again, this time in the company of a string of leggy Missouri mules that Ben recognized as belonging to Chuck Crane's pack string. The homely mottled-gray creature in the lead was unmistakable. There couldn't be another mule this side of the Mississippi River half as ugly as that one. Or half as dependable either. Ben set his tools down and began walking back to the house to greet his guests.

Chuck Crane ambled out of the shadows to join Ben at the corral rail. Ben's saddle horses and Chuck's mules were somnolent and silent within the enclosure, their bellies full and their eyes drooping closed.

"Looking things over before you turn in?" Ben asked.

"Ayuh. You too?"

Ben nodded.

Crane puffed on his pipe, the smoke from it pale in the moonlight as it wreathed his head. Crane was no more than thirty but was already balding. Ben had done business with him several times in the past and had come to like the young-old man from Vermont.

"Mind if I put my nose in your business, Ben?

Prob'ly my foot in my own mouth too, but dang it, Ben, I like you too much to keep shut."

"After an introduction like that, Chuck, I wouldn't think of letting you get away without me hearing the cause. By all means, man, speak up."

"Dang it, Ben, I know you've been friends with that Foster fella for a lot of years, and I hardly know the man. But your idea of leaving him in charge of the Ponderosa while you go off to New Orleans . . ."

It was something that Ben had worked out over the past couple days. He had to make the trip. There simply was no getting around that. And he couldn't leave Mr. Malloy to take care of the place. With Malloy's penchant for strong drink, that would be as good as a demand for disaster. Nor could he ask the boys to undertake a trip as rugged and uncertain as this one promised to be.

If Ben could take the time to travel across to San Francisco and then around the Horn by sea, that would be one thing. But the round trip would take well over a year by that route. He couldn't be away that long.

And there was no commercial overland route. Nor for that matter any real road to follow. From far western Utah Territory, where the Ponderosa was—not quite into California—a man could travel east or west easily enough, but there was no north-south road available. There were a few uncertain trails used primarily by Mormon emigrés, but travelers in small parties risked ambush by hostile Indians along those water-restricted paths. Ben believed the best and quickest way for him to reach New Orleans would be to take one of the Mormon trails south through the high desert to the tiny post known as Mormon Station, at the meadows the early Spanish explorers had called Las Vegas, and then turn east on the wagon route linking Las Angeles with El Paso del Norte and San Antonio, and finally, far distant New Orleans.

That way would be arduous, though, and potentially

dangerous. Ben would not consider exposing his sons to the dangers.

And so what choice did he have? Malloy was unreliable. Nearly everyone else Ben knew had their own affairs to worry over. George and Irma seemed his only realistic hope.

They had been quick to jump at the opportunity. At a suitable increase in pay, of course. So the plan was changed, and the store supplies were unloaded here at the Ponderosa. A notice would be posted down at the Truckee Meadows store site, and anyone wanting to buy or trade could make the climb to the Ponderosa. That way George and Irma would remain on hand here to oversee the ranch as well as the store. And, most important, to look after Adam and Hoss while Ben was away.

Two months each way, Ben hoped. Three at the most. Call it four to six months and he should be back.

"I mean, it isn't my place to be giving advice, Ben. Particularly advice that hasn't been asked for. But dang it, Ben, there's something ... I just don't think you should trust Foster. I'm sorry to say it, but I don't think you should."

"Oh, George isn't so bad, Chuck. I know he'll sneak a little here and a little there, but he's too timid to do any real harm, I'm sure. It's having a woman here to help with the boys that I'm really thinking about anyway. A woman's influence should be good for them."

"Maybe," Crane conceded, drawing on his pipe again. The glow from the active coal cut through the night and lent a cherry cast to his cheeks and jaw. "Something else you might consider, Ben."

"Yes?"

"I'm going back to San Francisco on the turnaround here, you know."

"Yes, what of it?"

"I was thinking you could write a letter and make up a packet. You know, the ring that Frenchy left and a letter to go with it explaining everything. I could post it for you.

You know you could trust me to do that, Ben, and I'd be glad to do it. I could post it United States mail, not just give it to some sailing captain or wagon boss but genuinely put it in the U.S. mail. You know? It would get to New Orleans in four, five months, or even less. Why, there's an outfit claiming two months assured delivery between San Francisco and St. Louis. And from St. Louis there's all kinds of traffic down the river to New Orleans. I'll bet the mail could have that package in the widow lady's hands inside of three months, Ben. It'd save you an awful amount of trouble."

"And what kind of trouble did Jean-Pierre worry about saving himself when there was a crazed bull trying to kill my boy Adam?"

"Aw, you know what I mean, Ben. No one would think a thing about it if you mailed that stuff. It's either that or take at least half a year out of your own life."

"I made a promise, Chuck, to a dying man. And I didn't tell him anything about mailing packages or sending messages. I said I'd find his widow and tell her what he said. And I'll find his son and hand the boy the ring too. That's what I promised, that's what I'll do."

"It was just a thought."

"I appreciate the thought."

"But you'll do as you told that Foster you would."

"I'll do as I promised Jean-Pierre I would, yes."

"I kinda wish you'd change your mind, Ben."

"I kind of wish I didn't have to make the trip too, Chuck, but a little inconvenience is hardly reason enough to break a pledge to a dying friend. Particularly one I owe as much as I owe Jean-Pierre."

"You're a good man, Ben."

"So are you, Chuck. Thanks for your concern."

Crane smiled. "Say now, bunions don't taste all that bad if you just chew on 'em lightly."

Ben chuckled and clapped the friendly freighter on the shoulder. "What say we go inside, Chuck? I think I know where to find a bit of well-aged brandy that you might like."

"I could stand the idea if you can, Ben."

"Then let's do it."

The two of them turned away from the corral and walked back toward the house.

CHAPTER 14

It had been years—sixteen? seventeen? something like that—since Ben last saw New Orleans. The great city had not changed much. At least not that he could see from the deck of the mail packet *Worley,* bound from Galveston to points east.

Actually, from Houston it probably would have been as efficient, or more so, to continue by coach to the delta city, but the opportunity to be at sea again was simply too good to pass by. He took passage aboard the *Worley* and frankly hoped for a squall to liven the journey. He did not get the foul weather he would have liked, but nonetheless was pleased with the feel of a hardwood deck slanting beneath his feet and the press of salt air against his cheek. The brief passage from Galveston to New Orleans was so exciting that it made him feel guilty to be taking such pleasure in the midst of so somber and serious a journey. After all, the tiny package containing Jean-Pierre's ring was heavy in his pocket, and the loss of his friend lay even heavier in his heart. Ben knew he was bringing an even deeper measure of grief to Jean-Pierre's unsuspecting family.

He stayed aboard the *Worley* as long as he reasonably could, enjoying each and every last small detail of warping the ship to her berth and securing the hawsers and, finally, off-loading cargo.

"Was there something you needed, Mr. Cartwright?" the first mate politely—and perhaps pointedly—inquired.

"No, Mr. Jonders, thank you."

"Bert, be a good fellow and help Mr. Cartwright ashore with his bags, will you?"

"Aye, sir."

The ship's officer took a step back and gave the passenger an abbreviated bow. "If we can be of any further service, Mr. Cartwright . . ."

"You and your people have been splendid, thanks."

"Glad you enjoyed your trip, sir. Good day now."

"Good-bye." Ben followed the sailor down the plank to shore. It was either that or remain on board the ship while his luggage went on without him.

"Take that bag, suh? Ver' good. You run 'long now, mon. The gennulmun an' me, we be fine from here, yes." A black man, short and wide of build, with a smile that was almost as broad as his shoulders and as bright as a crystal chandelier, plucked the bags from Bert—the sailor displayed no reluctance to rid himself of that particular burden—and took up position beneath Ben's chin like a porpoise tucking itself underneath the bowsprit of a cutter. "Whatever your need, suh, Henry Bloodworth be your answer. Guide, interpreter, bodyguard. Anything you require, suh, you call on Henry Bloodworth."

"And you, I take it, would be the estimable Mr. Bloodworth?"

"You, suh, are a mos' discerning gennulmun. I am indeed this fine fellow Henry Bloodworth."

Ben smiled. "And I am Ben Cartwright, Henry. It's a pleasure to make your acquaintance." Ben extended a hand, but the stocky man of many abilities shied away from it.

"You bes' know, Mr. Cartwright, that a white man shouldn't ought to be shaking no black man's han'. Not in this town he oughtn't."

"Thank you for the caution, Mr. Bloodworth, but I've become spoiled. I live in a part of the country where a man is as good as his actions and his word make him out to be. And where a man of color has every bit as much chance for fortune as any other. I fear I've gotten out of the habit of thinking it should be otherwise."

"Now, Mr. Cartwright, it ain't nice to tease an' titil- late like that. You like to get a man to thinking things that ain't healthful to contemplate. Black man get to thinking he good as white man, next thing he know, he neck grow six inches. Real sudden. Best to remember he place. You know?"

"No harm intended, Mr. Bloodworth."

"None done, Mr. Cartwright."

"If we might start over, Mr. Bloodworth, without the handshakes, I shall be needing transportation to a nice, quiet, respectable sort of hotel, something clean and pleas- ant. And then I shall be needing some help finding my way about the city. There are some people I need to see, and I have no idea where they may live."

"Mr. Cartwright, you come to just the right man to be your guide. Henry Bloodworth, he can find any soul who live in this N'Orlean. But first we go to your hotel. Sant' Hilary de Bruge. They have the suite waiting only for you."

"That seems a trifle premature, doesn't it, Henry, seeing as I've only just arrived and sent no notice ahead?"

Bloodworth grinned, his dark face bisected by gleam- ing white, and said, "No, you wait and see, Mr. Cart- wright. Henry Bloodworth never lies. Never."

When they arrived outside the tiny, rococo-decorated hotel front, the porter greeted them with fawning attention, snatching the luggage down from the roof of the cab and proclaiming, "You want me to unpack fo' you, Mr. Cart- wright? Be my pleasure, sir. Anyt'ing else you need? Press yo' clothes maybe? Don' you worry, sir, everyt'ing be jus' nice when you see it again. You jus' go 'long, sir, an' sign de gues' register at de desk, sir. You be upstairs in de back. Ver' nice suite. Overlook de cou'tyard, sir. Ver' quiet an' nice. Jus' what you like."

Ben chuckled. "Nice, Henry. Very nice indeed."

"What's that, suh?"

"I never spotted your church mouse."

"Suh?"

"Oh, I don't mind. Heavens, you're just doing a good job of things here. I'm certainly not offended. But I'm not taken in either. You had someone listening in. They overheard my name, of course. You tipped them about which hotel you were taking me to and to ask for a suite. Then the cab driver took us a few blocks out of the way. Not far. Just far enough to give your runner time to deliver the information so I could be greeted by name, with everything set just as nicely as if I'd sent word ahead myself. Hence this compliment, Henry. You did it all very nicely."

Bloodworth brayed with good-hearted laughter. "I knew there was a reason why I like you so much, Mr. Cartwright. 'Deed I did. And right I was, yes? Now come along please, suh. You can sign in at the desk an' see do you like you room. Then we be off to find these people you look for, yes?"

"I will sign in, yes, but I'm sure the suite will be just as I wished. We can press right along without bothering with that, Henry."

"Ah, Mr. Cartwright. If only all gennulmuns was so easy to please as you. You come right this way, suh. This won' take but a minute."

"Mr. Cartwright, Henry Bloodworth does not fail. Never. But, suh, this one time only, Henry, he be 'bout this much confused." Bloodworth held one hand up to show a gap between thumb and forefinger. The distance was no more than a fraction of an inch.

They had been driving around New Orleans for most of the afternoon with no success in locating Mrs. Jean-Pierre DeMarigny.

"I know she's here, Henry. She has to be. If only

Jean-Pierre addressed all the letters he wrote to her." Ben touched the package that lay next to him on the upholstered seat. Among Jean-Pierre's few possessions back at the Ponderosa, Ben had found this sheaf of letters, painstakingly written, each one dated and placed into an envelope, but none of them addressed and none of them mailed. The dates were up to half a dozen years old. They were written in French and all began *M' cher Marie, m' epouse, m' coeur* ... Ben did not have to speak French to believe that those words had special meaning to Jean-Pierre. The least he could do, he felt, was to deliver the long-ago written sentiments to Marie DeMarigny along with the message and, to her son and Jean-Pierre's, the ancestral ring. But if only there had been an address ...

"You wait here, Mr. Cartwright. I must ask more questions. Better you do not go into this place, though, yes?"

Ben smiled a little. Henry Bloodworth would have been appalled had he known some of the places a young and cocky Ben Cartwright had boldly ventured into. But that had all been in another time and place, and Ben had no desire now to precipitate the sort of brawl he used to actually think of as being fun. Now he would just as happily sit outside in the cab while Henry went inside to make his inquiries.

The cab tilted abruptly to one side and then bounced into a level position again as Henry jumped down from the footman's perch at the rear of the closed cab, which was little larger or better appointed than an opera buggy. It wouldn't have done for a black man to ride inside with a white gentleman; custom did not allow even the most pampered slaves that much privilege. A sliding passthrough at the back of the cab allowed conversation with servants on the footman perches. Another at the front permitted passengers to speak with the driver, who in this instance was a patient, silent man of café au lait hue whose services had been arranged by way of the ubiquitous Mr. Bloodworth.

As a matter of curiosity, Ben leaned forward and slid the front panel open. "John."

"Yes, suh?"

"How much are you charging for all this excellent service, John?"

"I wouldn't know 'bout that, suh. Best you ask Mista Henry when he get back, suh."

Ben chuckled, not surprised in the least, and returned the panel to its closed position. Henry had everything very much in hand here. It was a very good thing that Henry seemed a thoroughly trustworthy assistant and advisor.

The wait outside the place in question—Ben could not decide if the place was a saloon, a coffeehouse, or simply the residence of someone with a great many friends of questionable character—was relatively long, fifteen or twenty minutes of silence. Then Henry came out shaking his head. "We try one other place, I think. Then we know something."

One other place became two, two became three, three became half a dozen. Evening found them no closer to the answer that Ben needed.

"Best you go back to the hotel this time," Henry reluctantly conceded. "Tonight I know everything. I promise to you, Mr. Cartwright. This thing," he shook his head, "this thing mos' unusual. Tomorrow you have breakfast early, you hear? First thing then we go to where this widow lady she be. First thing. We pick you up right after breakfast. Then Henry Bloodworth, he show you how good a guide he can be. First thing."

The cab drove back to the hotel, and Ben stepped out with a bill already in hand to pay for this first day's efforts. Although at that he was only guessing at what Henry might care to charge. They never really had quite discussed that subject.

"No, no," Henry protested. "I have done nothing for you, suh. You don' pay till I do." John the cab driver would accept nothing either.

"Tomorrow," Ben told them. "First thing."

*   *   *

Ben breakfasted at first light and then took a seat in one of the plush and comfortable armchairs in the lobby to wait. It was quite a treat for him to be able to read a newspaper on its actual day of printing, so he was content for the moment.

Still and all, first thing in New Orleans must be something other than the California and Utah notions of first thing, because eight o'clock passed with no word from Henry, then nine, finally ten. Ben had long since finished that morning's New Orleans newspaper and was rather grumpily working his way through papers of varying age and condition from Mobile and Vicksburg and St. Louis. First thing indeed.

"Mistuh Cartwright?" The bellboy bowed and cleared his throat.

"Yes."

"There's a cab outside for you, sir."

"Thank you." Ben got up, the cartilage in his knees popping after sitting still for so long, and went outside. John was there sitting tall on the driver's box while Henry Bloodworth stood beside the iron step and an open door.

"First thing, Henry?"

"I am sad to tell you this, Mr. Cartwright. No place in all N'Orlean is there any home of a Jean-Pierre DeMarigny. No Marie DeMarigny. No young man name of DeMarigny. Only the old man Monsieur Guy DeMarigny. No other in all N'Orlean. And no Mrs. Marie DeMarigny living at the home of M'sieu Guy either. I talk with the slaves at that house. They tell me there is no Madame Marie. No Mrs. Jean-Pierre. If there was, Henry Bloodworth would find her. I am sorry, Mr. Cartwright. This woman you seek, this widow lady, she does not seem to exist. Not in all N'Orlean."

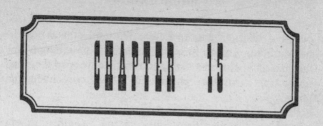

CHAPTER 15

"Mr. Cartwright, please. I do not think this is such a ver' good idea. You know? If only you would let me—"

"Thank you for your advice, Mr. Bloodworth, but my mind is quite made up. I am going. Alone if I must. But I am most certainly going."

"But Mr. Cartwright, you do no understand. Monsieur Guy DeMarigny is—how do I explain to you—he is of the old ways. He lives as if this is hundred years ago. And M'sieu DeMarigny is very rich, very powerful. An' very cruel. He is not a nice man. I, Henry Bloodworth, I tell you this. And Henry Bloodworth fears no man."

"I appreciate that, Henry. Thank you. John, drive on. The DeMarigny estate, if you please."

"If *he* pleases, Mr. Cartwright."

"I stand corrected, Henry. John, you will take me to see this Mr. Guy DeMarigny even if you do not please."

"Yes, suh. As you say, suh." John snapped his whip above the ears of his unmatched team, and the horses began to pull, jerking the cab into a sudden rocking motion that had Henry Bloodworth clinging for dear life to the uprights at his footman's perch.

The cab left the crowded, noisy, yet somehow intimate French Quarter and rolled through shabby streets and gracious residential neighborhoods, past small localized business districts and eerie aboveground cemeteries, finally gliding smoothly along a shaded, moss-hung lane that ran parallel to the dark and muddy waters of the great Mississippi. Out here where Guy DeMarigny lived, the homes were larger than most hotels. San Francisco had nothing to compare with these elegant mansions.

"You did say the gentleman was wealthy, didn't you?" Ben observed.

Henry Bloodworth did not answer. Ben decided he was probably sulking because his advice was rejected.

Eventually the cab pulled to a halt before a set of ornate wrought-iron gates hung between stone gate posts. Ben guessed that the huge, iron filigree crest that capped the gates stood a good eleven feet off the ground. The gate posts were almost that tall as well. A stone wall five or six feet high ran in broad wings in either direction for several hundred yards before melding into a four-rail wood fence. A gatekeeper's shelter was incorporated into the left-hand post wall. It was untended at the moment.

"Gate's closed, suh. We can't go no fu'ther."

"Nonsense. I don't see a lock. We can drive on to the house, John."

"Mistuh Bloodworth?"

"I'll get the gate, John. Go ahead and pull through." Ben felt the tilt of the coach as Henry got down. The freedman tugged the gate halves open, and John took his cab past them. Bloodworth latched them shut again and climbed back onto his perch. "Mr. Cartwright—"

"I know, Henry. I'll take responsibility."

"Yes, suh."

The lane leading to the house curved around to the right and then swung in a graceful arc back, the design of the driveway laid out so as to take best advantage of the foliage and sloping terrain and best show off the DeMarigny mansion, which was a massive brick structure with a mansard roof and eight gleaming white pillars—not true columns, but purely decorative things made of wood, Ben saw as they drew nearer—showcasing the entry.

Lest anyone mistake the wealth and ostentatious taste of the owner, the gardens surrounding the house were enhanced by the presence of statuary set on granite plinths, large pieces carved from stone, and smaller, more delicate ones sculpted in marble. Lions, wood nymphs, and half-dressed women in Grecian garb were prominent.

A host of slaves, little better clothed than the sculpted Greek ladies but dripping salty sweat in a way cold marble never could, were busy keeping the lawn and gardens trimmed to perfection. None of these people acknowledged the arrival of the cab in any way.

John brought the conveyance to a stop near the steps leading up to the broad porch that fronted the grand house, and Henry jumped down to open the door for Ben and help the gentleman down.

"You know, Mr. Cartwright, we could still turn around an'—"

But by then his point was moot in any event. The front doors of the house swung open and a gray-haired Negro in scarlet livery and a puff of lace swelling like a balloon at his throat came out to give the intruders a haughty sneer down the length of his nose. "Is the master expecting you, suh?"

Ben smiled and, not waiting for an invitation he was sure would not come, climbed the steps to the porch level so he could look at the aging retainer eye to eye. Taking his cue from his initial meeting with Henry Bloodworth, he did not make the mistake of offering his hand. He only nodded stiffly. "I am Benjamin Cartwright of the Ponderosa. Please convey to your master my apologies for not sending a note in advance, but my news is too important to allow the delay. Please tell him I request a brief audience."

"Would the master be familiar with your plantation, suh? This . . . Ponderosa?"

"He would not."

"And what would be the nature of your business with the master?"

"I have news for him about his son."

"You have been misinformed, suh. The master has no son."

"Has? Perhaps not. But I have reason to believe that he once had a son named Jean-Pierre. Is that not correct?"

"It would not be my place to comment on that, suh."

"Fine. Please tell your master that I wish to speak with him anyway."

"There would be no point, suh."

"I insist."

"Very well, suh." The old man turned and very calmly went back inside. He closed the door silently but firmly behind when he did so.

Ben waited where he was, once winking down at a rather nervous-looking Henry Bloodworth. Ben had no idea what Henry could be so concerned about. After all, what could Guy DeMarigny do to him even if the man were to become angry? More to the point, why would someone in DeMarigny's position bother with anything so petty as a disagreement with a simple freedman? Ben thought Henry was overreacting.

Ben waited.

And then waited some more.

After the passage of what seemed a rather considerable length of time, it occurred to him that the old Negro had no intention of returning with any response from the master of the manor.

Ben smiled. Fine. He had nothing better to do today than sit in the shade here at ... whatever DeMarigny chose to call this plantation. Ben faked a yawn, took his time about loading and lighting his pipe, then ambled over to two cane-bottom rocking chairs with an inlaid chess-top table between them. These were probably as uselessly decorative as everything else around here; it seemed entirely possible that he might have been the first person ever to use one for its avowed purpose. The chair proved to be quite comfortable, the day agreeable, and the pipe tobacco flavorsome.

Ben puffed away with contentment and began to rock slowly to and fro.

The door pushed open and the old Negro scuttled back out onto the porch before Ben hardly had time enough to find a rhythm in his rocking.

"The master wishes me to inform you, suh, that he declines your request for an interview," the old man said in a loud, clear, mildly artificial tone of voice. "Having no further business here, suh, I suggest you leave now or I shall be forced to take measures, suh. Serious measures."

The idea of this emaciated old fellow taking "measures" with a man half his age and ten times his vitality was ludicrous, of course. The threats did, however, reflect well upon the aging servant's willingness. Ben smiled and stood. "No measures will be necessary, uncle. If Mr. DeMarigny changes his mind—"

"The master does not change his mind, Mr. Cartwright. Ever."

"I see. More's the pity if a man can't accept reason and reality. But that is a cross he must bear alone, isn't it?" Ben said gently.

"I am sure I have no idea what you mean, suh."

"No, I'm sure you don't." Ben shrugged and made his way down the steps to ground level, the old Negro in his silken livery trailing behind.

When they were near the hansom and well away from the front windows of the DeMarigny mansion, the old man inched a bit closer and in a voice barely above a whisper said, "The young master, Jean-Pierre . . ." The old fellow was trembling now, glancing nervously over his shoulder in the direction of the open windows of the house but determined to follow through now that he had begun. "Lord love him, suh, would he be all right?"

"No, uncle, I'm sorry. That is what I came here to tell his father. Jean-Pierre died in my arms on the Ponderosa Ranch in far western Utah Territory not three months past.

He sent a message for his wife and a package for his son. I came here hoping to find them. Frankly, nothing was ever said about his father or any other family."

The old man's eyes squeezed tight closed from the pain of this news, and when he opened them again, they were unnaturally moist. "Did he ... did he ...?" The question was never fully articulated, and Ben could only guess at its content.

"He was honorable and honest and fine to the last," Ben said. "He died saving my oldest son's life. Jean-Pierre gave of himself so that my son would live. I buried him on my own land, and we Cartwrights will honor his memory for as long as the western mountains stand and the high meadow grasses grow."

"Yes, suh. Thank you, suh, for telling me."

"I wish I could tell his father too."

"I am sorry, Mr. Cartwright, suh. The old master ..." The servant shook his head sadly.

"I'm sorry too, uncle. For Guy DeMarigny much more than for Jean-Pierre."

"Yes, suh."

"Thank you for trying to help." Ben turned toward the steps into the cab, but the old man pressed closer.

"Suh."

"Yes?"

"The young master's widow."

"Marie, yes."

"She is living in the city under her maiden name, suh. Marie DuBey, she was then. The master ... requested ... that she not claim entitlement to the name DeMarigny."

"Requested," Ben repeated, struggling to keep his voice and expression matter-of-fact.

"Yes, suh. Requested." The elderly retainer, Ben thought, flushed a somewhat darker hue from embarrassment as he continued. "I believe you will find her, suh, in the quarter known as the Knackery. Rue le Pont' number twenty-five the last I knew of her, suh, although she may have moved since. It has been, I am sad to say, much too long since I asked after her."

Henry Bloodworth, no longer trying to pretend that he was not listening in, gasped. "Le Pont'? This house would allow one of its own, an' a lady at that, to stay there?"

"Do not turn your nose up at me, young man."

"Hah! You think you are better than you master? Hah an' hah. Not if these white folk do like that to they own." Henry made a rude gesture in the direction of the DeMarigny mansion.

"Quiet, both of you," Ben snapped. He looked at Guy DeMarigny's supernumerary. "Thank you, uncle. You've been a big help. Henry, I take it you know where the widow DeMarigny lives now?"

"Yes."

"Then I think we should go there without delay, don't you?"

"Yes, sir, of course."

"Thank you again, uncle, and good-bye. I'll not bother Mr. Guy again, I think."

"Suh."

"Yes?"

"When you see the lady. Tell her . . . tell her there are those of us who remember the young master. Those of us who still love him. Tell her we will light candles for him."

"I'll tell her, uncle."

From somewhere inside the house there was a shrill, insistent clanging of a small bell. Ben guessed that the master was becoming impatient with how long the old servant was taking to get rid of these unwelcome interlopers. Unwelcome indeed, Ben thought, because his own presence today must be a reminder to the foolish and bitter old man that he had rejected his own flesh and blood. Surely that must be a difficult thing for someone to try to justify, even to himself.

"You get out now," the liveried servant ordered loudly. "Go quick or I will throw you out."

"We're leaving now," Ben said just as loudly.

The old Negro winked at him, and Ben climbed into the cab. Henry mounted his footman's perch, and John eagerly set the team at a trot.

Ben was not interested in looking back at the cold grandeur of the mansion.

CHAPTER 16

B en understood now why the old Negro at the DeMarigny mansion was embarrassed and why Henry Bloodworth seemed so scornful. The part of New Orleans called the Knackery ... disgusting, to be blunt about it.

The poorly cobbled streets were little better than rabbit warrens. Rotting garbage and raw sewage stank in the undrained potholes and puddles underfoot. The residents were a mixture of impoverished whites and freed blacks living in squalid, unsanitary proximity. According to Henry, even the ordinary class of freedmen avoided this quarter if they possibly could. Most of the colored here, he explained, were former slaves who had been "freed" not from any sense of compassion or justice on the part of their former owners, but instead were manumitted when they became so old or infirm that their services were no longer valued. When their masters were unable to find a buyer for them and did not want the bother of pensioning them off, these sick or failing slaves were freed and dumped into this quarter to fend for themselves or else starve. And for Jean-Pierre's widow and son to be found here ... Ben shuddered at the conditions he saw around them. This was as bad as anything he had encountered in his sailing days, as foul as the most stinking Caribbean pesthole.

"We have to leave the cab here an' walk the rest of the way," Henry said, opening the door for Ben. "Sorry, but there won't be room enough further on an' no place to turn the horses 'round."

Ben stepped down, his nose wrinkling at the varied assaults upon it.

"If you have a gun wit' you . . ." Henry murmured suggestively.

"No, but I won't need one. If there is trouble, Henry, don't worry about me. Run, and I'll cover your retreat."

"Sir!" Bloodworth protested, genuinely affronted by the notion that he abandon a client.

Ben smiled. "Likely we'll not have to anyway, right?"

"Right."

"Then lead on, Henry." John, meanwhile, was busy backing the horses around and preparing the coach for a quick departure if need be.

"You don't go no place without us, John, or I whip all over you," Henry warned him.

The hack driver said nothing. Ben noticed that John kept his hold on the driving lines and made no attempt to block the wheels or give his horses any leisure while they waited here. The cab was prepared for a rapid departure indeed.

"We be right back," Henry said.

Ben followed Bloodworth into the odoriferous maze of tiny streets and alleys that was the Knackery.

The street where Marie DeMarigny was said to live proved to be mercifully close to where they left the cab. A signpost at the entrance to what looked like just another trash-strewn alley read Rue le Pont . . . something. The lettering at the end was faded and illegible. In this quarter it seemed possible that no one would so much as remember, or care, what the name of the impossibly narrow street was supposed to have been. Whatever the name once was, Rue le Pont' was what it had become.

"Number twenty-fi', the man do say. An' here it be," Henry said almost as proudly as if he had made a discovery.

Number twenty-five proved to be a doorway, its bolt plate smashed and hinges sagging, that led to an upper floor of a flimsy, brick-faced building that was leaning heavily on its neighboring structure to the east. Without the support of the building next door, number twenty-five would no doubt have collapsed before now.

Ben started up the stairs. The warped treads creaked and groaned with every step he took. The door at street level could not be locked, but no one could possibly climb these stairs without announcing himself. Ben supposed that was a protection of sorts.

At the top of the stairs there was a landing with a single door facing onto it. He hesitated only for a moment, then knocked.

"One moment." The voice was a woman's, clear but somewhat harried. After a bit Ben heard the approach of footsteps.

The door came open and he was confronted by a vision, an ethereal, unearthly vision. By, quite possibly, an angel, albeit a pale and ghostly sort of angel.

"Mrs. DeMarigny?"

The vision took a long, frightened look at the gentleman who had come to call.

And dropped into a dead faint.

"I'm such a silly goose. Please forgive me."

"There's nothing to forgive," Ben assured her. He had the lady—he continued to make the assumption that this fey and delicate creature was Marie DuBey DeMarigny, but he as yet had no confirmation of that as fact—reclining on a tattered sofa that constituted the principal furnishing in the front room of the apartment suite. "Truly." He looked across to Bloodworth, who was standing at the open doorway. "She's starving, Henry. I've seen the signs often enough in folks coming off the desert. Weakness of pulse, the peculiar scent on her breath. She needs food. Do you think you could scare up some warm broth? Chicken if it's available, otherwise pork."

"Down here, Mr. Cartwright, you give me five dollar, I can buy anything from a murder to a croissant."

"Chicken broth will do for the time being," Ben said. He fetched out a gold eagle and passed the ten-dollar coin to Henry.

"I be back real soon." Ben could easily hear Henry's progress down the stairs and outside.

Ben took his handkerchief out and gently wiped the lady's forehead. It was not so much that she needed the attention as that he wanted to give it. That he wanted to do . . . *some*thing for her, however limited that gesture might be.

"You're going to be all right now," he promised.

"Yes, of course. But please, you will forgive me for being so stupid? It is just . . . that name. It has been so long since I have heard it. You startled me. And I . . . so silly of me, I know . . . when you spoke that name I thought . . . I thought . . . I was afraid something might have happened to . . . you know. To the young Monsieur DeMarigny. So silly. Please forgive me."

"Are you Marie DeMarigny?" Ben asked.

"I am Marie DuBey. Once I was called Marie DeMarigny, but no longer."

Ben was frankly unsure whether he should tell Marie about Jean-Pierre's death at this point. She was entitled to the truth. There was no question of that. But she was so weak that he feared the shock of the news might be too much for her. He temporized by asking, "Where is the boy, Mrs. DeMarigny? Can I do anything for him while we wait for Henry to return?"

Marie bolted half upright on the sofa, her strength surging if short-lived. Her expression was wild-eyed and anguished. She cried out, the words in French and therefore incomprehensible to Ben.

Then once again she collapsed, falling back onto the sofa in a faint.

Good Lord, Ben thought. What have I done to this woman?

The shabby apartment was filled with aromas so rich and pleasant they almost drove away the thought and the smells of the vile neighborhood beyond the shuttered windows.

Henry Bloodworth had returned bearing a virtual feast of soft and easily palatable foods. There was chicken broth and a thin, rice-based concoction that looked like it had already been eaten once but which smelled positively divine. A creamy stew with bits of shrimp and oyster floating in the buttery broth. An apricot brandy that put color into the lady's cheeks, and a smooth duck liver pâté redolent with natural oils, capers, and spices. Croissants warm from the oven and so light they threatened to float off the plate unless something was done to weigh them down. A crock of sweet butter so fresh the droplets of pale buttermilk still oozed from its golden creases, and small pots of jam, strawberry and peach and pear preserves. Ben was thoroughly impressed that Henry would have been able to find so perfect a selection so quickly.

"You look better," Ben said.

"I feel better," Marie confessed. "But I am so ashamed. You should not have gone to this trouble, Mister . . . Caldwell, was it?"

"Cartwright, ma'am. Ben Cartwright."

"Yes, of course. Please forgive me." She sighed. "So much I must say to you that I am sorry, please forgive, no?" She sighed.

"As a matter of fact, you don't need to say any such thing. Not at all," Ben insisted. "Another bite?" He pinched off a bit of croissant and spread it thick first with butter and then with jam. The fat in the butter would give lasting strength while the sweet in the jam would provide quick energy. Because of the emigrants coming in off the harsh and unforgiving desert between Salt Lake and Truckee Meadows, Ben had had more experience with this particular debilitation than he ever wanted. Now, though, he was glad, because at least it helped him know how to begin rebuilding Jean-Pierre's widow's strength.

"I couldn't."

"Just this little bit, then." She ate it. "And one more sip of the broth." He spooned the rich, yellow chicken broth to her lips without waiting for the rejection he knew she would try to express. "There, that's better. I can see the color coming back into your cheeks already, and I'd be willing to wager your stomach feels warm and full now, yes?"

"But oui. How do you know?"

He smiled. "Oh, I am a very wise man for my years."

"Yes, I think this must be so," Marie said seriously. "Mrs. DeMarigny—"

"Please. You must call me Marie." She gave him a rueful smile. "We are not so formal in this quarter, Mr. Cartwright. The proprieties, they are seldom observed here."

"Oh, but with a lady such as yourself—"

"No." There was pain rising quickly into her eyes. "Please, no. I am not the lady, sir. No longer. Now I am . . . no one of interest or importance."

"I dispute that opinion, ma'am, and cling to my own," Ben said, half bowing from the stool he had drawn close to the sofa where Marie lay.

"You are kind."

"And you, madame, are a lady."

That brought a hint of smile to her lips and perhaps a bit more color into her sunken cheeks.

Marie was in no immediate danger, Ben could see, and now he had a moment in which he could appreciate her beauty.

Jean-Pierre's widow was small and naturally slim, her

current condition of emaciation apart. Ben could judge that with ease, thanks to the cut of her clothing, which barely sagged even in this period of extremis. She had dark hair, dark, lively eyes, and cheekbones that were high and delectably rounded. Her neck was long and elegantly slender, and her hands were delicate, with exceptionally long fingers and impossibly tiny wrists. Her nose was small and nicely molded, and her lips sensuously full if still pale from her entirely too close brush with starvation.

She was, Ben thought, quite perfectly lovely. A wraith. An angel.

And . . . he was still avoiding the hurt he would do to her when he explained the reason for his visit. He continued to try to put off telling her the truth. He did not want to hurt this ineffably exquisite creature any more than she had already suffered.

Once again he evaded the issue by asking, "Your son, Mrs. DeMarigny. Is there anything I can do for him?"

Marie gasped and turned her face away. But not so quickly that Ben failed to see the tears that sprang into her eyes.

"I . . . what is it, ma'am? What have I said to hurt you so?"

Her shoulders trembled and shook as she silently wept. Henry Bloodworth nervously cleared his throat and tiptoed out of the room and down the stairs to the street. Ben, having prompted this torment, did not have any such luxury. Instead he could only sit where he was on the stool, unable to offer the lady any comfort, and wish he had the answers that only Marie DeMarigny possessed.

It was hours later before it was possible to clarify the many shadings of truth that created the complex pattern of Marie DeMarigny's pain. And of Ben Cartwright's misconceptions.

He told her the terrible, hurtful truth about her husband, about where Jean-Pierre had lived and how he had died. And Ben gave her the package of letters that Jean-

Pierre wrote but never mailed. Ben also mentioned the ring that Jean-Pierre bequeathed to his son and heir.

At that point Marie had grown pale again, but this time she was able to maintain her control. Gracefully, regally, she rose, holding the bundle of letters to her breast, and asked him to excuse her while she read them in private.

When eventually she returned, the hour was late and the front room was in shadow. She moved with stiff and brittle poise, gliding from here to there and bending to light one candle after another until the room was bright again, if not gay. This humble, shabby little place could never be deemed gay. Finally she returned to the sofa and settled onto it as lightly as a puff of eiderdown floating to rest. She seemed composed and calm now, as she had not been earlier.

"Once again, sir, I beg you to accept my apologies. There is so much that you cannot have known."

"It is I who must apologize," Ben said. "I've brought you hurt, and I don't even know how. I never meant to. About my dear friend Jean-Pierre, of course. But in other ways too. For those I must apologize."

Marie sighed. "So much you did not know, M'sieu Cartwright. So much Jean-Pierre did not know. So much I did not know either. The letters, his letters, tell me much. And you had begun this tale when you came from him . . . I knew you were from him, you could not have been from those others, not and have treated me with such kindness . . . but you came from him and you asked about the child." Unspilled tears gleamed wet and shiny in the candlelight, but she did not give in to the impulse to cry.

"There is no child, M'sieu Cartwright. There never has been. When Jean-Pierre . . . left . . . he knew I was with child. He believed the child would have been a son. His son. Our son. And so, perhaps, this would have been. No one but God will ever know. I lost the babe only days after Jean-Pierre went away."

"I can't believe—"

"Please, M'sieu Cartwright. Do not judge Jean-Pierre. Do not be harsh with his memory. He was a good man. In those days he was not so strong a man as he needed to be. To stand up to his father, you see. His father is . . . a monster. I, Marie DuBey DeMarigny, have every right to say this of Guy DeMarigny. I if no other have the right. For what he did to my husband. For what he did to my unborn child. For these things much more than anything he may have done to me, oui? But of course, yes." She shook her head. "I will not speak of these things. There is no need." Absently she reached for a croissant and began buttering it.

"The point, M'sieu Cartwright, is that Jean-Pierre left here thinking that I would bear his son. And when he died, he still thought that I had. I am glad he never knew the truth. The thought of our son—the things he said to the two of us in those letters—they brought him comfort and helped to make the man of him that I knew he was even when he did not himself know. And I, m'sieu, was made to believe, you see, that Jean-Pierre knew of my miscarriage. I was made to believe that because of this he accepted the advice of that evil father of his and that my own dear Jean-Pierre rejected me. I am ashamed now. I should have known better, but I did not. If I had known, m'sieu, I would have flown to him. I would have found him no matter how far he fled from the lies his father spread about me. Those lies . . . it does not matter what they were. They accomplished their purpose. They divided husband from wife. They ruined my reputation. They destroyed my very will to go on. I have lived all this time in the shadow of those lies. Now, m'sieu, thanks to the truth that you have brought to me, now I can lift my face once more and look in the eye all those who have believed the lies and repeated them. Now I can become whole once more, m'sieu. For this I must thank you. For this I must thank my beloved Jean-Pierre most of all."

Ben did not know the specifics of Marie's story. He did not need to. It was enough that he could see the deep and dreadful pain that reflected within her eyes. And the staunch resolve that could be found there too now.

"Marie . . . you said I could call you that . . ."

"But yes, of course, m'sieu."

"Jean-Pierre was my friend much more than he was ever my employee. He died saving my son's life. I owe your husband a debt I can never repay. I would be honored, Mrs. DeMarigny, if you would allow me to . . . I don't know. Help you somehow. Any way you will accept. But, ma'am, I cannot, simply can not, leave here now and know that you remain in these circumstances."

"I ask nothing of you, m'sieu."

"I know you do not. It is I who offers, not you who asks."

"I will not take the charity, no. Marie DuBey DeMarigny will not take charity."

"No charity is offered. A pension, perhaps."

"I could not, m'sieu. No."

"Employment?"

She gave a grim smile. "Believe me, m'sieu, a gentleman such as yourself would not wish to employ the creature I have become."

"You have become, madame?"

She shrugged. "The creature this city believes me to have become. And is that not the same? Reputation is equally as bad as reality, no?"

Ben smiled. "As a matter of fact, Marie, no, reputation is not anything like as bad as reality. Reputation is only paint; it has nothing to do with the unblemished wood beneath."

"You are too kind, m'sieu. And you do not understand New Orleans."

"Nor do I have to, madame. Fie on New Orleans and on the fools who choose to accept Guy DeMarigny's lies, whatever those lies may be. You see, Marie, I intend to leave this city at the earliest opportunity. And I would like nothing better than for you to come with me. You can— Why, now that I think about it, I do need a housekeeper at the Ponderosa. Someone to tend to things. A woman's touch around the place. In particular a fine and genteel lady for my sons to know and to admire. Someone to help influence them beyond a man's hard frontier ways. I would pay you a fair wage, Mrs. DeMarigny, and consider it a privilege to do so. And if I might add, in all of Utah Territory there will not be a soul who has ever heard about Guy DeMarigny, nor one who would care about the man if ever they did hear of him."

"You tempt me, m'sieu."

"I mean to, Marie. I fully intend not only to tempt you, but to sway you to accept my offer." He smiled again. "Please?"

"I am sorry. It would not be possible."

"Not only possible, Marie, but sensible. It is the only sensible recourse open to you."

"No, I could not. New Orleans, it is all I have ever known. My roots are here."

"So were Jean-Pierre's, but sometimes even grand old trees begin to rot, Marie. Forgive me, but I can see that you have not exactly been . . . comfortable here." He looked pointedly around this room, tilted his head and listened to the cacophony beyond the shutters. He had almost become accustomed to the miasmic stench on the humid air, but now he was conscious of that all over again too. "This is not a healthful place, Marie. I cannot in good conscience leave you here. I owe Jean-Pierre much too much to permit that."

"We are at an impasse, m'sieu."

"We will speak again." He rose, took out his purse and laid five double eagles on the tray bearing the remnants of her meal. "For the necessities," he said.

"But I cannot—"

"It is not a gift and not a loan, Marie. It's an advance against your wages."

He turned quickly and left. He thought perhaps she was crying, but if so, she did it silently.

CHAPTER 17

The hansom rolled to a halt on the graveled loop in front of the DeMarigny mansion. Henry Bloodworth was on the driving box. His cousin John had refused to come this time. In fact, Henry had only agreed to come himself after Ben threatened to hire the services of another cab to make the journey.

"Wasn't it bad enough that we was out there yesterday?" Henry complained. "We oughtn't to go again, Mr. Cartwright."

"I have to make one more trip out there, Henry. I have no choice." He touched the lump in his coat pocket, the packet containing the DeMarigny family ring that Marie refused to take.

The ring had meant much to Jean-Pierre. He had wanted it kept within the family. If that dying wish were to be met, Ben had no choice but to once more seek an audience with the last remaining male DeMarigny. No matter how repugnant the old fool was.

Now they were there, and once more Ben found himself alighting onto what he definitely felt was hostile territory.

He climbed the steps to the broad front porch and approached the door. This time no one came immediately to greet him, and so he lifted the four pounds or so of brass knocker and let it clatter as loud and bold as it was able.

Two minutes later he knocked again. And a minute after that twice more. He was prepared to stand there banging on the door as long as was necessary.

Before he could knock again, the door was opened by a burly man—a white man this time, not a servant—who was scowling so hard his eyebrows practically met in the middle of his face.

"You are not wanted here."

Ben smiled at him. "To tell you the truth, friend, I am inordinately pleased to hear you say that. Frankly, I'd worry about anyone who was welcome at this door."

"If you think that kind of talk will—"

"I know, I know, don't bother trying to improve on my manners. And don't bother telling me that DeMarigny doesn't want to see me. I really don't have any desire to meet him either. All I want is to see his family's ring returned where it belongs." Ben pulled the packet out and tried to hand it to the man—bodyguard, overseer, whomever—who blocked the door.

"I don't know what you are talking about. But Monsieur DeMarigny wishes nothing to do with you or with anything you might have to say. Go on now. Out of here. Right now."

"I'll leave the ring for him, then." Ben bent and set the packet down on the porch floor.

"He doesn't want it."

"It was his," Ben persisted. "Then it was his son's. Now it is his again, like it or not."

"Monsieur DeMarigny has no son."

"I know. And more's the pity too. The real shame is that a man as fine as Jean-Pierre had no father. Good day." Ben touched the brim of his beaver and would have left, but the fellow came after him, grabbing him by the arm and jerking him back around.

"You left this package here."

"Yes."

"Take it with you."

Ben shook his head.

"Mister, you are going to take it with you."

Ben only smiled.

"If I have to beat you senseless and stuff it back into your pocket, mister, you will take it with you."

Ben laughed. "If you're man enough to do that, friend, then I'll agree to take it."

The man was half a head taller than Ben and outweighed him by at least fifty pounds. That was not the sort of response the man would have been accustomed to when he chose to threaten someone with a thrashing.

"Well?" Ben challenged.

The man thought it over. And backed off, shaking his head.

"Then good day to you, sir," Ben said jauntily.

"Monsieur DeMarigny doesn't like anyone messing into his affairs."

"Thank you for telling me. Good-bye." Ben touched the brim of his hat again and departed, Henry spanking the horses practically into a gallop the instant the cab door was closed.

Ben came down the warped and creaking staircase to find Bloodworth posted on the street with a scowl on his face and a conspicuous bulge under his coat.

"Whatever are you doing here, Henry? I told you I could find my way back to the hotel alone, didn't I?"

"You did, but there's rumors on the streets, sir. About you."

"About me? My, my. Think of that."

"You shouldn't take it s' lightly, Mr. Cartwright. Truly you shouldn't."

"All right, Henry. What are these rumors that have you so concerned?"

"Word is, Mr. Cartwright, that somebody don' like you messing about where you don' belong. Somebody don' like you visiting Miss DuBey so much. Somebody think you should ought to go home."

"And so I shall, Henry. Just as soon as I convince Mrs. DeMarigny to accompany me."

"Now you see, Mr. Cartwright, that right there is a big part of what cause this fuss. If you jus' call the lady Miss DuBey instead of—"

"I know, Henry. We've been over this ground too many times before. I appreciate your feelings on the subject, but I have my own. And I shall continue to refer to the lady by her proper name, which is Mrs. DeMarigny, if you please. Or if anyone else does either, for that matter."

"Yes, sir. Anyway, Mr. Cartwright, somebody—the rumors don' say who—somebody isn' real happy with you. The rumors say you be taught a lesson. In manners, like. They say you be beat upon and you looks mussed up more than a little."

"That's what they say, is it?"

"Yes, sir, it is."

"And what is that underneath your coat, Henry? A horse pistol?"

"No, sir, nothin' like that. It wouldn' do for a man o' color to be found on the streets wid a firearm. But a nice cosh with a quarter pound o' lead shot in the tip, no one object to that sort of thing, you see." Henry grinned.

"I see. Well, I appreciate your concern, Henry, and I thank you for the warning. But I'm sure your rumors are just that, rumors and nothing more. I think the 'somebody' in question will find that I don't frighten so easily, and then the old mon-sewer will slink away."

"I wish I believe the same as you, sir, but I don'."

"Then it remains to be seen which of us is correct, eh?"

"Yes, sir, it do."

"Yes, well, shall we walk together back to the cab? John should have had time enough to complete his nap by now."

"Yes, sir." They started off through the narrow, twisting streets that over the past week and a half had become all too familiar to both of them. "Miss DuBey, sir . . . I mean, Mrs. DeMarigny, she is feeling better now?"

"Considerably. Although she is just as stubborn as before. She—"

Ben's train of thought was shattered by a sudden rush of booted feet and the sight of two men leaping out of a recessed doorway with cudgels upraised and a great roaring issuing from their throats.

Ben understood the reason for all the commotion, of course. It's purpose was to so startle their victim as to render him immobile. And as a general rule of things it was a most efficacious method of assault.

Ben Cartwright, however, had been set upon by thugs more often than a little in his boisterous youth. The waterfront explorations of young sailing officers are given to certain hazards, and Ben long ago learned how to cope with bullyboys whose intent was to rob and maim.

Henry Bloodworth too proved to be no innocent awaiting his own slaughter. With a cry of his own, Henry whipped out his leather cosh, ducked a blow and rapped the attacker on the left a smart shot on the nose, pulping that appendage and sending a spray of bright blood into the muddy, stinking street.

That was all Ben had time to witness, as the thug on the right was coming on hard and fast.

Ben sidestepped that first rush, leaving one leg sticking out for the fellow to trip over. The man went sprawling into the filth on the ground, rolled and came up with a murderous glint in his eye.

"Not that easy, you don't," Ben informed him, and slipped underneath the deadly arc of the fellow's cudgel. Ben dodged the blow and came in behind it, flashing fists beating a sharp tattoo on the man's face until he could regain his balance. Then Ben danced back out of the way again.

The man roared in futile rage and blindly charged. This time Ben darted the other way, whirled and delivered a backhanded blow with a full sweep of his arm, his clubbed fist taking the man in the throat at full speed. The impact was hard enough to stop the fellow's upper body cold while his lower portions continued on with their momentum.

The man's feet went forward, his head and torso snapped back and he stretched out full length off the ground before he went down with a thump and a whoosh of breath forcibly expelled from his lungs.

The man hit the ground hard enough to need a few moments to gather wits and breath alike. Ben reached down and plucked the cudgel—a length of polished cypress knee with a rather attractive grain pattern and streaky red and yellow coloration—from the fellow's unresisting fingers.

"You won't be needing this any longer," Ben said.

"Hmm. It don' look like you need any help there, Mr. Cartwright."

"No, Henry, I think we have everything under control now."

"About them rumors, Mr. Cartwright—"

"Your judgment was sound, Henry. Thank you for coming to help."

"Yes, sir." Bloodworth looked rather pleased with himself.

"Would you be so good as to go find a constable now, Henry?"

"Sir?"

"A constable, Henry."

"Oh, but Mr. Cartwright, you won't want to be reporting this to no constable. Really you won't."

"Really I will, Henry. I insist upon it."

"Please, Mr. Cartwright. Don' do that."

"Henry! These two tried to split our heads open. Of course we shall have them carted off and put behind bars where they belong."

"But you don' understand, sir. Here in N'Orlean'—"

"... the law is still the law, just as everywhere else

in this country," Ben finished for him. Although he did concede, if only privately, that those words might not have been exactly what Bloodworth intended.

"Mr. Cartwright—"

"A constable, Henry. Please."

Reluctantly, Henry assented.

" 'Cartwright'? Spell that, please."

Ben did.

"And you claim that these two set upon you for no reason, is that it, sir?" The uniformed constable sent an ugly look in the direction of the two thugs who now sat leaning sullenly against a grimy, timbered wall, their wrists in manacles and legs in irons. Ben had the clear impression that incarceration by the New Orleans constabulary was not an event to look forward to.

"As a matter of fact, officer, this pair had a very good reason to assault me, and I know perfectly good and well what it was."

"I see, sir. Robbery that would be, right? I'll mark that down in the record and—"

"Constable—Sergeant, is it?—I am beginning to believe that you know more about this than you care to. Am I correct?"

"Now I never said any such as that. I'm only trying to be of help here, Mr. Cartwright."

"Yes, I am sure you are. But for the record, Sergeant—"

"Just constable, sir."

"Very well. For the record, Constable, these men set upon me and Mr. Bloodworth here at the express will and instruction of a Mr. Guy DeMarigny, who seems to find my presence in this city disagreeable. Perhaps because I remind him of his many shortcomings as regards his late son, Jean-Pierre."

The constable looked like Ben had just poked him with a sharp stick. "Mr. Cartwright. Please! Don't say things like that."

"I merely state the truth, Constable. Nothing wrong with that, is there?"

"You know what I mean, sir. Now please. For the record."

"For the record, Constable, I want the name Guy DeMarigny entered as the motive force behind this illegal and thoroughly reprehensible assault upon my person."

"Mr. Cartwright, you don't know . . . Sir, it would be better if we were to simply write down that these men attempted to rob you. Really. And I can assure you they will be most severely punished for it."

"They may be, but what about DeMarigny? He instigated the attack."

The constable looked at Bloodworth, who quickly threw up his hands and shook his head. "No, m'sieu, I know nothing of this. Nothing. One moment we are walking along. The next we are fighting for our lives. Beyond that . . . I know nothing."

The constable grunted. It was plain that he liked Henry's version much better than he liked that of the distinguished gentleman from Utah.

"For the record, Constable. Guy DeMarigny. I insist upon it."

"This I cannot do, Mr. Cartwright. I am sorry, but I cannot. And you must not ask me again. Please."

Ben frowned, but he had little choice. This, after all, was DeMarigny's town, not his.

Still and all, the message had been delivered. There were onlookers who were close enough to overhear. And the thugs themselves were taking it all in. No matter what else happened, word would get back to Guy DeMarigny. Ben Cartwright not only was not intimidated by the assault, now the visitor from the West was virtually thumbing his nose at the great man's power.

In a manner of speaking, that should be quite good enough, Ben decided.

"Call it robbery then, Constable."

"Thank you, sir. Thank you very much. And I can promise you, sir, these two will regret they ever saw you."

"I can believe that much at least," Ben conceded.

"Yes, sir. Thank you, sir."

"Can we go now? Thanks. Henry? Let's see if John is still waiting for us, eh?"

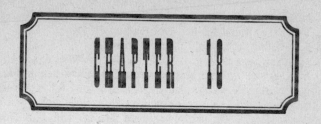

CHAPTER 18

B en sat alone at a table in the gentlemen's lounge attached to the hotel Saint Hilary de Bruge. His meal had been superb, and so was the brandy that he now held close underneath his nose so that he could inhale and fully appreciate the aroma that lifted from it. The evening was really quite perfect.

Yet if everything was all so damned perfect, why was he in such a foul humor now? He frowned and admitted that he knew good and well the cause of his displeasure. He was homesick. It was incredible. Ben Cartwright, the man who spent his early life roaming the distant seas, was homesick. He missed the mountains. He missed the high desert. He missed the huge trees and the hidden meadows and the brilliance of the vast western skies. Most of all, though, Ben missed his sons.

He did not regret coming to New Orleans. That was a debt of honor, and meeting the obligation was something he would never regret. But, dang it, he wanted to go home now. And he couldn't. Not so long as Marie DeMarigny remained in the state of genteel poverty in which he'd found her. He owed Jean-Pierre too much to risk ever again allowing her to starve. She had come so near to it when he and Henry found her.

Now she was out of immediate danger. But what

155

would happen to her if he left her alone here again? Nothing had changed for her. Not really.

If only she would listen to reason.

Ben was willing to do whatever she wished just so long as she allowed him to assure her future health and well-being. He would gladly establish a trust for her or a pension. Lord knew he owed Jean-Pierre that and a hundredfold more. Or, better, he would take her with him. He would employ her himself on the Ponderosa or see to her comfort in San Francisco.

He had explained this over and over to her, but to no avail. Day after day and hour after hour he pleaded with her. The stubborn, foolish woman would not budge. She insisted that anything he might give to her would be charity. Unless the gentleman was suggesting that she become a kept woman, and she would not agree to that either, thank you.

It had taken Ben some time to realize that Marie had been teasing him about that point. She had a quirky sense of humor, it seemed, and sometimes he was not entirely sure if she was serious about something or not.

At least he had finally concluded that all her mumblings and accusations about him trying to keep her were in jest. She was tugging on his leg so gently, he honestly hadn't been sure about it for quite a while.

As for the rest, though—her persistent refusal to accept any form of help from him—that she was quite serious about.

Dang her.

He was homesick, and there was nothing he could do to alleviate that until Marie accepted simple reason and acquiesced to one, any one, of the many offers and suggestions he put forward.

Ben sighed and lifted the brandy snifter to take a sip.

Before he could, however, someone walked into the back of his chair, jarring him so that the brandy splashed out of the snifter and onto his shirt front.

"Say now!"

"What's that? What's that?" roared the man who had just bumped into him. "Are you yelling at me? Well, are you? Damn you, mister, you shove your chair right into my way and then you have the temerity to shout at me? An apology, sir. I demand an immediate apology." The fellow's voice was loud and abusive.

Ben glanced down at his own shirt front, which was damp with spilled brandy, and then at the rude and abrasive chap who stood over him ranting and gesturing so as to call attention to himself from everyone in the vicinity. Deliberately so? It certainly seemed it.

After a moment Ben gave the man a rueful smile and, setting the half-full snifter aside, stood.

"Let me see if I have this straight," Ben said slowly and just as loudly as his accuser had spoken. "You walk out of your way to come around behind this table. You walk into my chair. And then you have the gall to complain to me because I am displeased with your stupidity. Is that about the size of it?"

"Damn you, sir. First you shout at me. Now you accuse me." The man gave his attention to the other gentlemen gathered in the room. "You all heard him, I believe." He looked back at Ben. "Sir, I have the honor to be Paul Alfonse Robelaird, and I demand satisfaction."

"Surely you jest."

"Jest? Sir, I challenge you. It is no jest. You will meet me on the field of honor, sir, or by your actions you will proclaim yourself a poltroon and a coward."

"My oh my," Ben said. "Why, you're all puffed up like a banty rooster, aren't you? And such a fine speech. Poltroon, indeed. It's a fine word, Mr. Robelaird, but I am afraid I don't know what it means."

"It means, sir, you are a wretch. A craven. A coward. Worse."

"Thank you for the instruction."

"You admit yourself to cowardice then, sir?"

"Mr. Robelaird, I probably shouldn't do this, but you've come along at a moment when I'm feeling just contrary enough to welcome your lunacy, sir. I accept your challenge."

"On the field north of the Madonna of All Souls cemetery then, sir, half an hour past dawn on the morning after tomorrow. I shall provide the services of a leech, sir, and a selection of weapons. Until then . . ." Robelaird took half a step backward, clicked his heels sharply together and bowed.

If the whole thing hadn't been so deadly serious, Ben realized, it would have been quite silly indeed.

But, damn it, he was going through with it. He really was. Because Guy DeMarigny was behind this unprovoked challenge. Ben was convinced of that. There was no other possibility that he could conceive for such as this.

DeMarigny was going to push and push and push some more, until Ben was able somehow to convince him that the pushing would do no good. Well, perhaps this was just the opportunity he needed for that, Ben thought. They would go through the stylized motions of this silliness, and then perhaps DeMarigny would be forced to conclude that honor had been fully served.

But, good heavens. A duel. In this day and age.

Robelaird sniffed haughtily, bowed again and marched stiffly out of the gentlemen's salon and away.

Ben shook his head in mild bemusement and returned to his seat, discovering that a waiter was there bowing and puffing with magical speed. More brandy was offered— from an even better distillation this time—and cigars as well. Apparently in New Orleans a duelist was entitled to certain perquisites whilst awaiting the moving finger of fate.

It was not yet dawn when Ben left the hotel. He had the torn and filthy remnants of an old sea bag slung over his shoulder, the accouterment in marked contrast to his clothing, which consisted of his best suit, yellow spats over freshly polished shoes, and a brand new low-crowned planter's hat in a pale dove-gray shade.

"I was hoping you get smart durin' the night an' not come out this morning," Henry Bloodworth complained when Ben joined him beside his cousin John's hansom.

"I said I would be there, didn't I?"

"If you say you gonna fly to the top of that tree yonder, do that mean you gonna do it?"

Ben smiled and touched the pouting freedman on the elbow. "Henry, my friend, I wouldn't tell you that unless I knew I could fly."

"Dammit, Mistuh Ben, you told that Robelaird fella that you meet him before you know what kinda man he is."

"I knew at the time that he was Guy DeMarigny's man. That was transparent enough. I had no reason to think a man like DeMarigny would allow himself to be represented by a simpleton."

"But Mistuh Cartwright—"

"I know, Henry. You've told me often enough, and I thank you. But I insist on going out there. It is going to work out. Trust me."

Most of the entire previous day had been spent with Ben adamant in his resolve to meet Robelaird on the field north of the cemetery—a site selection that Ben refused to think of as prophetic—and with Henry arguing against that determination. And he still was pressing his case that Ben choose discretion over valor.

According to Bloodworth, Paul Robelaird was a hothead and a snob. But a very deadly hothead and snob. Even though dueling was officially outlawed in New Orleans, it remained a socially acceptable—in some circumstances virtually a socially requisite—form of behavior. And Paul Robelaird was one of the local gentry who liked to avail himself of the unwritten code that demanded the spilling of blood as a proof of honor.

Robelaird had been four times to the dueling field in the past. Two of his victims died. One suffered the loss of an eye. The most fortunate of the four took a ball in his left hip and would walk with a slight limp for the rest of his days.

Never had Robelaird lost a duel or a pistol match.

"The man has the eye, Mr. Cartwright. He cool and steady and can't be ruffled. The time he fight M'sieu Brundage, I hear tell they reloaded an' shot again two times, three pistol volleys in all. M'sieu Brundage shot fast an' wild each time. M'sieu Robelaird, he was playing with M'sieu Brundage like the kitten play with the grasshopper. First time shoot beside the one ear. Next volley shoot beside that other ear. Finally M'sieu Brundage can't take it no more and start to blubber while he stand there with the empty gun an' wait for M'sieu Robelaird to shoot him. An' M'sieu Robelaird, he got no pity. He shoot M'sieu Brundage in the face. The m'sieu is lucky to only lose his eye. M'sieu Robelaird mean to kill him, certain sure, why else shoot the man in the face? He one bad man, Mistuh Cartwright. You one fine gennulmun, but you got no business here in N'Orlean facing a man like M'sieu Robelaird."

"I appreciate your advice, Henry, truly I do. But I said I would be there. I can't go back on my word, now can I?"

"Huh. Me, if M'sieu Robelaird come after me with one of them fancy pistols, I scamper like hell. Make that bunny rabbit look slow runnin' for its hidey-hole."

"Very sensible, I'm sure, Henry. But it is going to be just fine." Ben winked at him. "Trust me."

"Better this one time you trust me, I think."

"And I do, Henry. But I have to keep my word. Now let's be off, shall we? I'd hate to disappoint the gentlemen by showing up late."

Henry grumbled and mumbled some, but he opened the cab door for his client.

Ben tossed his sea bag in on the floor, the sack landing with a dull clatter of metal against metal, and followed it inside. Henry closed and carefully latched the door and climbed onto his perch at the back. "G'wan then, dammit.

Gennulmun won't listen t' reason. Won't take good advice. Won't—"

"Henry!"

"I shut up now if you like. But you know—"

"Henry."

"Yes, suh."

The cab tipped and swayed as John put the team into motion.

Off to the east the sky was beginning to take on a faint salmon color as the sun crept closer to the horizon.

Tendrils of pale mist floated here and there amid the dew-specked grasses, and the trees surrounding the small open field were draped with ghostly strands of Spanish moss.

Robelaird and his seconds had arrived first and positioned themselves so that Ben and his attendants—both Henry and John were black and therefore could not be considered seconds—faced the cemetery. Somehow Ben did not think that was any accident. It was just as well that the sight of the mortared stone crypts and ornately sculpted headstones did not dismay him. If anything, he thought them peculiarly attractive in the thin light of the dawn.

Ben was introduced to the physician, a gentleman who gave the impression of having qualifications tied more to his antecedents than to his accomplishments. He was bleary-eyed and puffy of face and badly in need of a shave. Ben guessed the gentleman had spent the night in celebration of something or other. If medical services were required, Ben thought, he would much prefer Henry's ministrations, or even those of John the cab driver, to anything this Dr. Heinrich would be capable of offering.

Still, the proprieties were observed. A physician—leech, Robelaird insisted on calling him, and that description might be more apt than it first appeared—was present and would be available to the loser of the impending contest.

Robelaird's seconds were two young gentlemen who carried themselves with solemn intensity and no small measure of self-importance.

"You are ready, monsieur?" Robelaird asked after Ben dismounted from the cab and, sea bag slung carelessly over one shoulder, ambled over to join the gentlemen in the center of the small field.

"If you are, yes."

Robelaird snapped his fingers and the younger of the two seconds stepped forward with a walnut case the size of a small briefcase. He held the case flat, laid over his extended forearms.

Robelaird grunted with anticipation and unfastened the brass latches, lifting the lid of the case to disclose a truly handsome pair of dueling pistols.

The barrels and locks of the identical firearms were heavily engraved and inlaid with curlicues of silver and gold. The wooden butt stocks were lightly checkered and were fashioned in the saw-handle grip style which would have been awkward in a weapon designed to be carried but which was an exceptionally efficient design popular with limited-use weapons such as these highly specialized dueling arms. The guns were caplocks. They had no provision for the attachment of loading rams under the barrels, as dueling weapons were expected to be charged at leisure by seconds who were not direct participants in the affairs of honor. The guns were, Ben had to admit, especially beautiful objects that nearly approached the level of an art form. They might have been crafted by a jeweler rather than a gunsmith, they were truly that handsome.

"Monsieur Tobias will load," Robelaird announced. "Then, sir, as the challenged party, you may have the first selection of weapon."

Ben gave the fellow a thin smile. "That's something I wanted to mention to you, Robelaird. As the challenged party I'm entitled to the choice of weapons. At least that's the way I've always understood it."

"To be sure, sir."

"Then I think you can put your pistols away. They aren't what I choose to fight with."

"No?" Robelaird did not look pleased. But there wasn't much he could say about it either. It was Ben's right to choose, not his. He turned and said something in French to the younger second, listened briefly to the fellow's response, and returned his attention to Ben. "Very well, monsieur. My friends have had the foresight to bring steel. I have a nicely balanced set of épées that I think you may like."

"No épées either, mister."

"Monsieur, really. I do hope you are not of the opinion that you shall be permitted to make a mockery of this affair. Surely you do not propose a farce, slapping at one another with powder puffs or tossing cherry tarts back and forth. You cannot with honor propose such silliness."

Ben smiled. "I agree. But I do insist on the choice of weapons. Steel, sir. Take your pick."

He upended the sea bag and dumped its contents to the ground with a clatter.

There, acquired the previous afternoon at a waterfront chandlery, lay two crude and ill balanced but deadly sharp cutlasses and a pair of black iron marlinspikes with the tips ground to pinprick sharpness.

"But monsieur—"

"Steel, Robelaird. My choice of steel. Now, sir, take your pick and prepare to defend yourself."

CHAPTER 19

Robelaird looked like he was ready to storm away in a huff. Which would have suited Ben just fine, actually. His intent and expectation were that Robelaird, being uncomfortable with the cutlass and marlinspike—a decidedly low class form of weaponry—would be relatively easy prey for a former seaman like himself.

Ben's plan was to thoroughly humiliate Robelaird, to teach the man a lesson, and then to nick his skin just enough to draw a few drops of blood and thus satisfy the demands of honor. Once that was done, he could withdraw and let Paul Robelaird stew in his own juices. And, by extension, Guy DeMarigny in his as well.

That was the plan. But if Robelaird wanted to refuse to fight, Ben would be willing to accept that alteration with equanimity.

"*Gentlemen* do not fight with," Robelaird sneered, "alley trash like this. If you want steel, we will fight with my fine épées. If you demand foils or sabers, I will send for them. But not," his lip curled, "*these.*"

"Do I take it you withdraw your challenge, Robelaird? Or are you showing the white feather?"

Robelaird turned purple at the suggestion of a cowardice. His face became so dark that for a moment Ben

164

feared the man might suffer an apoplectic seizure and keel dead away.

There was no such luck.

"Really, Paul," the shaky old doctor put in, "the chap's quite within his rights, y'know. Steel is steel, and the choice belongs to him. If you don't want to accept his choice of weapons, you have to withdraw. Only thing you can do, Paul. Quite up to you."

Robelaird gave the leech a murderous look, but Heinrich's bolt had found its mark, and the damage was done. If Robelaird refused to accept the choice of cutlass and marlinspike now, he would be branded a coward by those in New Orleans who cared about such things. Ben found this entire situation bordering on the ridiculous—somewhere between that and insanity—but Paul Robelaird and his ilk took it all most seriously.

With scowling ill grace Robelaird first kicked the cutlasses, then bent and snatched up the one nearer to his hand. He gave the marlinspikes a suspicious inspection, then picked up one of those too. It was obvious that he had no idea what he was supposed to do with the marlinspike, but since it was there, he supposed he should have one.

Ben provided instruction of sorts when he claimed the remaining weapons.

It had been years since Ben had had occasion to use either, but they felt surprisingly familiar in his hands now, even after all this time.

Unlike Robelaird's meticulously crafted pistols or, no doubt, the gentlemanly épées, these cutlasses were ugly, ungainly, brutal weapons. They were made cheaply, with brass handles and handguards and crudely hammered steel blades with too poor a temper to hold an edge. They made better bludgeons than swords, and promised neither grace nor glory to their owner. They were, however, devastatingly effective in the hands of a man who understood them.

The marlinspikes were not even weapons. At least that was not their intended purpose, never mind the ordinary seaman's penchant for grabbing them whenever a dirk was not handy. The spikes were nothing more than long, tapering bits of iron with a point at one end and a flare at the other. They were tools used for separating strands of hawser, line, or cable whenever such was to be spliced or repaired. Seamen from time immemorial, however, had found a sharpened marlinspike to be an excellent substitute for a fighting knife. And one, moreover, that no ship's officer could forbid in his crew's hands since the spikes were, after all, tools and not weapons.

When the two were used together, the cutlass was wielded in the right hand and was swung in long chopping strokes or was jabbed in wicked inside thrusts, and the marlinspike, flared end tucked firmly into the palm, was carried in the left hand where it could be used for stabbing in a clinch.

Ben handed his cutlass and spike to Henry, then calmly and without hurry began to strip to the waist, his hat and clothing being given to John to hold until this matter was ended.

Ostentatiously—Paul Robelaird was not the only one who could try to rattle his opponent in small ways—Ben bent low to flick the ends of a silk kerchief over his spats to knock the dust from them. He feigned a yawn and stifled it with one languidly raised hand, then looked at Robelaird for the first time in several minutes.

"Are you prepared, sir?"

Robelaird's answer was a look of frustrated fury.

"No?" Ben demanded.

"Yes, damn you. Yes, I am ready." Robelaird grabbed his cutlass and marlinspike away from the second named Tobias and gave Ben Cartwright a withering glare. "Damn you, sir, prepare to meet your maker."

Ben gave the man a smug half smile and took his own weapons comfortably into his hands. He shook himself, loosening the tensions that had been building in his muscles, then stepped forward to present himself before the challenger Paul Robelaird. "Dr. Heinrich, would you be good enough to give the command, sir?"

"Bow, gentlemen. Thank you. Now on my count of three you may have at it with a will. One. Two . . ."

Paul Robelaird came bounding forward, slashing and hacking with verve and energy if not with skill. The man understood the use of swords well enough. Better, in fact, than Ben ever had or ever would.

But as Ben had anticipated, Robelaird's knowledge of steel was on the order of the deadly épée, the graceful foil, and the manly saber. None of those skills translated well onto the short, chunky cutlass. And certainly none of them took into account the threat of the marlinspike.

Ben waited for Robelaird's attack with something close to amusement.

Robelaird stood off at arm's length, as he properly should with a saber, and flailed away in the direction of his opponent.

Ben gave the man a moment to realize—and become alarmed by—the ineffectiveness of this plan. Then Ben moved calmly inside the arc of Robelaird's wild hacking.

Ben battered Robelaird's cutlass aside with a sweep of his own heavy blade, taking punishment on the mild steel of the cutlass, which would have shattered the better tempered but more brittle steel of a saber, and with the flat of his blade rapped Robelaird first on the elbow and then on the ear, not hard enough to hurt him, but the insult of it was stunning.

Paul Robelaird believed himself to be the consummate duelist. Now he was being humiliated by a total stranger. And a Yankee stranger at that, not even an Acadian.

With a howl of rage, Robelaird slashed and cut, his steel whipping viciously through the air. But only through air.

Ben turned the first wild sweep aside, stepped away from the next and calmly, almost casually, moved to his left so that a backhanded slap with the flat of his cutlass spanked Robelaird on the gentleman's fleshy posterior. Robelaird screamed and spun madly about, his cutlass swinging like a scythe.

Ben knocked the blow down, stepped inside it and with the sharpened tip of his marlinspike compounded the insults by lightly jabbing Robelaird first in the side and then in the neck. At those close quarters, too near for either man to use his cutlass, Robelaird jammed an elbow into Ben's ribs and tried to grapple with him, dropping his quite forgotten marlinspike to the ground in the process.

"Here now," Dr. Heinrich scolded from off to the side. "We'll have none of that, gentlemen. Separate yourselves. Paul, you forget yourself, sir. Now move back. Both of you."

Ben stopped scuffling and took a step backward at once. Robelaird—Ben chose to assume that the man was acting in the heat of the moment and not out of craven impulse—took advantage of Ben's withdrawal to try to split his skull open with an overhand smash of Robelaird's cutlass.

Ben parried the stroke and gave Robelaird a cold glare.

"Paul!" the physician snapped, launching into a string of angry-sounding French that brought a flush of bright color into Robelaird's cheeks. After a moment, though, the Acadian said something in return and with his blade saluted first the doctor and then his opponent, lifting the hilt of his cutlass to his chin and bowing.

Ben returned the salute with his own cutlass and also bowed.

"Ready again, gentlemen?" Heinrich asked. "Begin."

This time Robelaird was not so quick to charge. This time he knew he had no pushover facing him. This time the two men circled warily round and round, cutlasses held ready, Ben with his left hand forward to show the fang of the marlinspike it held, Robelaird with his empty left hand tucked tight into the small of his back as if he were preparing to go into a fencing stance. Robelaird hadn't bothered to retrieve his marlinspike when they paused.

Right foot forward, Robelaird shuffled a few steps ahead. He was trying to use the cutlass like an épée now instead of a saber, thrusting and probing with it as he came.

Ben gave Robelaird room for error and then struck, waiting until the Acadian was too close to withdraw and then, with a lightning strike, smashing Robelaird's cutlass aside and, again with the harmless but insulting flat of his blade, bopping the man on one shoulder and then the other. Had Ben chosen to strike with the edge of his cutlass instead of the flat, Robelaird would have been instantly crippled by the blows and would have lost the use of both his arms.

Robelaird shouted something in French and tried to retaliate, only to find Cartwright dancing around to the other side of him and once more administering a pair of taunting, teasing strokes with the flat of his cutlass, this time on the head and again to his belly.

"Damn you, sir." Robelaird sounded close to tears with the depth of his frustration.

He held his head down and cutlass up and blindly charged.

Ben ducked aside and tripped the fellow as he ran harmlessly past. Robelaird sprawled face forward into the dirt, losing his grip on his virtually useless cutlass as he fell.

"Damn you," he repeated, his voice cracking and his face contorting in an agony of humiliation. "Damn you!"

"Hold, gentlemen," the doctor ordered. "Monsieur Robelaird, you have been felled. Do you yield, sir?"

"Never." Robelaird scrambled to his feet, hastily brushing the dust from his trousers and retrieving his cutlass from the ground. At this early hour it was still admirably cool, but runnels of sweat streaked Robelaird's torso and beaded his forehead.

"I would withdraw if you will," Ben offered.

The man snarled something in French that, from the sound of it, Ben was just as pleased to not understand.

Robelaird lifted his cutlass and tried again.

Ben knocked the blade aside and spanked him once more.

Robelaird spun, lost his balance and toppled into the dirt for a second time. He was openly weeping now. He grabbed his cutlass in a two-handed grip and launched himself at Ben's knees.

"M'sieu Robelaird! For shame, sir."

Ben backpedaled away from the poorly conceived threat and shook his head. "This has gone far enough," he said.

"Oui, m'sieu. Enough." That was one of Robelaird's seconds. "Enough."

Paul Robelaird was on hands and knees, shaking and moving slowly from side to side like a bull buffalo run to ground by a pack of wolves. "No," he said.

"Come, Paul. You are beaten."

"No."

The man said something more in French, and Robelaird's other second added to it. Robelaird reluctantly and slowly came to his feet. He staggered for a moment, then caught his balance and came forward.

Ben nodded and transferred his cutlass into his left hand along with the marlinspike, so he would be able to shake hands with the vanquished Acadian. He had no intention, though, of complimenting Robelaird on the fight. This had been anything but a good fight, and everyone present had to know it. Still, Ben would not be churlish in victory. He would shake the man's hand and hope to forget the affair as quickly as possible.

Robelaird came forward with his right hand extended as if to shake and his left hand behind him as if resuming a fighting stance by habit.

"M'sieu," he said, "you are a cheat and a coward."

Ben blinked. This was not what he had expec—

"Now, sir, you die."

Robelaird's left hand flashed into view.

Ben caught a glimpse of color. The brown of dark wood, yellow of brass, gray of steel. The object in Robelaird's hand was small, no more than five or six inches long. Comprehension flashed a warning.

Too late.

The stubby derringer in Robelaird's hand bloomed a bright, fiery blossom, and Ben felt a giant's punch slam into his body. He lunged forward, knowing he was grievously wounded but trying to fight back.

Before he could strike with the thrusting blade of his cutlass, a red fog closed in over him, enveloping him, lifting and bearing him lightly into the clouds that had somehow mysteriously descended to fill the tiny and ever tinier field of honor where he was. Where he had been. He felt himself rising. Floating. Drifting free of all earthly fetters.

With a sigh and a brief flickering smile, the last tenuous thread of reality parted and Ben Cartwright was gone.

CHAPTER 20

A h, it hurt. It hurt so very much. The pain was bad, and yet he embraced it, clinging to it, savoring its every nuance, for pain was the only point of reference he had in a world that had turned into mist and shadow.

He floated in and out of a murky half sleep, surfacing and then receding like waves gently lapping a marshy, insubstantial shore.

And the pain was the only constant through all of it. The pain. Dear Lord, the pain.

"M'sieu Cartwright. Swallow for me. Try, m'sieu, just this one time."

An angel's voice, thin and sweet. Surely the angels sounded exactly so. But with a French accent? How odd.

Hot. Wracked by fevers and trembling. No not hot, cold. Shivering and gasping. Sweat pouring from his flesh. Chills shaking his bones.

He felt the scrape of wool across his burning flesh as he lay beneath a heavy blanket, shaking and shivering.

Fingers of ice stabbed deep inside his body while the surfaces burned. He cried out aloud. Felt the touch of a cool hand on his brow. Relaxed, smiling, and let the shadows claim him once more.

Water rocked him to and fro like a babe in its cradle. Soothing water. He could hear it slap and gurgle against wooden hull planks. A hull. A boat. The gentle, rhythmic rocking. It was all too natural to question.

His eyes remained closed, and his soul was at peace. He was at sea and all was well.

His eyes fluttered and came open.

Marie DeMarigny sat close by. She was smiling at him. She held something in her lap.

"Hello." Her voice was cheerful and bright. The tones were bell-clear and melodic. An angel's voice. Why did he have the impression this was not the first time he'd had that thought? He could not remember.

"H . . . H . . ." He cleared his throat and tried again. "Hello, yourself."

"You are feeling better, yes?"

He nodded. His neck felt stiff, and every part of him felt like it had been long unused. Movement was difficult. He was out of practice.

He dimly remembered having been in pain, but that too seemed a long time gone. Now there was a sensation of heaviness in his chest and a low, dull ache, but nothing particularly acute.

"Where . . . what . . . ?"

Marie's smile was gentle, kind, angelic. "Soon. I will tell you all very soon. First you must eat. Here. Please try to swallow, yes?"

It was a bowl she held in her lap. Broth. He could smell it when she dipped a large spoon in and held some for him to taste. The broth smelled wonderful. Rich and aromatic. Chicken, he thought. Why was it he remembered chicken broth in connection with . . . of course. But then he had been the one feeding it to her. Now their roles were reversed.

He allowed her to spoon the broth into his mouth. His mouth was dry and it was hard for him to swallow, but the warm broth trickled through his throat and brought a delicious sense of warmth into his stomach. Bright buds of flavor burst across his tongue and over the roof of his mouth.

"More? Please?"

He nodded. He smiled.

And without any sense of transition, he lapsed into sleep.

"My, m'sieu, you do look ever so much better now."

"Thank you."

The bowl of broth that had been in her lap was gone. Now she was holding a scrap of lace that was in the making and a shiny tatting shuttle that she was using to make it. He would have preferred the bowl, actually. He was ravenous, his belly gurgling and rumbling with its demands.

"Where are we?" One glance was more than enough to tell him that they were not in her apartment. Nor were they in his hotel room. He was sure he had never seen this room before—the walls were crude planking warped and papered with pages torn from illustrated magazines—and there was no city noise coming through the shade-dappled window.

"Ile de Fortesque. Do you know it?"

He shook his head. That was a mistake. The movement brought on a headache so violent he winced.

"What is wrong?" She moved so quickly that he could not follow her motion. One second she was in the chair. The next she was bending close, so very close, above him with her hand pressed to his forehead.

"Nothing. Really."

"You are hungry?"

"Yes."

"I will bring food. Then you sleep more. Then, next time you wake, I will tell you all."

That seemed quite good enough for the moment.

This time he was able to get down nearly an entire bowl of broth before his eyes sagged closed and he floated away again.

"This place, once it was used by smugglers—what your people called pirates, although they were not—now there is a sort of village. No one comes here who is not invited. You know what I say? No . . . police. No sheriff or marshal or hired assassin."

Ben had no idea why that should seem important to her. Or to him.

"It has been not quite two weeks since you kill Paul Robelaird, and—"

"Wait. What did you say? Robelaird is dead?"

"But of course. You do not know?"

He shook his head. This time, mercifully, there was no headache.

"He shoot you. You fall. You stab him. The doctor, I forget his name . . ."

"Heinrich."

"Yes, of course. Dr. Heinrich, he say you both will die. He does what he can, but say you both will die. About M'sieu Robelaird he is correct. That one dies in the grass like the dog he is." She turned her head and made spitting sounds, although without, Ben believed and hoped, actually spitting on the floor. "He was without honor, that one. All New Orleans heard what he did. He deserved to die. But you, the doctor say you will die too. He cut out the bullet Robelaird shot into you, but you lose so much blood, and the bullet, it is so close to the heart. The doctor gives you no chance. He shrugs and goes away.

"Henry Bloodworth, he does not know what to do with a dying man, so he brings you to me. He also helps himself to your purse, m'sieu. You should know this. But do not be hard on Henry. In his own way he is a good man. He pretended not to see the money belt that he himself wrapped inside your shirt. He robbed only enough so he can feel good about himself as a scoundrel and a man of the world, no?"

Ben smiled. "I see what you mean. No hard feelings."

"Anyway, it is only fair that I help you to die in peace after you do so much for me. So I say I will take care of you. Then soon I begin to think you will not die. And then I have another problem, because then Henry returns and tells me that the police, they would arrest you."

"Arrest me. Whatever for?"

"But, m'sieu, for murder, what else."

"Murder!"

"*Certainement,* m'sieu, what else do you think? Dueling, it is forbidden. And Monsieur Robelaird, he is dead. Besides, that evil old man Guy DeMarigny demands that they arrest you and charge you with the murder. So they look for you. They cannot find you at your hotel. Henry swears to them he does not know what became of you. He tells them probably you die, no? Says they should speak with the doctor who tended to you. But if they find that you are alive, m'sieu, if they find you ... poof. Into the jail. And there you surely must die. So once more Henry help you. Help me with you. At night we carry you away from the place where we hide you. Put you on the boat. Bring you to this place where Henry Bloodworth has friends. Freed men and women of color. We are the only whites here. But that is good. No one will look for you here. To the police in the city you are already dead. So far as Guy DeMarigny knows, you are dead. And now," she laughed gaily, "now you fool them all an' you are alive, no?"

"I am alive, yes," Ben agreed.

"You are hungry again?"

"Starving."

"Wait. I be right back." She bounced lightly to her feet and was gone in a rustling swirl of crinolines and skirts.

Ben let his head fall back against the slightly musty pillow where Marie had propped him. He was weak, he was hurting, he was hungry . . . and he was most definitely alive.

And this time he even felt strong enough to remain awake while he waited for Marie's return.

CHAPTER 21

Recuperating is not the same as recovered. It was nearly two full weeks more before Ben was able to leave the bed where he had awakened, and during that period his activity was largely confined to conversation, and that largely confined to Marie DeMarigny, although Henry Bloodworth did come by once, ostensibly for a visit with his "cousin" Achilles MacGregor who lived in the smuggler's village.

Ben came to know, and to like, Jean-Pierre's widow all the more during that time. At first, perhaps because it was the only subject of interest they shared, they spoke almost exclusively about Jean-Pierre. Later, more comfortable in each other's company, the talk was apt to veer and wander.

"Jean-Pierre was a good man, and I loved him. I think we could have been happy together except for his papa, that wicked man. The lies, oh the lies. Jean-Pierre believed some of the lies. The letters you brought to me show that he did. He believed them but was willing to forgive. He never knew how much of what he was told was lies. But he had grown. He had learned. He was a better man when he died than he was when he ran away from

New Orleans to escape from being caught between his love for me and his duty to his papa."

"It's sad that he never knew there was no child."

"No, m'sieu, it is not so sad as you think because it was his regard for the son he believed he had that made him think of what it is to be a father and what it is to be a man. It is the son he never had who helped him to grow into the goodness his papa tried to keep from coming out in him."

"The child. Would it have been a boy?"

Marie did not answer. Not in so many words. But her shrug and her sad, plaintive sigh said no, the stillborn babe had been a girl child.

"Down on the ground? Helping to pull a calf from inside the mama cow? *Non*, monsieur, *non*. Not my Jean-Pierre."

"Oh yes. He was quite a mess, let me tell you. Soaked to the skin from his waist up and reeking of ... well, it is really quite a messy process, and Jean-Pierre had been into the affair literally to his shoulders with both arms. But proud of himself? You should have seen him. He looked like he might claim to be the calf's daddy himself, he was that proud of the little thing. And of himself for delivering it. Why, he made me promise that we could keep it on the ranch for breeding and not sell or butcher it for meat. It's still there too. A heifer, thank goodness. I'll be breeding her to my new bulls this year. Just think. Poor Jean-Pierre is going to be a grandfather."

"So beautiful. Not at all a silly, skinny, ugly thing like me. I wish you could have met her, m'sieu. You would have loved my mama. Everyone did. Truly." Marie made a face. "M'sieu this and m'sieu that. Would it be scandalous of me to call you Ben? *Non? Merci*, Ben. And now you must call me Marie." She extended a small hand, an impish expression lighting her dark eyes, to seal the pact with a shake.

                    *   *   *

"Oh, Ben, I hope Adam does not blame himself for
what has happened. Little boys, they do that, you know.
They take so much upon themselves. So much fault. So
much blame. I hope Adam does not. He sounds like such
a sweet boy." She smiled. "And Hoss with the funny name
and so much love. I think I know them already and I have
never met them. But from the way you speak of them, it
is almost that I do know them. I could see them on the
street in a strange, far city, and I think I would know them
even in a crowd because of all you have told me about
them. How much you love them. How very much you
must have loved their mothers. Tell me about their mothers, Ben. Tell me about the two women you loved enough
to marry."

"Nothing but Indians and eagles," he said. "But that
was before the big rush to California, of course. Now you
see a dozen wagon trains a week. Sometimes more in the
height of the season. For us that would be late in the summer when the trains have had time to make it out from the
States. Up the Platte River and across the mountains, then
across the desert and on to the Sierras. Everyone tries to
make it past us and across the Sierras before winter.
Mostly they do. But it was the land I was telling you
about. Oh, Marie, you can't imagine anything so beautiful.
Or so completely different from New Orleans and the
swamps and bayous here. The Sierras are the most stunningly lovely . . . mind, I haven't seen much of the Rock-
ies, but I can't believe anything could compare with the
grandeur of the Sierras . . . and the lake near the Ponderosa. Tahoe, it's called. It's huge, miles and miles from one
end to the other, and very cold. The mountain peaks surround it, so that when you stand on a hilltop and look
down on it, you see the snow-tipped peaks reflected in the
surface of the lake like it was a gigantic mirror." He
smiled. "Sometimes I think that anything that perfect must

be a mirror. It must be what God uses when He wants to bend close and examine His whiskers for strays."

"Ben! Don't say that, it's blasphemous," Marie squealed. But she was laughing when she said it.

"Blue. I've thought it over, and my favorite color is most definitely blue. Not a dark blue, though. Not like a royal-blue or even a navy-blue. Sky-blue. That's it. Sky-blue. I used to own a scarf that color once. Something happened to it, though." She shrugged. "Still I have the memory. Nothing can take that from me."

Ben's heart ached for her. So small a thing. A scarf. And even of that she had only a memory. Yet there was no hint of self-pity in her expression or her tone. She asked not a whit more than she possessed. And her voice when she spoke to him about the color blue was full of life and joy and appreciation. She was a rare girl, Marie DuBey DeMarigny. Jean-Pierre had been a lucky man to find her. And a damnably foolish one to have left her.

"I have to start thinking soon about the trip back," Ben said. "Goodness, the boys must think I've abandoned them. Do you think you could find some writing paper and ink, Marie? I should write them a letter, at least. A letter should travel in, what, six, or eight weeks. Certainly it would go quicker than I can. I'll explain to them ... well, not everything that's happened here; I wouldn't want them to worry ... but at least I can explain to them that I've been delayed. Let them know they needn't worry about anything. With luck I still might be able to make it home before winter sets in. And it won't matter if the passes are closed or not. I'll stay on the eastern slope and cut straight north from Mormon Station. There shouldn't be any real difficulty except in finding forage along the way."

"The journey, it is hard?"

"More tedious than difficult."

"And there are wild Indians to waylay one?"

"I can't say that would be impossible, but the likelihood is really quite small. I think you'll mostly find that Indians are like anyone else. Good neighbors for the most part, but with a few bad apples to be avoided or if necessary met with force. Our neighbors at the Ponderosa are almost all Indians, and we get along fine. They are as welcome in my home as I am in theirs. Did I tell you that they saved my life that first winter I was there, after Inger died? Oh. It's a bad sign when a man starts repeating himself, or so I'm told. Anyway, if you would find me the implements, I'd like to write a letter and assure the boys that everything is all right. Thanks."

It felt good to be able to get out and walk around some. Also a little frightening. He was so weak and unsteady that he worried constantly about falling and opening the wound again. He was sure he could not bear the delay if he had to start healing all over again now.

Still, it was good to be able to move around a bit without help except for that of the stave Henry Bloodworth's cousin Achilles gave to him.

The first day he could manage a journey that far, Ben leaned on the stave and hobbled along the dirt path that served Ile de Fortesque as a main street. He found the shanty that was Achilles MacGregor's home and was admitted by a stunningly beautiful woman with a café au lait complexion and the lithe grace of a doe.

"Come in, M'sieu Cartwright. I am Andromeda."

Ben removed his hat. "My pleasure, ma'am."

"Thank you. Sit there, please. I will tell Achilles you are here." Her voice was a husky, curiously deep melody that was very pleasant to listen to. She smiled and glided away into another room. Shortly, Henry's cousin appeared. He was barefoot and bare-chested and carried a small, sturdy knife in one hand and a block of pale, fine-grained wood in the other. He found Ben standing in a corner looking at the pieces of a chess set arranged on a shelf there.

"Hello," Ben said with a smile. "I came to thank you

for the staff. It's a big help. But I couldn't help admiring these chessmen. They're exquisite. I take it you play?"

"No, I don't play the game, m'sieu. I only carve the pieces."

"Pity," Ben said with a shrug. "I was going to challenge you to a game. You do wonderful work, though. A man with all that talent should have been a sculptor instead of a . . . what is it you call it here anyway?"

"Wood carver," Achilles said with a straight face.

"Yes, of course. Ile de Fortesque is well-known as a village of wood carvers, I'm told."

"Was there something else you wanted, m'sieu?"

"No. Only to thank you."

"And so you have."

"Have I done something to anger you, Achilles? I didn't mean to. If I have, I will be glad to apologize."

"You have—"

They were interrupted by Andromeda MacGregor, who stepped briefly into the room and, filling the place with the warmth of her smile, offered tea, or if their guest preferred, something stronger.

"Nothing, thank you. I won't be staying long."

"How sad." She made a face, then brightened. "Perhaps you will come again? We have very few callers here."

"It would be my pleasure, ma'am." Ben's balance was not good, but by holding onto the back of a chair for support, he was able to manage a shallow bow.

"Good-bye, then." She swept out of sight again, leaving a vivid impression behind.

"Your wife is very lovely," Ben said when she was gone. "The two of you make a handsome couple."

He intended it as a compliment, but Achilles jerked like Ben had just prodded him with a sharp instrument.

"Achilles, I wish you would tell me—"

"I shouldn't. I wasn't going to. Henry told me you are different, but you aren't. You come into my home and you mock me."

"Mock you? Achilles, however have I mocked you?"

"You say things about my wife. I know what you are thinking. You think we have not seen this before? The white master come, look at the nigger wench, say, 'You boy, you too black and musky to lie with that nigger girl. I take her into my bed. You bring her to me. And mind you smile when you tuck your wife into my bed. Smile, boy, or I have the meat whipped clean off your nigger bones.' I hear that plenty before we run away. Now you come into my house. You look at my wife. I know what you are thinking. Best now for you to leave, I think, else I do things I promise not to do."

"If any tiny part of that were true, Achilles, you would have more than enough reason to hate me. And I suppose I can't blame you for doing it anyway. You can't see into my heart any more than I can feel the pain that's in yours. But it's a shame we can't. When I said you and your wife make a handsome couple, Achilles, I meant it. She is lovely. And she is your wife. Why, I can't imagine the sort of man it would take to . . . never mind. You cannot only imagine it, you've experienced it. More's the pity that you have. But that kind of man is not representative of my race, Achilles. Not any more than the oaf or the scoundrel is representative of yours. Thank goodness we are all individuals, Achilles. Perhaps someday we'll be allowed to think of each other one by one and not feel we have to lump everyone together the way we do now. Until then, please accept my apologies. I meant to cause you no harm. Not even the pain of bad memories. I'm sorry that I have, but don't worry, I'll not bother you again."

Ben bowed again, not so low this time, and began hobbling away.

"Cartwright," Achilles MacGregor said before Ben reached the door.

"Yes?"

"Henry, maybe he know what he is saying. You know?"

Ben shrugged again.

Achilles cleared his throat. It was obvious he would have liked to apologize for his outburst but did not quite know how. Not, at least, in so many words. "Look, um, those chess pieces?"

"Yes."

"If you want to play one game . . ."

Ben smiled. "I'd like that."

"Sit down if you like. There. I will tell Andromeda to bring tea and scones. You like scones?"

"Very much."

"She makes better scones than any you ever taste before this day. I guarantee it."

"Tea, scones, and a game of chess too?" Ben smiled. "I think I'm glad I came out today."

Achilles MacGregor, smuggler, wood carver, and runaway slave, proved to be an excellent match at the chessboard. He and Ben developed the habit of playing a game or two nearly every afternoon after that. Three games on Sunday afternoons when the World Championship—or so the opponents proclaimed—was at stake, two games out of the three to determine the supreme honor.

Ben set his coffee cup down and, frowning, cleared his throat loudly.

"Are you going to tell me now, Ben?" Marie asked.

"Tell you what?"

"Whatever it is you have been working up to telling me for the past two days."

"I didn't think it showed."

Marie did not bother to answer that absurdity.

Ben cleared his throat again, hemmed and hawed a few moments longer. Finally he spoke, in a very low voice. "I've talked to Achilles."

"And this is your great news? You talk with Achilles every afternoon. The two of you sit on his porch surrounded in pipe smoke and wisdom, and you talk and you move your little wood things around that board and you talk some more. Ben Cartwright, if you want me to become excited just because you have spoken with Achilles MacGregor—"

"I asked him to take me in the boat on Saturday."

Marie paused, her hands frozen in the act of drying a tin plate with a small towel. "You ask him to take you," she repeated.

"It's time, Marie. I'm healed."

"You are not."

"Almost as good as new. Good enough."

"But you should . . . three, four more weeks. You need more time. The place in your chest, it could still break open. You could begin to bleed again. If the journey is hard, the coaches poorly sprung—"

"I'm fine. You know I am."

"It is too soon," Marie insisted.

"If I don't go now, I'll be caught by the hard winter. It could be spring before I get back to the boys and the ranch. I have to leave now Marie or stay until next year."

"It is too soon."

"Saturday," Ben said.

Marie nodded, her expression fixed and disinterested now, and resumed drying the dishes.

"Marie."

She didn't answer.

"I still want you to go with me." This was ground they had gone over and over and over again in the past. He had been reluctant to bring it up again now. But confound it all anyway . . .

"I know what you've said about that before. But think, Marie. Think about what I've said. Think about Utah and the Ponderosa. It isn't charity I'm offering you. It's a decent life. A fresh, clean start in a fresh, clean land where there are no memories and no lies, where no one will know anything about you except what you choose to tell them. More important, people there will look at what you *show* them. People in the West are anything and any-one they are capable of being. No one there has a past. And if you tried to go back to New Orleans now, why, who knows what might happen. If the police find out that I'm still alive, they could arrest you for harboring a criminal. I'm still wanted there, you know. For murder. That's an awfully serious charge, Marie. They could turn right around and charge you with abetting my escape. Even if there is no official attention, there might be rumors again. With some small basis for truth, even. You know and I know that nothing untoward has happened between us, but would people in New Orleans believe that? You've nursed me back to health for all this time, and we two have lived under one roof while you've been engaged in doing it. Things like that have a way of becoming known, if only in whispers. And those whispers would not be kind, Marie. The rumors would start up again, Guy DeMarigny would see to it. You know he would hurt you if he could. This would only give him more weapons to harm you with.

"And think about it, Marie. I've heard you say over and over again that you would like to see the Ponderosa. You want to see the Sierra Nevadas and Lake Tahoe and the ponderosa trees. You've said you would like to meet Adam and Hoss. Meet my Indian neighbors and be invited to dinner in a wickiup. See San Francisco. See the high desert and the plains and prairies. Breathe air untainted with coal smoke and the stink of the cities. See the wildflowers in the high meadows and drink water cold and sweet from the mountain streams. Snow. Good heavens, you've never seen snow. You would see so much snow you wouldn't believe it if you come west, Marie.

"And it isn't charity I want you to take, Marie. It's opportunity. It's . . . Marie, why are you smiling like that?"

She laughed. "I am smiling, Ben, because you have been so very intent on trying to sell your idea that you have not been listening."

"Did you say something?"

"I could not, Ben. I could not get the words in, as you Yankees so quaintly say, edgewise."

"What, um, was it you wanted to say?"

"The last time you asked me to go to the West with you, I said I could not consider it, no?"

"Exactly. But you see, that's what I want you to think about now. Just pay attention to all the things I'm telling you, Marie, and—"

"Ben."

"Yes?"

"You be quiet for one second, please?"

"Certainly."

"The last time you say I should go with you to the Ponderosa, it was a month ago."

"Yes, that sounds about right."

"I have had much time since then to think."

"I'm glad you're being receptive to the idea now, Marie, because—"

"Ben."

"Sorry."

"I have changed my mind, Ben. If you still want me to go with you, I will go."

"But . . . that's wonderful, Marie. Why didn't you say so to begin with?"

She put her dish towel aside and began to laugh. "Because, you goose, you did not give me a chance, what else?"

Ben felt a surge of quick pleasure at the knowledge that Marie, beautiful Marie, angelic Marie, would be going with him. He would have her company that much longer.

But would the pleasure of her company be enough?

It was absurd. He was ten years Marie's elder. He had half-grown sons. And she was the widow of a man who had been his friend.

But the simple truth was that Ben's feelings toward Marie DuBey DeMarigny were not all platonic. He was, bluntly, attracted to her. Not that he would ever let her know that, of course.

A girl as lovely as Marie could have her pick of men. In California she would be a flame the moths would swarm to. Men of all stamp would covet her, court her.

Handsome men. Rich men. Men who spoke the language that was her birth tongue. Men who understood women far better than Ben Cartwright ever would. Those men would seek her out, and Marie would be attracted to one of them as she never could be to a simple man like him, and then . . . he frowned. Then he would no longer have the joy her companionship brought him.

That thought was painful but brief. After a moment he brightened.

Today he did have the pleasure of her company. And tomorrow and for quite a good many tomorrows yet to come.

Rather than dwell on that far distant future, better to savor the present.

"Could I have a little more coffee, please?"

"But of course." Quickly she moved to serve him.

For reasons he did not bother to elaborate, Achilles chose to take Ben and Marie to the small and relatively inaccessible port of Anahuac rather than on to the much more logical port at Galveston. Ben decided in this instance it was best to accept Achilles's judgment and to ask no questions. After all, Achilles MacGregor was a well-known . . . wood carver, and could be presumed to know what he was doing.

One thing was sure, he was an accomplished sailor. Ben thoroughly enjoyed the journey along the coast from Ile de Fortesque to Anahuac.

Marie, on the other hand, would have been much happier if they had allowed her to go ashore and walk the entire distance. Or swim it if she had to. Anything other than bob about at the whim of wind and wave. The raven-haired lady's only view throughout the duration of the trip was that of the water's surface, seen from a very short distance while she leaned over the lee rail, whichever rail that happened to be at a given moment.

In fact, part of the business of tacking Achilles's delicate sloop proved to be the task of moving Marie from one rail to the other with each change of direction. Ready about. Uncleat the jib. Clear. Hard on the tiller. Sheet in the jib. Shift Mrs. DeMarigny to the new downwind rail. Trim the main. It became a part of the routine.

The girl could scarcely support herself upright by the time Achilles finally ghosted to a berth—he had no trouble making his landfall at night here—at the old East Texas town of Anahuac.

"Will you be coming ashore?" Ben asked.

"No, better I do not."

"I'll miss our chess games," Ben said. He smiled. "And you."

Achilles looked embarrassed. "I never thought of a white man as a friend before. Never expected to, you know?"

"I know."

"Yes, well . . ."

"I still think you and Andromeda make a handsome couple, you know. I'll go a step farther. I think you are one very lucky man to have so beautiful a wife."

Achilles laughed. "Thank you. I'll tell her you said so, Ben."

"If you ever come west . . ."

"If you ever come back this way . . ."

Both men smiled. Ben brought out a cloth poke that was heavy with coin. "I don't want to embarrass you, but I want you to take this. Share it with Henry if you wish. Buy something pretty for your lady."

Achilles felt the weight of it and shook his head. "This much silver, Ben, it is much too much. You owe me nothing. For a friend, this little trip, it is nothing."

"For a friend this is a gift of appreciation, not a payment for services." The coins in the bag were gold, not silver, but Achilles did not know that.

"You will need money to travel."

"I can get more at the bank in Houston. They already know me there. I deposited a draft on my San Francisco bank with them when I was coming east. I have to cash the rest of it now anyway, and if I carry too much on me, I'm asking for trouble from bandits. Save me from that fate, Achilles. Help me out by taking this off my hands."

"For you, then. I wouldn't do it for anyone else."

"Now that's a spirit of genuine cooperation if I ever saw one."

Achilles took Ben by the elbow and, in a serious tone, said, "Take care, my friend."

"And you."

"You remember where I told you you can arrange for the coach to Houston? And if you see police, Ben, you are not to worry. This is Texas. Guy DeMarigny has no influence here, and in Texas they do not care what is said about a man in Louisiana. Here you and the lady both are safe from him. Remember."

"I remember. You've been a wonderful help, Achilles. Thank you."

"Go with God, *ami*."

Ben jumped lightly from the gunwale of Achilles's boat to the wharf and gave Marie the support of his elbow. By the time Ben's boots left the planking and were on solid earth again, the narrow, swift sloop was standing well out into the harbor, her sails filling with the night breeze and her stem slicing swift and proud into the dark waves.

"*Vaya con dios, amigo,*" Ben mumbled under his breath to the now barely visible craft, the Spanish words only dimly remembered yet somehow seeming appropriate to this time and place. "*Vaya con dios* may we all."

CHAPTER 22

Stagecoach service between East Texas and points as far west as Los Angeles was irregular but available. The rolling stock on the various stage lines was as irregular as the scheduling. Passengers might be asked to ride in almost any sort of conveyance that could be dragged from one point to another.

In the staid and settled Northeast, travelers might ride from Boston to Braintree in a leather sprung Concord coach that was as sturdy—and as comfortably heavy—as a walk-in bank vault, pulled by a handsomely matched Percheron six-up.

In the Southwest those same travelers might suffer for long days and nights riding in a cast-off army ambulance with canvas sides, dry rot in the floorboards, and seats made out of unpadded oak slats, with extra splinters added for spice. If the passengers were lucky, such a rig might be drawn by a biting, kicking, contrary collection of Spanish mules, no single one of which would weigh as much as a decent keg of beer and no group of which would—or so one would think—be capable of pulling an ambulance full of people and baggage more than ten minutes without stopping to rest.

Yet the stage-line operators managed to get the job done. The ungainly vehicles rattled and bounced day and night, somehow without falling apart. And the ill-mannered and ugly little mules cantered and complained for mile after mile without ceasing, and still had mettle enough at the other end to bite at their hostlers and kick at one another when they were let out of harness.

Marie accepted it all as a great adventure and squealed every bit as loudly as the little mules did, her outbursts, however, being expressions of enthusiasm rather than complaint. She observed everything with a fresh and delighted outlook and was excited and pleased by each new experience.

"Oh look, Ben, what are those red things hanging down off that post? Peppers? Truly? Whatever would anyone do with so many of them? But how quaint. How pretty. And look there. That baby wrapped in the shawl. Doesn't she have the biggest, saddest eyes you ever saw in your life? Isn't she adorable?"

Ben, who had traveled across most of the western hemisphere at one time or another, felt almost like he was traveling for the first time. He mentioned that to Marie when they were clattering westward aboard a surrey somewhere between Seguin and San Antonio.

"You are making fun of me, no?"

"No," he assured her, "I most definitely am not."

"Just because you have been everywhere and I never before this trip have been outside of New Orleans."

"What?"

She sniffed. "Call me a liar, then. It is true I was as far from the city as Ile de Fortesque. But only when Henry take the both of us there."

"That is the farthest you've ever been from New Orleans?"

"Oui, that is so. One time, when I was small, my mama and papa and I went onto a barge. It was a big barge. Bright blue it was with red and yellow on the canopy. There were tables where we could eat and benches where we could sit, and Nigras on the shore with ropes pulled us along the levee and we had a most wonderful time. I remember all of that so very well. But I do not think we went very far. I do not think that would count as a trip out of the city. Except for that one time," she shrugged, "nothing. I have never been so far before that I could not see the smoke from the rooftop chimneys in the French Quarter."

The idea that someone, anyone, might virtually live a lifetime of growth and struggle and eventual decline and never once travel more than a day's foot travel from the place where that person had been born ... it was something he had heard of before, but something he did not understand. To one of Ben's questing, inquisitive nature, such a thing was beyond being alien.

It bothered him to think that anyone could or willing would stay so firmly implanted in one lone spot. He couldn't quite grasp it. He could, however, very much appreciate Marie's wide-eyed enthusiasm for every new sight and sound and experience.

In San Antonio they bought cheese and tortillas— Marie had never tasted the flat corn cakes before and fell instantly under their spell when Ben first suggested she try one—and walked out along the banks of the stream that was locally, and with a straight face too, referred to as a river. Marie found that to be most amusing. But of course her sole experience with rivers before this trip had to do only with the Mississippi. Ben pointed out to her with considerable logic that the comparison was hardly a fair one.

"Mmm, Ben. This is good. I love goat cheese. Here, take some more. But Ben, you must help me finish it. If you do not, I will eat it all and be fat and ugly and it will all be your fault. A tiny bit more ... better. Now I will only become a little bit fat." She smiled, swallowed, followed the cheese with a huge wad of crunchy, greasy tortilla. She grinned and wiped her mouth on the back of her wrist. "Very much longer and I think I shall forget all the manners my mama ever taught to me, no?"

He started to say something, but Marie's eyes got

large. And then sad. He turned to see what she was looking at.

"Do you see, Ben? These Texas people, they are so
bad. They let even their churches fall to ruin. You see
there? Such a shame. I think it must have been pretty
once. Now it has become ugly and awful. Someone should
tear it down, don't you think? If they do not need a church
there anymore, they should use some of the stones to make
a shrine. Churches should not be allowed to become like
this though, Ben. It is all much too sad to look at."

"It's even more sad than you know," Ben told her.
"That old church is the place they call the Alamo. It's
where Texas independence was born. Or so some say."

"Really? Tell me about it, Ben. Please?"

And so they ambled on along the river, and Ben told
her what little he knew about the Alamo and the things
that had happened there.

The whole trip was like that, Marie questioning and
Ben pontificating to the point that he felt embarrassed to
be the one who was talking all the time. And yet he enjoyed it too, being able to talk with her, having such a
beautiful young woman focus her time and interest on
him, knowing that she accepted as fact whatever he chose
to say. Quite frankly, it flattered and pleased him simply to
be the center of Marie's attention for so very much of the
time.

Anyway, he enjoyed watching her enthusiasm. In a
manner of speaking, he was able to share it through her
eyes.

At a relay station some days west of San Antonio,
while one set of scruffy gray mules was being exchanged
for another, Marie clapped her hands and practically
jumped up and down in her excitement.

"Ben! Look, Ben. Are those Indians? Are they really?"

"Mm-hmm."

"They won't . . . scalp us or anything . . . will they?"

He smiled and shook his head. In a louder voice he said, "Hello. You there. Do you speak English?"

The Indian pretended not to hear.

"No? Oh well. I wanted to make a gift. Tobacco. But never mind."

The Indian scowled and came closer. "You swap?"

"All right."

"Swap woman?"

"I don't think so, thanks."

"Yes?"

"No."

" 'Bacco?"

"Yes." Ben pulled out his pouch of pipe tobacco. The Indian made a face and spat. "You want plug tobacco? This cut leaf is all I have."

The Indian said something in a language that sounded like he was in grave danger of choking to death. He reached under his blanket and pulled out a bright and shiny silver object that, upon closer inspection, proved to be a virtually new cigar trimmer. "Swap?"

"All right," Ben agreed. He handed over his pipe tobacco—he had more in his bag—and accepted the cigar cutter from the Indian. "Thank you."

The Indian grunted. He turned, stopped, turned back again. Giving Marie a long, insultingly specific looking over, he said, "You sure no trade? Give ten horses, ten and ten and ten buffalo robe. Big price. You swap? Eh?"

"Not right now, but if I change my mind I'll let you know," Ben promised.

"I wait. Ten horses and two horses and all so many buffalo robe?"

"I'll let you know."

The Indian grunted again and walked away.

Ben stifled his laughter until the fellow was quite far. But he could control it only so long. "Mighty big price, Marie. I was tempted."

She poked him in the ribs. Then she too began to laugh.

On a hot afternoon in El Paso, where no one seemed to know that winter was approaching, Marie came to him with an expression of deep concern lining her pretty features.

"What's wrong?" he said, quick alarm sending a pang of anxiety through his chest.

"Oh, Ben. It's awful. Just awful."

"What is?"

"I never thought . . . I mean I should have thought . . . but I never did, and now . . . Ben, I may never eat any Cajun food again."

"What?"

"I was doing some shopping, Ben. Or trying to. I wanted to make a really nice supper for you for a change. But . . . oh, Ben, I can't find *any*thing here. No file. No prawns. No oysters or crawfish or okra or . . . or . . . or just *any*thing. Nothing but old tortillas and beans and chili peppers. A little rice, but what does that matter when none of the rest of it can be found? Ben, what am I going to do if I can't get the things I need to make Cajun food?"

He laughed. "You'll survive, Marie. At least I think you will. Besides, in San Francisco you can buy anything."

"Even Cajun?"

"I don't know for sure, but we'll certainly find out, won't we? We'll get my factor working on it first thing."

"Thank you, Ben."

He hoped he hadn't started something that he wouldn't be able to finish. Even if he had, though, he could always send to New Orleans for whatever strange things she was talking about.

Later that evening as they sat in the courtyard of the hotel after dinner—a non-Cajun dinner, to be sure—Ben asked her, "Tell me something?"

"Yes, of course."

"What does it mean, 'Cajun'? I've heard you mention it, and others back in New Orleans, but I don't really quite understand what Cajun is."

She smiled. "You know Acadian?"

"Certainly. Jean-Pierre was Acadian. You are Acadian. It has something to do with being French and being from someplace called Acadia, right? Someplace in France, I suppose?"

"Nearly so. Acadia was a colony of France in Canada. Then a long time ago some damnfool—excuse me but is true—some damnfool, he give 'Cadia to England. Big mistake. Some 'Cadians stay and now they kiss-kiss at that silly old queen. The smart 'Cadians leave Canada and come south to French colony at New Orleans. Except we not so smart after all, and some other damnfool Frenchman give that colony to the United States. Us poor 'Cadians, we get stuck no matter what, no? But what you ask about is Cajun. Cajun is the lazy-tongue way to say Acadian. Acadian, 'Cadian, Ca'jun. You see? Is just the same, Acadian, Cajun. Just the lazy tongue and the slow talk."

"Simple," Ben said. "I should have thought of it myself."

Marie shrugged. "You think the store near the Ponderosa sell Cajun stuff?"

"No," Ben said. "But I think it's entirely possible that it will next year."

"Good." She yawned. "Too late now." He couldn't tell if she was referring to her shopping experience in El Paso or to the hour of the evening. "Good night, Ben."

"Good night, Marie."

At Walmsley's Ferry on the Gila in Arizona, they abandoned the comforts—however uncertain—of the stagecoaches, and Ben purchased two riding horses and three pack mules, two of which were gentled to saddle use and could be relied on as spare mounts if need be.

"But Ben, I do not know how to ride."

He grinned. "By the time we get to Mormon Station you will."

"What is at this Mormon Station place?"

"That's where we leave the California road and strike

out north for Utah and the east slope of the Sierras. Once we find the mountains, all we have to do is follow them until we see Adam and Hoss standing at the front door waving to us." He winked. "More or less."

"In that case I must learn to ride very good so we will be there soon."

By the time they had gone ten miles, Marie seemed comfortable in a saddle. By the time she'd spent two days on the road, she could ride better than Ben. Light as she was, and agile, Marie proved to be a natural equestrienne. Apart from her balance and ability, she had a particular affinity for horses as creatures to be petted and enjoyed. Ben regarded a horse as a useful means of getting from here to there when a ship, coach, or train was not available. Once she began riding on them, Marie came to regard each horse or mule as a companion and plaything that should be pampered and showered with affection. In any event, it took amazingly little time for her to become quite perfectly comfortable on horseback, and after a few days, if either one of them could be accused of slowing the other's progress, it would have been Ben who impeded hers and not the other way around.

They reached Mormon Station with the weather holding dry and sunny. The air was crisp and chilly at night, but the days were pleasantly warm and there was no hint of approaching storminess.

There was no reason at all, Ben decided, why they should not leave the well-traveled California road and turn north from here. The alternative would have been to go on to Los Angeles and then home by way of San Francisco and the high passes. Following that route would almost certainly mean they could not make it back across the mountains before the spring thaws, though.

"Eat hearty tonight, Marie, because from here on we'll be on our own. The only cooking we'll have after tonight is what we cook for ourselves."

She made a face. "And to think I still have found no Cajun food."

"If that's our biggest worry, I think we're going to be all right," he told her.

Oh Lord, they were in trouble. Big trouble. Ben hoped Marie had no idea just how much trouble.

He didn't know just exactly where they were, but wherever it was, there was no place to run, no place to hide. Whatever was coming—and it was a great monster of a something—it was coming fast and it was coming cold, and they needed to get the hell out of its way.

Having grown up with the sea and sailing ships as man and boy, Ben's lifelong habit was to remain attuned to the weather around him. He frequently scanned the horizon, noting color and cloud in all directions without so much as consciously thinking about it. It was simply something that he did.

And now . . .

The towering wall of roiled and murky slate-gray cloud was descending from the west by nor'west at an astonishing rate. Even as Ben watched, the front swallowed up his view of a pointed, yellow hilltop and swept across the barren flats ahead.

They needed shelter. They needed warmth if possible.

There was nothing.

In order to travel with some degree of comfort and speed, it was necessary to remain on the relatively smooth going of the lowlands, avoiding the rugged, rocky, virtually impossible to traverse hills to the west. Yet it was only in those hills that there was any hope of finding shelter. The only terrain feature within a half hour's gallop that Ben could see was a salt marsh to the east by northeast. There was no shelter there. Only icy muck and salt-white mud and a chance to drown before you could freeze to death. As an alternative, it seemed slim pickings indeed.

"Marie."

She had been walking her horse, Louie the Bold—

she'd insisted on naming it, just as she'd insisted on making a pet of it—and now she quickly drew rein. Ben stopped his horse beside hers.

"I don't want to alarm you, Marie, but—"

"I know, Ben. I have been watching it too."

"We're going to have to stop."

"Where? There is no place."

"Here."

"But there is no break from the wind."

"There will be." He dismounted and began stripping saddles and packs from the animals. Marie joined him.

When their gear was all piled as high as possible, Ben walked one of the mules close and picked up its near foreleg. He tugged on the thin and ratty excuse for a mane, and the mule was forced onto its side.

"Ben!"

"What, Marie?"

"Shouldn't you turn him loose? He might freeze if he cannot move. Would it not be better to let them go so they will save themselves?"

Ben shook his head. "If we do that, Marie, it won't matter if we survive the storm or not. Without something to ride, we would die out here anyway. We have to keep them with us and hope at least one of the five lives. And if we're going to do that, we might as well make use of them as part of the windbreak. Now lead Louie the Bold over here, please. We'll put him in close and hope he makes it. And hand me that rope there, please."

Marie became pale. But she brought the horse to him and did not protest when Ben eased it onto the ground and tied it so it could not rise again.

Surrounded by horses, mules, and equipment in as good a nest as they could create under the circumstances, and burrowing beneath all the blankets and clothing they possessed, Ben and Marie waited for the onslaught of lashing wind and blowing snow that was only a few miles distant and coming hard.

*   *   *

"Ben."

"Yes?"

"If I do not ... you know ..."

"Don't talk like that. We're going to be fine." He had to speak loudly and directly into her ear lest the howl of the wind drown out his words. The wind moaned and shrieked and sought out any tiny gap that would allow it to cut beneath the blankets in search of living flesh to freeze.

"No, Ben, I want to say this."

He did not want her to think in those terms, but neither could he deny her any comfort, however small it might be. If she wanted to tell him something, to accuse or vilify or condemn, he would listen and let her vent her emotions.

"Thank you, Ben."

"What?"

"You have let me see and do things I never thought could exist in the world. You have taken me away from the rumors and the hurts of the city and given me happiness and freedom and a whole new life. Just this much and you have made me so happy. I ... want to thank you."

He squeezed his eyes tight closed and fought back the impulses that were within him. It was insane, of course. Stupid and cruel and crazy. Here they were in a desert blizzard, probably dying, and Ben Cartwright was finding himself attracted—very forcefully attracted—to Marie DeMarigny.

They lay underneath the piled blankets, the two of them pressed close together, and instead of the cold that surrounded them and the weight of the snow that was threatening to bury them, all Ben seemed able to think about at the moment was the feel of Marie's slim and trembling body pressed so tight against his own.

He could feel strands of her hair tickle his nose and could smell the sweet and delicate scent of her flesh and could feel the warmth of her cheek so near to his chin.

He wrapped his arms closer about her, sheltering her,

trying to give his own body warmth to her, and instead of thinking about saving her from frostbite, all he could think of at this moment was the seductive womanly shape of her. He shifted a little, fearful that she might sense his reactions to her nearness, and blushed with embarrassment. The blush brought a brief glow of heat to his neck and cheeks and almost made him feel warm for a moment. He moved again and held Marie even closer. If only he dared kiss her while she was within the scope of this embrace. But, dammit, this was not an embrace. Not by her consent or knowledge. It was only a means to keep her warm. So far as she believed.

But, oh, if only . . .

"Marrrrie?" It was difficult to speak. His chin trembled almost uncontrollably, and his jaw ached. He was losing feeling in his nose and ears, and his hands felt numb and clumsy. It was almost as hard to think as it was to speak. They were close to death, and he knew it. Yet there was no sign that the storm was anywhere near abating.

Ben had no idea if it was day or night. It had been hours, perhaps a full day, perhaps even longer, since he had tried to peer outside the icy cocoon they shared beneath the blankets.

If only the snow had been allowed to pile up on top of them, it would not have been so bad. Ben knew that. A few feet of snow would actually have acted to insulate them from the cold, and they could have easily survived, with the temperature a bit less than freezing because of their own body heat inside a snow cave.

But the wind, the damnable wind, whipped the snow away from them before they could benefit from it. The wind, the incessant, interminable, howling, awful wind had crept insidiously beneath their blankets to find them and to leech the warmth from them and then to carry that warmth away to be wasted out in the deadly open.

Deadly open. Equally deadly where they were. The difference seemed only a matter of time.

"Marie?"

She was limp in his arms, and there was no answer from her sweet lips.

He gently shook her, but there was no response.

He tried to convince himself that it was only the exhaustion, that she was merely sleeping.

He tried to convince himself, but he failed.

Sobbing, Ben played the lone last card that he knew of.

He fumbled with stiff and clumsy fingers and, bracing himself but knowing there no longer was any choice to make, he began to hack and saw at yielding flesh, flesh that might still have been living . . . or might not. At the moment, he neither knew nor cared.

"Ben."

"Yes, Marie?"

"I feel warmer now."

"Yes."

"Am I dying?"

"No, Marie. I won't let you die."

"Ben."

"Yes, Marie?"

"Before I die, there's something I want to tell you."

"Yes, of course."

"I don't want to upset you, though."

"Nothing you could say would upset me."

"I . . . I know there is no reason why you should . . . feel anything. There are many reasons why you should not, a man so handsome and fine as you. But . . . Ben . . . I love you. Since those wonderful nights at Ile de Fortesque when we sat and talked and talked and talked. I began to love you then. I have grown to love you more each day since then. That is why I changed my mind to come with you. And Ben . . . I am glad that I came. I would rather die here with you than live there alone. Do I embarrass you? I am sorry. I should not have said anything. I just wanted . . . you know."

Ben's chin quivered and he tried not to cry. Oh, Lord. To think . . .

He moved closer. Rested his cheek against hers. He really did not want to weep. Not even with happiness. Because if he did, he was sure the tears would freeze on his cheeks.

"Ben."

"Yes."

"How is it that I feel so warm now? Is it that we are dying together, my dear?"

"No, my darling." He kissed her. Very gently, for the first time, he pressed his lips lightly to hers. "We'll talk about it later, dearest."

He did not want to tell her that she was lying inside the stomach cavity of her pet horse Louie the Bold. The animal's body heat would last for hours. And if that heat lasted longer than the remainder of the storm, that heat and that of the rest of their animals, they might yet have a chance to live.

But he did not want to tell Marie. Not just yet.

He kissed her again.

And, oh, how very much he wanted now to live.

CHAPTER 23

T he mule reached the top of this latest incline and Ben pulled it to a halt to give the faithful animal a breather. Marie stopped beside him, and he reached over to take her hand and give it a gentle squeeze.

"Just another mile. You can see the smoke from the chimneys there."

"This city . . ."

He smiled and shook his head. "Hardly a city. Genoa barely is big enough to be called a settlement. It's mostly just a trading post and a few cabins. It's also as close as we have to a town in this end of Utah Territory."

"There will be a priest in this Genoa place?"

"Not likely, nor a preacher either. They come through now and then, but there isn't a regular church established here yet. The preachers we see around here are just circuit riders and wandering padres who cover hundreds of miles in search of a flock to feed. What we can find here in Genoa is Sid Yeltner. He's a justice of the peace appointed out of Salt Lake City, and as much civil authority as there is on this side of the mountains."

"He can marry us?" Marie asked.

Ben squeezed her hand again. "Yes."

"Then let us hurry, please."

Ben laughed and bumped his mule forward into a walk again.

The mules were tired, but they were managing nicely, had been ever since the storm abated. Neither horse had survived—Ben never would know if he killed Louie the Bold or if Marie's pet mount had frozen to death already by that time—but all three mules were able to stagger and wobble onto their feet, shake themselves briskly like so many oversized dogs, and then, clumps of ice and snow still clinging to them, begin placidly to search the ground for forage.

That was all four days back. At this point the fears and furies of the brief but vicious storm seemed only a bad dream to be dimly remembered. How close he and his precious Marie had come to death then. How very little that seemed to matter now that it was behind them. The important thing now was what lay ahead. And an entire lifetime of talk and tenderness was what Ben could see for the future they two would share.

He still found it incredible, quite perfectly beyond reason, that Marie DuBey DeMarigny, soon to be Cartwright, would—could—see anything in him. But, oh, his heart leapt with joy at the knowledge that this unlikely, magnificent turn was true.

Grinning like a man who had personally, and quite recently at that, invented love, Ben Cartwright rode forward into the rude and tiny settlement south of the Ponderosa.

"What do you mean Sid isn't here?"

"I mean like you can look but you won't find him, Mr. Cartwright. I mean like Sid don't live here no more. He's sold out an' gone back to New Jersey."

"New Jersey?"

"Ayuh, that's where Sid is from. Said something about wantin' to see his old woman again."

"He had a wife in New Jersey?"

"That's what he said."

"What about Ivy?"

"Sid sent her back t' her folks. Ivy and them didn't mind. He sent 'bout half the stuff in his store with her. They've got beads an' blankets enough to last 'em for years now."

Marie tugged silently at Ben's sleeve. For a moment there, as he tried to grasp all these odd changes in Genoa, he had almost forgotten she was with him. He turned to her.

"Sorry, dear. The justice of the peace I was telling you about? Jenkins here tells me he's sold out and gone. Left his Indian wife here and went back to his real wife at home, apparently."

"But what about the man to marry us?" Marie asked.

Harley Jenkins, a bent and arthritic old fellow who trapped and prospected and somehow eked out a livelihood, snatched his hat off and stepped forward. "Marryin', Ben? Is that what I heard the lady say?"

"Yes. We'd hoped Sid would be able to marry us. But seeing that he has gone—"

"There's another J.P. if its a wedding you want, Ben."

"Who?"

"Don't know as you've ever met 'im. He showed up a few weeks after Sid left. Brought a justice o' the peace commission from them fellas in Salt Lake, came in, built him a place an' commenced dealing out law an' cards, whichever a man is of a mind for. It's that new cabin on the hillside yonder." Jenkins pointed. "You want I should introduce you, Ben?"

"Please. And please excuse me, Harley. I've forgotten my manners here." Ben performed introductions between Marie and Jenkins.

"Come along, folks. We'll get you married right up," Harley Jenkins promised.

Word of the impending nuptials spread quickly. Not by any particularly mysterious means, though. Harley Jenkins, who seemed every bit as pleased and excited by the prospect of the wedding as either the bride or the groom, shouted the news to all who were within the range of his voice. And they in turn shouted the news on in relays of noise and excitement.

By the time they reached the new justice of the peace's establishment, there was a laughing, joking, light-hearted procession trailing behind them that must surely have included the entire population of Genoa, Utah Territory, a population which was considerably larger than Ben would have thought possible. The settlement had bloomed and blossomed since he had last been here. Now he guessed there must be several hundred residents in Genoa. And apparently each and every one of them was going to stand witness at the wedding.

"Come out, Larry, come out, you got duties to do," someone shouted.

The crowd took it up as a chant. "Out, Larry, come out. Out, Larry, come out."

The cabin door opened, and Ben could see half a face and one eye peeping out.

"Out, Larry, come out. Out, Larry, come out."

"What the hell . . . oh, excuse me, ma'am, I didn't see you there. Now, uh, what is all this about?"

Larry was no taller than five-three or -four, but probably tipped the scales at two hundredweight or better. He was short, beefy, florid of complexion, and wore spectacles with wire rims and lenses little larger than postage stamps. His hair was dark and there was plenty of it, not remarkably so on his head, but a coarse furry mat of it extended over his neck and could be seen puffing out of his shirt at the throat. Tufts of it poked out of his sleeves at the wrists, and his beard, although freshly shaved, looked like a wire bristle brush with the wires worn short.

"What is it you want here, eh?"

"Larry, this here is Ben Cartwright of the Ponderosa. I know you've heard of Mr. Cartwright. Ben, this is our new justice of the peace, Lawrence Jessup. And Larry, the lady here is . . . I forget her name now, something French and pretty . . . point is, she's here to marry up with Ben. And as J.P., Larry, you're to do the honors."

"Cartwright? Ben Cartwright?" Jessup looked puzzled. "I thought you were dead."

"Not that I'm aware of," Ben told him.

Jessup cleared his throat, gave Ben a suspicious stare, then shrugged. "I suppose if you aren't dead, it isn't anything that will hurt my feelings."

"Am I supposed to understand that comment?"

"What? Oh, uh, no. Never mind." Jessup's expression lightened. He clapped his hands and in a loud voice said, "Who's standing treat for this wedding party here?"

"That would be my responsibility, I believe," Ben said.

"Good. Drinks for everyone. Leon, you and Morey bring out the keg in the far right corner. Not the one with the green paint on it, mind. Roll out the good stuff. Mr. Cartwright is buying. And bring out some food too. Pretzels, crackers, that wheel of yellow cheese on the top shelf in the pantry . . . oh, and the jar of pickled eggs. Don't forget the pickled eggs."

"Wait, wait," someone shrieked from far back in the crowd. "Don't nobody do nothing yet. I gotta run fetch my squeeze box."

"Carl? Has anybody seen Carl? He needs to get his fiddle and get down here quick."

"Three cheers for the bride. Huzzah! Huzzah! Huzzah!"

Ben looked at Marie and winked. He leaned down and whispered, "I hope you don't mind. . . ."

She giggled. "It's wonderful. Sort of."

The whole thing was growing quite out of hand. Ben's and Marie's intention to have a nice, quiet little marriage ceremony had suddenly developed into a great, grinning, community party with all of Genoa invited. Whether they'd been invited or not, actually.

Within minutes there were kegs of beer and cider, foods were being served, music was playing and the womanless men had begun to dance enthusiastic if inexpert jigs and clogs and reels, half the dancers clomping and stomping their way through the male roles and the other half with neckerchiefs tied around their arms to indicate that they were the "lady" dancers. It was all very much the glorious affair, set out of doors on a crisp and brilliant autumn day.

The justice of the peace disappeared momentarily. When he returned, he was dressed in tie and tails and a stovepipe hat that was nearly as tall as its wearer. J.P. Jessup looked and acted most solemn and dignified, as befit such an occasion.

Someone dragged a table out of the city hall/saloon/ living quarters that was Larry Jessup's cabin. Others helped the bearlike little man onto it so that he could be seen above the crowd. After a few moments people caught sight of him. The music died away and the dancing and celebrating slowed and finally stopped.

"Mr. Benjamin Cartwright, Miss Marie ... Du, De, uh, um ... Miss Marie, will the two of you folks come over here, please, that's right, right there will do. . . . Now, do the two of you, standing before this company of citizens and good folk, do the two of you ..."

Jessup launched into a wedding service that touched now and then on the tried and true old phrases but which also added its own original touches. Ben, for instance, never would have thought to include in his wedding service anything about Marie pledging to honor and make good any of his gambling losses. For some reason, Jessup seemed to find that one a necessity. There were a few others of similar nature; but nothing Marie was not willing to agree to and nothing Ben chose to shy away from either.

When Jessup finally reached the point of announcing in a strong, clear voice, "I now pronounce you husband and wife," an ear-piercing roar went up from the crowd.

Hats were thrown in the air. Hands were shaken. Drinks were downed. And men filed shyly past to have a close look at the beautiful bride while they offered Ben their congratulations and Marie their best wishes.

All in all, Ben decided, it was a wedding a man could be happy with.

Before very long, with the music once more ringing out and the dancers once more bouncing and tugging at one another, Ben and Marie slipped away.

"Oh, Ben. Never have I seen anything so very beautiful."

Marie's voice was hushed with wonder. They sat in their saddles on the top of a hill. Lake Tahoe lay spread out at their feet like a great, brilliant jewel. A sapphire of immense proportion and complete perfection.

The peaks, with their mantels of purest white, rose in majestic splendor on the distant California side of the lake. Their beauty was mirrored in the still, blue waters of the lake below.

This was Marie's first look at the lake, and it fairly took her breath away. "Oh, Ben." She began to cry.

"What is it, darling? What's wrong?"

"But nothing is wrong, my sweet. I am just so overcome with the beauty that it is too much to hold inside. That is all."

"I hope I'm not expected to understand that." She didn't answer, so he moved his mule closer to hers and leaned out so he could put an arm around her shoulders and comfort her.

Marie sniffled and sobbed a bit, but when she took her eyes off the splendors of God's beauty for a moment so that she could look at him instead, there was a beatific smile on her face and deep joy in her eyes. He felt better then, knowing she was all right.

"Thank you, Ben. Thank you for bringing me here."

He nodded and would have kissed her, but his mule chose that moment to take offense at something Marie's mount did. The animal snorted and shook its head and, with its ears pinned flat, sidled away from Marie and her mule. Ben could either let the mule carry him away or fall off trying to stay close to Marie. He chose to stay in the saddle.

Marie laughed. Then she sobered. "Ben."

"Hmm?"

"Could we . . . rest here a little while?"

"Yes, if you like."

"I would like." She dismounted, and he did the same. Ben tied the two saddle mules and the one that was carrying their few remaining packs—most of what they had brought with them from New Orleans and points closer had had to be abandoned back on the desert where they'd suffered through the blizzard—and followed her to a soft bed of needles beneath one of the towering pines. He sat beside her and gazed out upon the lake and the forests and the rugged, magnificent mountains.

"So strange," Marie said. "So little while back we almost died in that storm. But here the only snow we see is many miles away on those mountaintops. There is nothing on the ground here."

"It can be like that at this time of year sometimes. It will snow, and then in another day or two it's all melted away and gone. And who knows, there might not even have been a storm at all here. It could have skipped over the Ponderosa completely." He smiled. "We'll ask the boys when we get home."

"Home," Marie whispered. "I want very much to reach home."

"Our home," Ben said. "Yours and mine and the boys'."

"Yes." She touched his wrist, then moved closer, snuggling in beneath his arm and resting her face warm against his chest. "So long . . . I have never had a home of my own. Not really."

"No?"

She shook her head. "But do you know what, my darling?"

"Tell me."

"It was worth waiting for, this first and last and only home of my heart."

"I hope you'll think so."

"Already I do, my darling." She lifted her face to be kissed, and he accommodated her.

Later, both of them filled with the happiness of love, they stood hand in hand while Marie once more looked out over the lake and the mountains with such intensity that Ben thought she must surely be trying to memorize each and every line or shadow of the wonderful scene before her.

"May I ask of you a favor, my darling Ben?"

"Anything."

"If I die before you, Ben, would you bury me on this hill? I would like that, you know. To spend all eternity with God's most pretty handiwork in front of me. How nice that would be," she said.

"Marie! Don't talk like that."

She looked at him with life and love in her eyes. "I do not mean to be morbid, my love. I will not die. Never. I promise."

"That's better."

"Come, then. We will go home now, yes?"

"We will go home now. Yes indeed."

They returned to the mules and followed the gentle contours of the hills down to the ranch. To the Ponderosa. To home.

"I hope ... you aren't disappointed," Ben said. "It isn't much. Just a bachelor kind of place. But we can build a proper home, Marie. For our family. We can build any kind of house you like, whatever you want."

"Anyplace you are is my home and my castle," Marie told him. She looked at the long, log cabin they were approaching. "But perhaps a change here, a tiny improvement there. What you think?"

He laughed. "We'll build a grand house. Just exactly the way you want one to be."

She winked at him. Then, turning back to the Ponderosa, she said, "But the boys, Ben. Where are your sons? I am so anxious to meet them."

They rode into the ranch yard, and Ben called out a loud, cheerful hello. Edgar Malloy came to the front door, a pan of dishwater in his hands. He saw Ben, gaped, and was so startled, he dropped the pan of water instead of flinging it into the dusty yard, then turned to bolt back inside the house.

"What the—"

Malloy edged back outside, pointing. And behind him came George Foster and his wife Irma. George held a shotgun gripped so tightly that his knuckles showed white against the dark wood of the gun stock.

"Hello, George. Irma. Where's Adam? Where's Hoss?"

George looked nervous. Irma said something too low for Ben to hear. Judging from her expression, it was something sharp and snippish. George cleared his throat and glowered.

"You get out of here, Ben Cartwright."

"What did you say to me, George?"

"You heard me, Ben Cartwright. We heard you was dead. I reckon you ain't, but that don't change nothing. You get out of here."

"George, where are my sons? And what do you think you're doing trying to tell me to get off my own place?" Ben demanded.

"You heard me right, Ben Cartwright. This here is *my* land. And you ain't welcome on it. Now get off. Git. Quick, afore I lose my temper an' shoot."

Foster, incredibly, brandished the shotgun for Ben and his bride to see.

"Git, I told you. Get off my Ponderosa land or I'll shoot you down for trespass."

"Dammit, George." Ben rode a few steps closer. "I won't have you—"

Foster, his eyes wild with fright but his jaw set with

grim determination, lifted the shotgun to his shoulder and took shaky aim.

"I warned you, Ben. Now I reckon I'll do what I got to do."

He pulled back on the big, earlike hammers of the double-barreled scattergun. The twin tubes each looked big as a hawse pipe.

"Get off my land, Ben. The Ponderosa belongs t' me now."

Ben felt sick to his stomach.

"Where are my sons, George? What have you done with my boys?"

Foster's only response was a near frantic waggling of the barrels of the shotgun.

"I should have shot him down like the vermin he is," Ben complained.

They were standing in the warm, fall sunlight beside a rocky promontory overhanging the road. It was only a mile or so from the Ponderosa. Ben had stopped there only because it seemed a likely spot. And because he wanted, quite desperately just now, to hold his young wife in his arms. And because he did not know where else to go.

He felt . . . empty. Confused. His world had turned topsy-turvy and he didn't even know why.

"The ungrateful son of a bitch," he grumbled. "After all I've done for him, to try and take my home away. But that isn't the worst of it. The Ponderosa, the livestock, all my books and furnishings and everything . . . that isn't the worst of it by any measure. All those are just things, you see. The worst, the very worst thing possible, is that I don't know what he's done with my sons. Where are Adam and Hoss, Marie? *Where are my boys?*"

Marie, understanding the magnitude of his pain, did not try to give false comfort or to make easy promises. She simply wrapped her arms tight around him and held him as close as was humanly possible.

After ten or twenty minutes, Ben took a deep, ragged

breath and squared his shoulders. "All right, damn it. This isn't the homecoming I planned for you. That one will just have to wait a little while longer. For now, dear, the first thing we need to do is find my sons. Then we'll tend to that ingrate George Foster. Whatever that takes."

Marie smiled and kissed him tenderly at the corner of his mouth. "Wherever you go, my dearest Ben, I will follow. Whatever you say, I will do."

"Thank you."

It wasn't exactly the introduction he would have liked for Marie's first meeting with Ben's old friends the Pah-Utes, for this entire set of circumstances was very little to his liking.

"Marie, this is Doheetsu, headman of this band and a very old and dear friend. Doheetsu is the son of Ma'hundi, who saved my life long ago and who taught me much. Doheetsu and his people are always welcome in my lodge, eh, Doheetsu?"

"Yes, Sees Far, many yes. All same as you are at home when you are here."

"Doheetsu, this is my wife Marie. My woman."

The Indian grinned and turned to shout the news to the others who were gathered behind him. An approving roar went up from the score or so people who made up the roving band. Some of the women crowded close and began very shyly to touch and pat her, as if wanting to examine her or perhaps to take or impart some magic or meaning from the physical contact.

"Mrs. Ben. Good," Doheetsu said happily. "Many sons, yes?"

"We hope so, Doheetsu, but first we must find Adam and Hoss. Have my boys come to stay with you?" Ben found it particularly interesting that Doheetsu referred to Marie now as "Mrs. Ben." The Indians tended to attach their own names to people, and until this moment Ben hadn't ever really been sure if they grasped the idea of his true name or not. Apparently they did. They knew he was

Ben Cartwright even if they did not care to call him by that name.

"No, Sees Far. Thinks Much and Big Small Boy are not here. You lose them?"

"Yes, I think so."

"They are not lost in mountain to not find way home. Thinks Much can no be lost. I teach him good. Not lost."

"No, I don't think so either. But I don't know where they are, Doheetsu. I'm worried about them."

"Little man with gun and much fear chase them away?"

Ben knew he really should not bother being amazed any longer that the Indians always knew so much about what was happening at the Ponderosa even though they so seldom visited. Apparently they observed much more than they were observed. Even by Ben, whom they trusted as if he were their own brother.

"I don't know, Doheetsu. What do you think of the little man who lives in my house now?"

"Don't like. He try to cheat. Not even good cheat. Put thumb on scale. Stupid."

"He should try playing Hand with you," Ben said. "Then he would learn some lessons about cheating."

Doheetsu grinned, obviously proud of his exploits, including any that might rely on a bit of cheating to accomplish. "Little man have cold winter then. Only have own skin for to keep him warm if he play Hand game with me, Sees Far. I try to get him to play once, but he say no."

"Too bad," Ben said. "Will you look for the boys, Doheetsu? Help me find them?"

"We look. All our people."

Ben nodded. No more was needed on that subject. If Doheetsu said it, it was so. This band and all the others they talked to would be on the lookout for Adam and Hoss.

"You want Mrs. Ben stay with us now, Sees Far?"

It was something Ben hadn't thought of before, but it might be a good idea. If not now, then perhaps later, depending on what he had to do to resolve his problems with George Foster.

First, though, he still had to find the boys.

"Maybe," he said. "We will see."

"Winter camp. You know where to find."

"Yes, thank you."

Doheetsu turned and said something to his people— Ben's command of the language was poor, but he could manage the gist of things—and the women reluctantly abandoned their inspection of Sees Far's new woman.

It was a very good thing that Marie did not speak the Pah-Ute tongue. The women had been vociferously sorting out Marie's strength, endurance, and probable child-bearing capabilities. Her ears should have been burning by now.

Men and women alike clucked with concern when Doheetsu told them that Adam and Hoss were missing. If the boys were anywhere in the territory covered by Doheetsu and his people during their hunting, they would soon be found.

But if they were elsewhere . . .

"Come along, Marie. I think we better go talk to Larry Jessup again. He's the closest thing to law we have this side of Salt Lake City."

Marie seemed actually reluctant to leave the Indians. She was enthralled by them and already was well on toward developing a friendship with a young woman whose belly swelled with a soon-to-be son or daughter, this although neither woman spoke a word of the other's languages.

"Good-bye, Sees Far."

"Good-bye, Doheetsu."

CHAPTER 24

The justice of the peace at Genoa peered at them over the tops of his undersized reading glasses. "I understand your plight, Mr. Cartwright. I even sympathize. All I can tell you, though, is that I acted in good faith. A petition was presented to me as a notary. I attested to the signature. Beyond that, sir, I cannot say."

"But you tell me these people claim they had my certificates of title invalidated by a court in Salt Lake City?"

"I am only telling you what was told to me." The furry J.P. shrugged and sucked on the stem of an empty pipe. "Mr. Foster made an appearance before me in the official conduct of my duties. His identity was affirmed to me by two witnesses, one of them being your former employee Mr. Malloy. They mentioned an article in a San Francisco newspaper announcing your death as the, ahem, result of a duel in which both participants were alleged to have perished. They also said something about seeking a resolution of settlement with your estate."

"Neither my factor, DeShong, nor my attorney, Kendall, would allow anything like that, newspaper account or not."

Jessup spread his hands and sighed. "I declaimeth not, sir. Like I say, I am only repeating what was told to me. Mr. Foster said your claims were invalid, not I. He

220

said new and correct filings were being entered. I notarized his signature and attested to his documentation as necessary."

"Did you mail it on to Salt Lake, then?"

Jessup shook his head. "I did not. I returned the documents to Mr. Foster. They were not complete at that time."

"No? What was missing?"

"The name, or names, of the owner of record."

"But—"

"Mr. Foster made the filing application. It does not necessarily follow that the filing must be made in his name. In this case, although it was not my place to ask, nor did I do so, I received the impression that another party would be involved, indeed that this separate party might be the sole owner of record. That is to say, Mr. Cartwright, I believe your Mr. Foster was acting on behalf of another."

Ben shook his head. "This makes no sense, Mr. Jessup. None."

"I cannot dispute you, sir. I only relate what little I know." The J.P. gnawed on his pipe stem for a few moments, then said, "I've heard something of your reputation, Mr. Cartwright. At that time, I must confess I'd never heard of you. I have heard a great deal about you since that time. And, um, some few things about Mr. Foster and Mr. Malloy too. If I may suggest . . . ?"

"Please do."

"You obviously have legal counsel."

"That's in San Francisco."

"Nonetheless, inform him at once. Also your attorney in Salt Lake City, if you have one."

"I'm afraid I don't. Salt Lake is so far away, and all my business affairs lie to the west in California. Having our governing body so far to the east has been only a minor annoyance in the past."

"Would you like me to suggest a firm in Salt Lake?"

"Yes, if you would."

"I have, if I may say so, some very good friends there. I am sure there will be someone among them who could be of assistance. Further, I would be pleased to send a letter of recommendation on your behalf. It would be particularly helpful if you could produce your documentation. You know, certificates of title, fee simple deeds of record, preemption filings or land purchase documents or whatever. I could verify those and make sure they are entered on record in support of your counterclaim. Which I am assuming you will want to file."

Claim, counterclaim, it was all so very confusing. And at the moment all so very unimportant. Where was Adam? Where could he find little Hoss? *Where were his sons?*

"You are being very helpful, Mr. Jessup. I appreciate it."

"Glad to help if I can, sir. Do you have your documents with you? I could start on them right away."

"No, they're—" Ben stopped in the middle of the sentence and barked out a short, bitter laugh. "The documents you sugget, Mr. Jessup, are in my safe. Which is in my bedroom, back at home on the Ponderosa."

"Oh, dear."

"Exactly. At the moment it seems George Foster holds possession not only of my home, but of the papers I need to prove that it really *is* my home."

"Dear me," Jessup said.

"I had wording a trifle stronger in mind myself," Ben admitted.

"Yes, I would think you very well might. My goodness."

"I believe, Mr. Jessup, I would like to buy a drink now. Something with some authority to it."

"Oh my, yes indeed." And by the simple process of walking from one side of the long room to the other, the man changed from being Judge Jessup, justice of the peace for Genoa, to smiling and genial Larry, saloon keeper and all around hale fellow.

Ben trailed behind Jessup with a heavy heart. Where were Adam and Hoss?

Ben sent letters both to Alton DeShong and David Kendall in San Francisco. Rather than wait for the generally dependable but abysmally slow postal service—from Genoa to Sacramento could require three or four weeks for the passage of a simple letter—he paid young Charley Berwick to act as a courier and rush the messages west.

"Will we be going to Salt Lake City like the judge suggested?" Marie asked.

"No. I'm sure Judge Jessup's advice was good, but his thoughts were on our property. My concern has to be with the boys. We'll worry about them first, then George Foster and his shenanigans afterward."

Marie squeezed his hand tight in hers, and the two of them mounted the mules once more, even though Ben owned a score or more of fine-blooded saddle horses that were only a few miles away on the Ponderosa, where Foster and Malloy waited with guns and stubborn stupidity.

They had to have shelter, someplace to live, especially since at this time of year one could never know if the day that began in sunshine would end in more sun or in a howling blizzard. Storm fronts could materialize over the Sierra Nevada peaks so close above them to the west and turn a bright and brilliant day into bone-numbing cold virtually within a span of minutes. It was not uncommon for a single hour to see a change in temperature of forty degrees in either direction. And much as he worried about his sons, Ben did not want to risk his bride to any further danger. He had to place her under cover somewhere.

With the Ponderosa Ranch headquarters denied to him, and both Genoa and the Pah-Ute camp much too far away for his purposes, he took her to the stone-walled half dugout that served as his part-time store in the lowlands at Truckee Meadows.

This time, for the first time that he could remember, he did not immediately go to the knoll to visit Inger's gravesite. It was something he hadn't yet had a chance to discuss with Marie, and he did not want to hurt Marie's feelings now by showing his abiding love and respect for the woman who preceded her in his heart and in his bed.

"This is . . . very nice," Marie said when she saw the rude quarters he had in mind for her.

Ben laughed. "Darling girl, if you can say that with so straight a face, then I shall have to start questioning your honesty."

"But it is nice, Ben. Sort of. I mean . . . it's cozy."

"If you mean it's little, then I have to agree." The inhabitable part of the dugout was no more than a dirt-floored, stone-walled space of eight by nine feet or thereabouts. A door of heavy planking hung on rusting iron hinges at the front, and a low-roofed root cellar had been gouged out of the hillside at the back of the single room so that supplies could be stored safely away from freezing or pilferage. The front door opened directly to the outside, since this particular place was intended for summer use only. Had it been expected to be used the year around, a wall would have been erected in front of the door to block snow and wind.

No stove or chimney was in place, but a gap had been left in the roof at a back corner, and a slab of wood was laid over it to keep dirt and snow from falling in. Ben walked up on the roof and removed the plank, creating a rough and ready sort of smoke hole there. A fire laid in that corner could be expected to vent itself through the hole in the roof, providing the front door was left open a crack to allow for the flow-through air movement, and providing the winds were coming from a direction that would not drive the smoke back inside. The arrangement was somewhat iffy, but it worked more often than it did not.

"There's a crane and hook here, see—where you can hang a pot over the coals—and there are some pegs here for clothes or whatever and—"

"Ben, the way you are showing me how everything

works—it sounds to me like you will not be here with me. You aren't going to . . . do something foolish, are you?"

"Take a gun and go after George Foster?" He smiled and shook his head. "I don't say that the man doesn't deserve it. And don't think that I wouldn't like to do exactly that. But I couldn't, dear. I just couldn't do a thing like that. No, we'll depend on the law to take care of George and Edgar and whoever it is who has egged them into this nonsense. What I must do is go into the mountains and look for Adam and Hoss. I know George well enough to know that he wouldn't have the stomach to harm children even if someone ordered him to. There aren't many men who would. I have to believe that the boys are somewhere up there, probably hiding from George and waiting for me to come home and find them. Well, that is exactly what I intend. And I don't want to risk you—no, don't stop me, please, I know what you are going to say; you are going to give me that whither thou goest speech, and I know you mean every word of it. So let me confess one more thing, please. It isn't just your health that I'm thinking about. It's the boys too, Marie. If you come with me, then I have to spend part of my time thinking about you, about your safety and your comfort and your health. If I travel by myself, I can move as fast as I dare and concentrate on nothing but looking for Adam and Hoss. Those mountains are rugged, dear, and unyielding. They nearly killed me before I learned to cope with them. Knowing you were with me, knowing what was being risked, it would take too much away from my search for the boys. That is why I want to leave you here with food and wood enough that I won't have to give thought to your comfort until I either find my sons or give up looking for them up there. Can you understand that, Marie? Do you?"

Her answer was to come into his arms, pressing herself tight against him and giving him a fierce, proud hug.

"You go on then, Ben. Do what you must to find your boys. You needn't worry about me, I'll be fine here. And when you come back, my darling, my heart, we will be a family, all four of us together, and together we'll do whatever we have to to regain the home you worked so hard to build." She gave him a kiss and a push toward the door. "Go on, Ben. Go."

He paused for a moment to look at her, taking in every curve and color and texture of her so that he could capture her in his thoughts when he wished to. And then he turned and went outside to the waiting mules.

There was a brisk bite in the air, that peculiarly clean and snapping scent of fall. Today the promises carried on that chill were frightening to him in their implications. He had to find his sons quickly, before the next storm came raging down upon them.

He had to unite his family or it truly would not matter to him what happened to the Ponderosa.

It was nearly two weeks before Ben came riding down from the mountains to the lush beauty of the meadows along the Truckee.

Marie ran to him as he slowly, painfully dismounted. His right leg was stiff, his trousers cut open, and a length of cloth wrapped around his knee for a bandage. "Ben! What happened?"

"Stupid," he said. "Stupid. I slipped, took a fall. That was . . . I'm not sure, four days back? About that long. I was up by the rock formation we call the Cat's Head. Adam knows it. He was following a wounded deer up there once and found an ancient campsite with stone arrowheads of a kind we'd never seen before. I thought he might have taken Hoss there now to hide. It's high, though, and hard to get to. I slipped on some loose rock and took a tumble. Banged this knee up some. Darn thing swelled up like a frog's throat in the courting season. It took me the rest of that day and into the next to crawl back up to where I'd left the mules. Had a heck of a time getting mounted again too. Then I started down. I . . . don't recall quite everything from then until now."

"Ben! Oh, Ben. There is blood in your hair too. You hit your head when you fell."

"Really? I never noticed."

She ducked beneath his arm and insisted that he put his weight onto her shoulder so that she could help him inside the dugout. She placed him on the blanket-covered grass pallet that she'd fashioned for a bed, and covered him with a quilt that her mother made, one of the few things they had salvaged from the storm in the desert to the south those weeks earlier.

"Sleep now, darling. You are safe now."

"But the boys . . . Adam . . . Hoss . . ."

"Shh, darling, shh. Sleep now. We will find the sons later. Now sleep."

Ben protested no more. His eyes fluttered and closed, and within seconds he had fallen into a deep and healing sleep.

Marie placed a kiss, gently so that she would not disturb him, then went back outside to tend to the animals. For a girl who had never before been outside a city's environs, she was learning to cope very quickly.

But then she had to.

"Are you sure you feel up to riding again? You are not dizzy?" she asked with concern.

"I'm fine. Really."

"You don't look fine. You don't sound fine."

"See how appearances can deceive?" He managed a weak smile.

"All right. But if you feel dizzy—"

"If I do, we'll stop."

"Promise?"

"Yes, I promise."

"All right, then." She let go of his hand, giving him charge of his own mount, and went to her mule to climb onto the saddle.

Since his return from the mountains, throughout a too brief period of recuperation from the fall, Ben had fretted and fumed over this delay in his search for Adam and Hoss. Marie was afraid if he did not resume looking soon, he would go mad with the unrelenting anxiety.

Ben insisted that he had to do something and do it quickly. The days were becoming colder and colder, and there was a hard freeze each night now. Youngsters, anyone for that matter, could not survive in the open in weather like this without adequate food and coverings. And when the snows set in, it would be even worse. Ben knew he had to do something soon or his sons might die of exposure in this high, harsh country they all loved so intensely.

He was not yet well enough to go back into the mountains to look for them. Much as he hated to admit it, he needed some days more to recover before he would be up to that.

But he could not lie in bed with tea and broth and do nothing while his sons were somewhere out there alone. The only thing he could think of now was to return to the Ponderosa.

He would ask George Foster what he knew about Adam's and Hoss's intentions. How they left the Ponderosa and why. And did George know where they were now? Ben would appeal to George's humanity. Surely Foster had some spark of decency left in him. Some small grain of gratitude for all he had done for him and Irma in the past.

If not . . .

"One thing, dear," Marie had told him. "No, two. First thing, this time I want to go with you. No, don't look at me like that. You are still weak. Your balance is terrible. I see how you have to lean on the wall just to get from the stool to the bed or back. You could fall and be hurt again. I want to be there with you, just in case."

"All right," he agreed, "you can ride along."

"The other thing, my darling, I want you to leave your gun here. Do not even take it with you. Not the rifle and not the pistol thing. You leave them both here so no matter what that awful M'sieu Foster does, he will not tempt you into something you later would regret. No?"

Ben sighed, then nodded. "All right. I won't carry any sort of weapon when we see George."

It seemed a harmless enough promise. After all, there were no predators, animal or human, between the Truckee Meadows and the Ponderosa. He remembered—so very long ago, it seemed now—assuring someone of that very thing. Mrs. Hamer was it? That was only last spring. And it was Adam and Hoss who rode ahead that day to tell Edgar Malloy they would be having guests for supper.

How different things were now. How wonderful they had been then. If only he had known and had appreciated the difference . . .

"Are you ready, Ben?"

"Yes, dear."

"Then let us go speak with this M'sieu Foster and see can we do something to find the boys, yes?"

"By all means, yes."

They started up the road at a slow and gentle walk so as to avoid jarring Ben's throbbing, still not quite healed head injury.

CHAPTER 25

I told you before, Cartwright, you got no business here. This is my place now. I own it, nice an' legal, and you ain't welcome. Now clear off or I'll shoot. I swear I will, Cartwright. I'll shoot." Foster brandished the shotgun again. He was scowling and making faces, and this time he seemed less nervous and blustering than he had the time before. This time he sounded as if he believed it all himself.

"It isn't the ranch I came to talk to you about, George, it's the boys. Forget the Ponderosa. We'll worry about that later. Just tell me what you know about my sons."

"I don't know nothin'," Foster snapped.

"You do, George. Please tell me. I know you didn't harm them. No one is accusing you of that. Why, we've been friends a long time, George. You've known Adam and Hoss since they were babies, practically. They've always looked up to you, George." That was an exaggeration of the first water, but a harmless one under the circumstances. "You taught Adam how to make a willow bark whistle, George. Why, you were there when Hoss got his first long pants. I know you never meant any harm to my sons. So let's just forget about the Ponderosa for now. Tell me when they left here and what they took with them.

Did Adam say anything to you? I won't hold any of it against you, George. I know you meant them no harm. But tell me. Help me, please. Any little thing you can remember . . ."

"I don't . . . I just—"

"No, Foster, wait. Don't send him away so quickly. Perhaps we can make a bargain here." The voice was a new one and one Ben did not remember. Certainly it was not Edgar Malloy who called out from the shadows of the doorway.

Ben frowned.

Then this whole, insane situation became understandable when William Dunnigan stepped outside to stand beside George Foster in the ranch yard. Dunnigan, whose schemes for wealth and power Ben had scotched. Of course. The article in the San Francisco newspaper. Dunnigan thought Ben was dead and intended to move in and scoop up the Cartwright holdings for himself. Abandon one dream and replace it with another, stolen from the man who had ruined the first.

"Hello, Bill," Ben said calmly.

"Don't call me by my first name, you son of a bitch. You call me Mr. Dunnigan and you say it nice and respectful."

"Very well, Mr. Dunnigan. What is it you have in mind?"

"Those kiddies of yours. You want them back, right?"

"That's right."

"My good friend and partner here is willing to negotiate with you, Cartwright."

"That's what I came to ask him to do, Mr. Dunnigan."

"He'll tell you everything he knows, Cartwright."

"And in return?"

"You sign a quit claim giving up all your interest in the Ponderosa land holdings."

Ben grunted. "You know, of course, what you've just told me, Mr. Dunnigan."

"What's that, Cartwright?"

"You've just let me know that your claims, whatever they were, depended on me being dead in New Orleans. Without me here to contest whatever it was you told the authorities in Salt Lake City, you could take title. But as long as I am alive to dispute your game, you can't possibly get away with your plan. Thank you for the information, Mr. Dunnigan."

"Damn you, Cartwright, you're only guessing, and you're guessing wrong. I've already invalidated your deeds. I know which ones and where to find the filings because you were thoughtful enough to leave all your papers in your safe. Why, the safe wasn't even locked."

"The safe was intended to be protection against fire. To tell you the truth, Mr. Dunnigan, it never occurred to me that I had to worry about protecting myself from my friends." He was looking at George Foster when he said that. "What was it, George? Did Mr. Dunnigan here flatter you? Promise you riches? A share in the Ponderosa, perhaps, and a lifetime position as general manager? Something very much like that anyway." Foster scowled but attempted no denials.

"And poor old Malloy," Ben went on. "All you had to promise him was a steady supply of whiskey. What about Irma, George? What did she say to all this?"

Irma stepped out of the cabin. "Don't think you can sit there all smug and mighty now, Ben Cartwright. You've lived high from the sweat of our brows for all these years and never gave us a chance. Now the worm has turned. Now how d'you like it?"

"Is that the way you remember it, Irma? How sad for you, because you sound like you really believe that drivel."

"You're getting away from the point, Cartwright. Do you want to deal or not? Everything my man Foster here knows about your sons, and all you have to give us in exchange is your signature."

Ben sat for some time looking square into Bill

Dunnigan's eyes. Then his face twisted with disgust and he turned his head and spat into the dust.

"Bargains are something that happens between men of honor, Mr. Dunnigan. You don't qualify. Besides, it occurs to me now that I'm looking at George and you face-to-face that my boys are smarter than to tell anything important to anyone as low and sneaking and no-account as the pair of you. Wherever Adam took Hoss and whatever those boys are up to, they never said anything about it to either one of you. I'm wasting my time here today. Good-bye." He reined the mule's nose around and would have spurred it forward.

"Cartwright. Hold it right there!" Dunnigan's shout was punctuated by the sound of a gun hammer being cocked.

Ben motioned surreptitiously for Marie to ride away, but he himself reined back around again to face Dunnigan and the Fosters.

"I can't let you leave here now, Cartwright."

"No?"

"You said it yourself. You know there's a flaw in my plan. That flaw is that you are alive to give testimony counter to my claims. But if I correct that one little flaw . . ."

"Murder, Dunnigan? Is that it?"

"It wouldn't be the first time, Cartwright. And this time it will be a pleasure."

Wild Bill Dunnigan leveled a revolver and aimed it at Ben's chest. Ben's thoughts were racing. If he tried to spin around and run away, he would surely be shot down. What he needed to do was to attack. If he'd been on his horse, he would have spurred it into a jump straight at Dunnigan and hope the man's first shot flew wide from being startled. But this mule, although patient and willing enough, was really only a pack animal being pressed into service under saddle. And a mistake at this point would be fatal.

Worse than that, however, if Dunnigan succeeded in killing him, he would be forced to murder Marie also. That would be the only way Dunnigan could prevent her from bringing the law down on him. And know it or not, the Fosters would surely be next in line. A man as brutally cold as Bill Dunnigan would not give them a club to hold over his head when in the future, as they surely would, they became greedy. No, Ben thought, today Bill Dunnigan had to kill him and Marie, and soon he would kill George and Irma and probably Edgar Malloy too.

Unless . . .

Ben bent low and with a roar stabbed the mule in its flanks. His heart leaped into his throat. And then dropped precipitously into the pit of his stomach. Instead of charging forward into the muzzle of Bill Dunnigan's pistol, the slab-sided mule bogged its head and brayed in protest of this unusual treatment.

Dunnigan's pistol barked, a spear point of flame and smoke bursting out of its muzzle. Ben heard a high-pitched, sizzling sound, not unlike the world's biggest and angriest yellowjacket, snarl past his ear as the pitching, bucking mule jumped and twisted.

Dunnigan shouted something and cocked his revolver to try again. Ben let go his grip on the mule and sailed off its back. He landed hard on his side, his injured head pounding, and tried to scramble onto hands and knees so he could throw himself at Bill Dunnigan in a bare-handed assault.

Before he had time to leave the ground, Dunnigan took aim.

The sound of a gunshot rang out.

Bill Dunnigan blinked. And dropped his pistol. Blood coursed down his arm and over the hand that had been holding the gun. He cursed and bent to retrieve the weapon with his other hand. He hadn't time enough for that, however. Before he could grasp it, Ben was on him.

Wounded man or no, Ben pushed Bill Dunnigan upright, positioned him with his extended left arm, and with his right fist delivered as true a punch as he had ever landed to another man's jaw.

Dunnigan's eyes rolled back until only the whites were showing, and he dropped to the ground with no more life or resistance than a sack of milled flour falling off the tailgate of a wagon. He was out as cold as a trout.

Ben looked frantically around.

George Foster was standing near the cabin door with his shotgun on the ground at his feet and his hands flung high into the air. He looked stunned and his eyes were shifting wildly from left to right as he searched for some glimpse of whoever it was who had shot Bill Dunnigan. There was no sign of Irma Foster now, nor any of Edgar Malloy, who hadn't been seen at all today.

Ben looked back at Marie, but her hands were empty too. He had thought for a moment that she had brought a gun with her, but that was not the case.

Then who . . . ?

A flurry of movement beyond the barn caught his eye, and a moment later Adam and Hoss burst into the yard.

Adam was carrying the cut-down Pennsylvania squirrel rifle Ben had given him some years before. Little Hoss was armed with a slightly crooked stick that the boys had sharpened with their knives and then held over a fire to harden the tip.

"Pa! Pa!"

"Boys." Ben ran, his arms held wide, to grab his sons in a bear hug.

"I didn't want . . . I was scared, Pa. I knew it wasn't right to shoot nobody. But that man, he was trying to hurt you and the lady here and—"

"You did the right thing, son. You did just right. You did too, Hoss. You boys couldn't have done any better than you did today. No one could have done any better."

Ben motioned Marie close. She was smiling as she came near. She stopped a few paces distant and stood there.

"Boys," Ben said, "this is your new stepmother. Her

name is Marie, and I hope you will come to love her as much as I do."

Marie gave them one of her sweet smiles. "I am so happy to meet you. Your papa talks of little else. He says you are wonderful boys, very close to one another. I hope you will be as close to your baby brother or sister when it is born."

Ben jerked. Then relaxed. No, of course not. It was much too soon for Marie to be sure of anything like that. She was only speaking rhetorically, about something she hoped would happen sometime in the future. Of course that was all there was to that. But he would have to remember to ask her about it later.

Ben gathered his sons close to him. There was so much he needed to ask them. For the moment, though, he had to think about what to do with Bill Dunnigan and the Fosters. And with Edgar Malloy, if he was still around somewhere.

Ben heard a faint rumble like distant thunder, and looked up to see a cloud of roiled ocher dust rising over the road to the west. Moving figures came into sight beneath the dust. Horsemen. Lots of them. Dozens of them. Ben's heart leaped again. If these were some of Bill Dunnigan's bullyboys come to plunder on behalf of their master . . .

But they weren't. As the horsemen drew nearer, Ben began to smile.

"Honey," he said to Marie, "you are going to have the opportunity to meet some of our friends. Lots of them, in fact."

For the horsemen proved to be a self-appointed delegation—or posse, or quite possibly mob—that had left San Francisco upon receiving news from Alton DeShong that Ben Cartwright and his boys were in trouble.

Ben had done favors for them in the past. Now they had turned out to help him in return. Several score of them, wealthy businessmen and laborers with grime beneath their fingernails, miners, bakers, and storekeepers.

All those of Ben's friends who heard the news dropped their own affairs and rode east into the mountains unmindful of the conditions they might find there. Ben Cartwright was in trouble. Ben needed them. They were going.

They rode into the Ponderosa now with guns and knives and even a few rusty swords strapped around their waists and dangling from their saddles. Some of these men had not been mounted on horseback in a dozen years or more, but they rode as hard as they could come, with Alton DeShong and Dave Kendall leading them.

"Is it true, Ben?" "Are you all right, Ben?" "What is it that's happening here, Ben?"

The questions issued from dozens of throats all at the same time. It took a while to sort things out and bring some measure of order to the scene.

George and Irma Foster were forcibly dragged out of Ben's bedroom, where George was trying to hide and where Irma had been making a last-ditch effort to fill her apron pockets with stolen items of value.

Edgar Malloy was passed out in the root cellar with a nearly empty liquor jug beside him. He was rudely wakened and brought out to be put with the others.

Bill Dunnigan was bandaged, somewhat reluctantly, and chained to the wheel of a wagon. That one, David Kendall assured everyone, would be seen to by the force of law. Not San Francisco law, he didn't think, since the man's crimes occurred here in the mountains. Nor Utah law either, as Salt Lake City was so very far away. A miner's court in one of the Mother Lode gold camps should be able to handle the matter. Half a dozen men quickly swore the whole thing had taken place in California. They were certain of it. After all, they hadn't yet passed any signs saying they were entering Utah Territory, had they?

Bill Dunnigan quailed and begged for mercy from the hard-eyed friends of Ben Cartwright, but no one seemed much inclined to extend him sympathy or goodwill.

"Don't you worry none, Ben," Arlen Whitcomb said

solicitously. "We'll take keer so's this rascal don't bother you or yorn ag'in."

Ben believed they would too.

The men cheered Marie when they were told she was Ben's new bride. They cheered again when Adam, timidly at first and then with eager enthusiasm as he came to enjoy being the center of all this grown-up attention, related his story and Hoss's.

The boys had been hiding in the mountains for the better part of the past two months. They'd slipped away from home in the middle of the night after Bill Dunnigan returned to the Ponderosa from a trip to Salt Lake City. Hoss had overheard Dunnigan and George Foster talking. He hadn't understood much of what they were plotting, but he knew it was bad. Hoss had warned Adam, and the two boys together had eavesdropped on the plotters.

As soon as they realized Dunnigan intended to steal the Ponderosa, they knew they would be in danger sooner or later. Adam got his rifle and powder, and the boys made up packs with blankets, knives, flint and steel, burning glasses, everything they would need to survive in the manner Doheetsu had taught them.

They had spent nearly the entire time within a mile and a half of the ranch, hiding out and watching nearly every day while they waited for their father to return and make things right again.

They hadn't seen Ben and Marie come that first time. They could only assume that they must have been away hunting that day. Adam and his rifle had kept them supplied with meat. "And Hoss too, Pa. Hoss is getting real good with the rifle, aren't you, Hoss?"

For their other needs, salt and soap and whatnot, they crept in at night and stole from the pantry. The Fosters and Malloy never had caught on to the pilferage.

Ben had had no chance to find them in all his searching because he hadn't thought to look for them practically within the shadow of the Ponderosa. He had been combing the distant slopes while Adam and Hoss were close enough to the house to smell bacon on the griddle. Neither Ben nor Doheetsu and his people went anywhere near the ranch in their searches.

Today the boys had been in their usual hiding spot beside the barn when they observed the confrontation with Dunnigan.

"I wasn't trying to hit him in the arm like that, Pa," Adam confessed. "I was just trying to hit him. His arm kind of got in the way, and I'm glad it did. I wouldn't want to kill anybody. Not even him. Not after . . . you know." It was obvious that the memories of Jean-Pierre still haunted Adam.

Ben squeezed his son's shoulders—a hug would never do with all these men looking on—and told him once more, "You did exactly the right thing."

"You want we should hang these other three along with Bill Dunnigan, Ben?" someone asked.

"No, I don't, Tyler. I'd like you to take them back to California with you. I don't want them around here anymore. But I won't be party to any hanging, and I don't want any of you to be either. Just take them back and turn them loose. And then talk about them to everyone you see. Make sure everyone in the Mother Lode country knows what kind they are. I think that will be punishment enough for them. As for Dunnigan himself, well, I don't know what to think."

"I told you, Ben. The law will take care of him. We'll see to it."

"California law, Dave? How could that apply?"

Kendall grinned. "Why, Ben, the man was in California when he conspired to steal from you, wasn't he? Of course California law should apply."

"I think I'll leave that to you, then."

"Boys, we came here looking for a fight, but Adam and Hoss took care of that for us," DeShong said loudly. "I say if we can't have a scrap, then we need to have a shivaree for Ben and his pretty bride Marie. What do you say?"

Their answer was a rousing cheer.

Ben, grinning until his cheeks hurt, stood with Marie on one side and his two fine sons on the other and his friends—oh, how impoverished a man would be without friends—before him.

CHAPTER 26

Joseph Burns Cartwright came into the world late that following summer. He weighed five and three-quarter pounds, had a shock of jet-black hair, a red, furious complexion, and lung power enough practically from the moment of his birth to announce his troubles.

Marie adored him. So did Hoss and Adam. So, in fact, did his proud father, Ben.

"Three sons and the most beautiful wife in the world? What more could any man want?"

"Some part of that new silver discovery on the other side of Sun Mountain, I suppose," Marie told him from the nest of covers where she lay nursing her newborn son.

"Bah. That's only money. What I have here with you and our sons ... this is the truest form of wealth." He winked at her. "And anyway, dear, we do have interest in several claims over there."

"I do hope there isn't going to be a big rush and lots and lots of people coming into the country now, Ben. I've come to love it just like it is. I'd hate to think everything will change."

"I'm afraid change is the nature of things. There's already a town taking root at Truckee Meadows. Now there likely will be another one spring up around the silver mines. I've heard a rumor that there's gold in the ore bodies too. If there's gold, then the rush will start for sure. But we'll be all right, Marie. You'll see. We won't let any of that affect the Ponderosa."

"Promise?"

He smiled. "I promise it will affect us as little as we can manage, anyway."

"That will have to be good enough."

Ben reached down to touch the palm of the baby's hand. The infant took hold of his fingertip with a tight and tenacious grip. Ben *knew* the response was no more than a reflexive action, but the feel of it thrilled him anyway, and his heart filled with love and pride.

"Ah, little Joe," he said. "You have so much wonder and joy and beauty ahead of you. I hope your years will be rich and full and long."

"And ours too, my darling?" Marie asked.

Ben moved his hand very carefully so as not to dislodge little Joe's grip while he found Marie's hand and squeezed it at the same time. "You've already made my years rich and full," he said.

Marie's eyes welled full of glistening but unspilled tears as she looked from her husband to her son and back again.

"I think he's finished eating now," she said. "Just a second ... there ... now you can let Adam and Hoss in to see Joseph again, if they like."

"Like? I think I can hear them out there getting ready to batter the door down if we don't open it again soon."

"It looks good to me, Mr. Cartwright."

"Good isn't good enough, Charles. This tree has to be perfect. This one will be the primary support for the house, and I want this house to be perfect."

"Yes, sir, perfect it shall be then. Tell Mrs. Cartwright I said so."

"I shall, Charles. I certainly shall."

Charles Wilcox was foreman of the Cartwright timber operation which normally supplied the shoring needs of mines in the new and burgeoning Comstock district, but now the loggers were concentrating their energies on the grand new home Ben was building for his beloved Marie and their three boys.

The house would overlook Lake Tahoe, of course. It would be protected from the fierce winter storms. Mostly it would be Marie's, a fitting replacement for the low and rather crude log cabin that had been good enough for a bachelor's nest but which was hardly suitable for a gracious lady.

Besides, Ben liked knowing that he could build for his family anything Marie might desire. She had chosen not an elegant mansion in the New Orleans style—although certainly he would have been pleased to give her one if such had been her desire—but a two-story house of native timber and stone. Something she said would be mete and proper for this Ponderosa she had come to love so very much. Something that sprang out of this soil. Something that belonged here as much as the rocks and the forests did.

The design was hers, much more masculine in appearance than Ben would have expected her to want.

They had had plans drawn by an architect who came to them all the way from St. Louis and who was highly recommended. It had been one thing for him to huddle in close consultation with Marie. After all, that was why he had traveled here. But the poor man had had to perform his task while an utterly fascinated Adam peered incessantly over his shoulder. Adam seemed to find architecture a matter of magical attraction. Hoss, on the other hand, was more interested in gathering up the discarded stubs of colored pencils that the gentleman from St. Louis sometimes made available. And Joseph, who was coming to be known as Little Joe by his brothers, was content to chew on the gentleman's pant legs whenever he was left alone long enough that he could crawl underneath the man's chair. Ben never did understand the attraction that led to

Joseph's passion for masticating the woolen cloth, and that cloth in particular.

Whatever, the house would be glorious, and there was no lady Ben could think of who better deserved to preside over a manor of her own design than his own Marie.

"If you'd care to come down this way, Mr. Cartwright, I have some more trees marked for you to look at."

"Only the best, Charles. You know I want only the best for this job."

"Yes, sir, I sure do know it."

Ben nodded and smiled and followed his foreman down the slope through the stand of mature and mighty firs.

"They finished the foundation? Oh, Ben, I can't wait to see."

"Careful now. The path hasn't been cleared yet. There are still all sorts of rocks and roots in the way."

"Hah. You just know I'll beat you there. And I will too. Last one home has to do the dishes tonight, Ben."

Marie tossed her head, her black hair gleaming in the sunlight, and quirted her favored skewbald pony on the flank. The horse snorted and raced madly up the path the workmen's wagons had carved into the hillside.

Ben, caught unaware, took a moment longer to react, so that Marie's flying mount was a good four lengths and drawing farther and farther ahead as it carried her slight weight, while Ben's much more heavily burdened bay struggled vainly to keep up.

The sound of Marie's laugh floated back to Ben as his wife raced him to see the foundations of their new home. The sound of her laugh. And then a cry of alarm.

Her horse stumbled. Momentarily lost its footing. Lurched hard to one side and then up again.

The horse raced on, but Marie's balance had been broken. She slipped, made a frantic grab for the saddle horn and missed. She fell and hit the ground hard. She spun, raising a cloud of dust on the path, and tumbled over and over again, arms and legs flailing loose and out of control.

"Marie!"

She had tumbled many times, of course. Anyone who rode could and would be thrown one time or another. But she had landed hard this time and didn't seem to be doing anything to stop her rolling.

Ben hauled his horse to a stop and threw himself out of the saddle. He ran to her. Dropped to his knees at her side.

"Marie?"

He gathered her slight, still body into his arms.

There was no resistance. She lay limp as a child's doll in his embrace.

"Oh, God. Oh, Marie. No."

He kissed her eyes, her lips, her temple. There was no response. No flutter of lashes. No tremble of lip. Nothing.

"Dear God, please no."

There was a slight—so little, so horrid—depression on the back of her skull above and behind the left ear. The skin was not broken. There was no blood, not even a bruise.

"Marie!"

Ben lifted his tear-streaming gaze toward the distant heavens and cried out the loud and anguished plaint that has daunted mankind through all eternity. "Why, God, why?"

There was no answer.

He stood on the knoll overlooking Tahoe. It was a gloriously beautiful day. Marie would have loved it.

He hoped somehow she knew.

Once, in passing reference, she had said this was where she would want to be buried. It was where she rested now.

And Inger down at the Meadows, at the place some were beginning to call Reno.

And Elizabeth, ah Elizabeth, all the way back in Boston. He doubted he would ever see sweet Elizabeth's grave again.

But then he did not need that reminder for him to call her back so dear to mind.

He had been blessed, he knew. For all his sorrows, Ben Cartwright was a man who was blessed. He had his sons. Adam. Eric. Joseph. No man could want for finer sons. He had this land, these mountains. He had the friendship of men who were honest and good. He had no right to regret.

And if now he wept, so be it. He missed her. He missed her now and he would miss her for as long as he lived. He knew that. He could accept it without in any measure liking the necessity for it. But he could accept it.

And the Cartwrights and the Ponderosa would go on.

Marie's sons—she had loved each of the three of them; they were all her sons, Adam and Hoss as much as Joseph—would grow here and prosper, and the Cartwrights would go on.

Ben Cartwright stood surrounded by the majestic Sierra Nevadas, the mirrored Tahoe reflecting their splendor, the sounds of carpenters' hammers reaching his ears on a vagrant breeze.

He stood alone beside a simple stone marker, face lifted heavenward and tears streaking his face, but a tenacious determination filling his breast too.

He was not alone. He was *not*.

And no hand would ever move him from this land, for the vast Ponderosa was the legacy he would leave to his sons.

"Good-bye, my love," he whispered, and turning, went down the mountainside.

The Cartwright saga continues!

If you enjoyed THE PONDEROSA EMPIRE
by Stephen Calder, be sure to look for the
next novel in his BONANZA series,
THE HIGH-STEEL HAZARD,
available in spring 1993 wherever Bantam
titles are sold.

Turn the page for an exciting preview of
the next stirring adventure of Ben,
Adam, Hoss, and Little Joe.

Ben looked up with a smile. Adam was home. It had been—what?—six days Adam was away. Ben had missed him. He got up and gave his eldest a hug to welcome him back. "How did everything go down south?"

"Fine, pa. We marked all the timber they need to fill this contract. You won't hardly notice what they take out."

Ben nodded.

"There's a lot of good forest down there, pa."

Ben lifted an eyebrow. Knowing Adam he felt fairly sure there was more to this than idle chatter.

"While we were cruising timber for Mr. Tobin, pa, I got to thinking. There's no reason why we shouldn't start a little milling operation of our own down that way. One small steam donkey engine and a few teams of heavy horses for skidding the logs, some hand tools and a couple wagons for delivering lumber down to the rail siding, that's all we'd need. Call it a crew of six on the engine and saw and sixteen, maybe eighteen men cutting trees and hauling timber. Those and a few more men to haul the milled lumber. I think we could make a nice profit and still not harm the forest. In fact, it needs thinning. What we would take out would only let in more light and help the younger growth. And, Pa, there's quite a market for lumber. Quite a market."

"Have you thought your idea through yet?"

Adam shook his head. "Not yet. I didn't want to do that until I mentioned it to you first, pa."

"You know I'll trust your judgment," Ben said. And that was the simple truth. Adam had a fine head for business. More so in many ways than did his father. Except for his one basic rule of demanding decent and fairness in all trade, Ben tended to let business affairs run their own course. But then Adam, being young, was still intent on trying his wings. If Adam had his way about things the Cartwright family would diversify their interests to the point that none of them would be able to remember all the ventures they were into. It was hard enough as things were, with Ben and his sons owning bits of this and snippets of that from old investments and—much more often—old involvements with the businesses of friends. From his earliest years in this country Ben had had a policy of helping his friends whenever and however they needed. He often was repaid with small percentages of his friend's affairs so that now he owned fractional interests in, quite literally, more ventures than he could keep straight in his mind. He really didn't want the family affairs to become that fragmented too. But on the other hand he truly did trust Adam's judgment in most matters. Hoss's inclinations might be swayed by sentiment and Joseph's by emotion, but Adam's thinking nearly always was cool and precise and carefully reasoned. "Give it a good looking over and make your estimates, then we'll talk again," Ben said.

Adam nodded and helped himself to a seat in one of the leather armchairs in his father's office-cum-study. "What is it you're working on there, pa?"

"This? Just a letter. Do you remember Mr. and Mrs. Shannon?"

Adam smiled. "Mrs. Shannon is the lady that makes the gooseberry tarts, isn't she?"

Ben had forgotten that. Obviously Adam hadn't. Lord, that had been a good many years ago. "That's right."

"We haven't seen them for a long time," Adam said.

"We got a letter from Les just after you left to go down to Packsaddle."

"If you got the letter that long ago and haven't answered it yet then he's asked for something harder for you to deal with than just an exchange of news or the borrow of a simple loan," Adam correctly interpreted. Adam's perception pleased his father.

"It isn't a loan he wants exactly," Ben said. "Les has invited us to invest in a railroad scheme he and some other fellows are putting together. I've thought it over, though, and I don't think I'll go in with him. Johns Bend has been a strong, steady source of good ore bodies. That whole area has been. It hasn't been a boom-and-bust cycle over there. But you never know when the veins will pinch out and just disappear. I don't know that the investment would be that good."

Adam grunted and stared into his steepled palms.

"What?"

"Oh, I was just . . . thinking."

"Yes?"

"That area has been producing for more than twenty years, right?"

"That's right."

"And there still isn't any railroad in that part of the country, right?"

"True."

"So all the gold shipped out of there has been processed right there, right?"

"Yes. What's your point, son?"

"I've been doing some reading, pa. Did you know that a small stamp mill like I bet they have in Johns Bend only extracts thirty, maybe thirty-five percent of the gold that's in a given piece of ore?"

"I don't suppose I ever heard that, no."

"It's true enough. And another true thing is that modern ore processing can extract fifty-five, even sixty or sixty-five percent of the available mineral."

"Is that so?"

"Yes, sir." Adam looked up from whatever it was he'd been seeing inside the grasp of his hands. He smiled. "Think about it, pa. Twenty-odd years of discarded mill tailings are lying there, and only half the recoverable value has been taken out of them so far. Why, it's kind of like free gold lying there on the ground and nobody wanting it, nobody thinking it's valuable. The only thing that keeps anybody from being able to haul those old tailings to a smelter for reprocessing with these better extraction methods is the problem of transporting all that bulk economically."

"What you're saying is . . . ?"

"Oh, I'm not saying anything, pa. Not exactly. But it's like with me and my idea for a sawmill down south. I think it has enough merit that maybe it ought to be looked at a little closer before a decision is made."

Ben scratched the side of his jaw. "We do have stock holdings in the first three mining properties Les developed there," he mused aloud. "We grubstaked him when he and Chloe were starting out. Les gave us five or maybe it was ten percent of those claims. You could say that we already own a good amount of the tailings dumps over there."

"I would think a person could buy up tailings pretty cheap, pa. About all he might want."

"Not once people understood why they were suddenly valuable."

"I wasn't suggesting. . . ."

"I know you weren't, son."

"Anyway, pa, I don't think you should turn Mr. Shannon down without looking into his railroad a little closer. I mean, a deal like that wouldn't only make those ore bodies and tailings more valuable, it would also mean steady traffic for the railroad too, wouldn't it?"

As usual, Ben thought, Adam was seeing the situation clearly. "Perhaps," he said, "I should write and tell Les I'll swing by Johns Bend and take a look at this railroad idea of his the next time I'm traveling through."

"Sounds sensible to me, pa."

"I have to admit, son, that isn't the letter I'd planned to write."

"Whatever you think, Pa. You know I won't argue with you."

"No, you probably have a good idea here. The next time I go to San Francisco I'll make a detour up to Johns Bend. It won't be all that much out of the way."

"Yes, sir." Adam stood. "I better make sure Hop Sing knows I'll be home for supper."

Ben frowned. "Maybe that will calm him down a little."

"What's Hop Sing mad about now?"

"Oh, you know how he is. He planned supper with Joseph in mind, then Joseph begged the afternoon off and rode down to see some girl that has him all google-eyed and his palms sweating."

Adam laughed. "That sounds like Little Joe, all right."

Ben wasn't laughing. "I'm not sure that I approve of this one, Adam. Her father is a snake oil barker, and the girl dances in the tent show. I hope that's all she does. I . . . don't want Joseph to wind up being hurt."

"You know, Pa, Joe *is* almost grown. He hasn't seen much of the world outside of Virginia City and a few other places just as rough and crude and crazy. The wonder of it is that he hasn't been taught a hard lesson by some phony flirt already."

"I suppose you're right, Adam."

"Do you want me to talk to him?"

"No, that would only make him all the more determined to see this girl for what she pretends to be but isn't. You know Joseph. Let him hear the word 'can't' and he won't rest until he's proven you wrong. Or until he's battered himself bloody from trying to prove himself right."

"Yes, sir, that's Little Joe, all right."

Ben shrugged. "Sorry. I didn't mean to put any of this onto your shoulders."

"You didn't, Pa. And look, if you want to read up on the new gold recovery techniques I can find some journals for you to look at. It's very interesting."

Interesting. Ben gave his oldest son a wry smile.

Bless Adam's heart, he really did find such dry subjects as mining and metallurgy to be of interest.

"I'll let you know, son, thank you."

"Yes, sir." Adam grinned and went off in search of Hop Sing while Ben returned to his letter writing. But the letter he was composing now was not at all the one he would have written had Adam not returned home when he did.

"Up a little more, little more, little . . . hold it. Now down. No, too much. Up . . . there!" With a grunt that was as much satisfaction as it was effort—after all, Hoss was providing the bulk of the effort involved here—Ben slid the heavy wagon wheel back onto its axle. "Hold it just a few seconds more, son, and I'll have this . . . there." He spun the hub nut onto the threaded steel at the end of the axle, working quickly while Hoss continued to hold the back corner of the wagon off the ground. "Are you doing all right, son?"

"Just fine, Pa. Except for my nose itching something awful. I wouldn't mind if you was to hurry it up just a little 'cause of that."

Ben chuckled. And hurried. He tightened the nut until it was nicely snug, then said, "All right, Hoss, ease it down nice and slow."

"Whew!" Hoss let the weight down carefully. The new spokes on the old wheel creaked and groaned a little as they carried a load for the first time, but Ben's workmanship was sound and there was no danger the wheel would buckle now.

Ben looked up in time to see Hoss vigorously scratching the side of his nose. He began to laugh.

"What's the matter, pa?"

"Nothing, son."

Hoss scratched some more, sniffed twice and shrugged. "You want me to get a wrench an' tighten that nut the rest o' the way, pa?"

"No, I can do that while you go wash your face."

Hoss gave his father a questioning glance.

"Look at your hands, son."

The question on Hoss's broad face turned to astonishment when he looked down at his own massive hands. "Now where in tarnation . . . ?"

Both his hands were liberally smeared with thick, black, gummy grease the same approximate color and consistency of caulking tar. Obviously the grease had been on the frame of the wagon Hoss lifted.

"If you think that's bad," Ben said, "you should see your face. One side of your nose is covered with the stuff."

"You're funning me, pa. Ain't you?"

"It was only a suggestion. You don't have to wash if you don't want to."

"Pa!" Hoss looked down at his hands again, then gingerly felt his nose. There was already dark grease liberally smeared there. Hoss's investigations only made it worse. "Pa, do I really . . . ?"

Ben grinned. "Yes, son. You really."

Hoss sighed. Then smiled. Hoss's entire personality shined through into plain view whenever he smiled, and those smiles were as big as his heart. Ben always loved to see his middle son's good natured smiles. "I think I'll go wash my face now, pa."

"Good idea, son."

Holding his hands well out to the sides lest he touch anything—a clear case of locking the barn too late—Hoss ambled across the ranch yard toward the house.

Ben stepped inside the equipment shed and plucked a hub wrench down from a wall peg, then went back outside and began tightening the big nut. The wheel needed to be snug or it would wobble and cause undue wear on hub and axle alike.

Ben was nearly done when he heard the clatter of hoofs on hard earth and the crunch and grind of iron tires on gravel. He straightened, a sharp pain briefly reminding him that he wasn't quite as young as he used to be, to see a light rig rolling into the yard. He recognized the outfit. The wagon body was painted maroon trimmed in black while the tarred canvas top was black with maroon fringes. The wheel spokes were mud-splattered white. The wagon belonged to Jeremy Isley's livery stable in Virginia City. The man driving it—it took Ben a few seconds to recall his name; he wasn't someone Ben normally did business with although they had met on several occasions—was Armand Blauhaus. Blauhaus was a pawnbroker.

Blauhaus did not look entirely comfortable handling the reins of the hired horse. He leaned back to pull against the sweating brown's bit and pleaded more than ordered, "Whoa, horse, whoa."

Ben stepped out from behind the wagon where he'd been working and intercepted the brown, taking hold of the bridle cheekpiece and uttering a few soft, soothing murmurs for the benefit of the horse. Blauhaus appeared quite relieved. He let go of the reins and removed his derby to mop the sweat from his brow even though at this elevation there was rarely a day that was warm enough to make a man sweat in the absence of hard labor.

"Thank you, Mr. Cartwright. I thought I was having a runaway."

The horse hadn't been close to running away, Ben knew, but it would have been impolite to mention the fact. "No harm done, Mr. Blauhaus. Would you care to step down?"

"I would do, thank you." Blauhaus climbed carefully to ground level and seemed rather grateful to be there once his feet were safely ensconced on firm earth again. Ben let go of the brown's bridle and found a hitch weight behind the seat of the buggy. He clipped it to the bit ring and set it down to secure the horse in place, then turned to offer a handshake to his guest. Blauhaus, anticipating the convention, was fussily removing his driving glove. Ben had a moment to look his unexpected visitor over.

Armand Blauhaus was a slight, short slip of a man, probably somewhere in his mid to late fifties and with only a few strands of graying hair remaining on top of his pate. He made up for the lack on high by cultivating a Vandyke and mustache. His whiskers, however, were invariably neat, tidy and closely trimmed. But then Armand Blauhaus was meticulously tidy at all times, about his person and—so Ben was told—his accounts. He was dapper if not always fashionable, preferring the tried and true to any impulsive extremes of fashion. Today he wore black trousers, gray cutaway, cream brocade waistcoat, maroon puff cravat—surely, Ben thought, that was coincidence; surely the man hadn't actually coordinated his wardrobe with the paint on Isley's rental buggies—and cream-colored spats over a pair of ancient but freshly blacked and polished lace-up shoes. All he needed to make the ensemble complete would be a malacca cane, Ben decided. Even as Ben was thinking that, Blauhaus reached into the driving box of the wagon and brought out a cane. Malacca. With a brass duckbill head. Of course.

"Welcome to the Ponderosa, Mr. Blauhaus. Would you care to come inside?"

"I would." Blauhaus inclined his head a fraction of an inch. "Thank you."

Ben led the way, showing Blauhaus to a comfortable chair in the huge sitting room that dominated the ground floor. "Excuse me for a moment, please."

Blauhaus nodded again, and Ben went back to the kitchen. In comparison with his dapper visitor he felt positively grimy. He quickly washed and asked Hop Sing to bring tea. It was much too early in the day to offer anything stronger, and Ben had the impression that this guest would prefer tea service to mugs of coffee. There was no sign in the kitchen of Hoss, which meant Hoss must have seen Blauhaus drive in and—for some reason as yet unclear—slipped out the back way. Curious, Ben thought. More and more curious. He dried his hands, decided not to worry about anything further and returned to the sitting room.

"I've asked my cook to bring tea," he said. "I hope that's all right with you."

"Very nice, very thoughtful, thank you." Blauhaus bobbed his head. He cleared his throat, removed his other glove and laid cane and gloves aside. He was sitting on the forward few inches of his chair, his back as stiff and straight as if he were a military cadet at attention.

"So, um, what can I do for you, Mr. Blauhaus?"

"I know you are a busy man, Mr. Cartwright. I will proceed to the point at once, yes?"

"Whatever you wish, Mr. Blauhaus."

"I think so, yes."

"Very well."

"It is to save you time and difficulty that I come here, you see."

Ben did not see, yet, but he had hopes that he soon might. He smiled and nodded pleasantly and waited for Blauhaus to get on with it.

He had to wait a bit longer because Hop Sing chose that moment to come in bearing a tray with formal tea service for two in ornate silver, their very best, complete with canned milk and refined sugar. Hop Sing, Ben saw, was putting on the dog here. But then Mr. Blauhaus seemed to have that effect on people, perhaps because of his own fastidiousness. Hop Sing put the tray down without a word and scurried off again, returning moments later with a plate of tarts that Ben hadn't known they had. Obviously Hoss hadn't known it either or there wouldn't have been any for company to share.

"Thank you, Hop Sing," Blauhaus said when Hop Sing poured the tea. Which was another thing Ben found to be of interest. He would not have suspected that Blauhaus would know the Ponderosa's Chinese cook. Nor, for that matter, vice versa. Hop Sing said something in Cantonese and bobbed his head, his pigtail flying. Blauhaus smiled—now surely the fellow didn't speak Chinese, Ben mused—and accepted a tart. Hop Sing finished serving the guest and passed tea tray and tarts to Ben with somewhat less ceremony.

"Now," Ben prompted when Hop Sing had gone, "you were saying something about the, um, reason we have the pleasure of your company today?"

"So I was, yes." Blauhaus smiled. "I came to you, one loving father to another as it were, to discuss your son's account."

Account? One of Ben's sons had an account with the local pawnbroker?

Ben felt his jaw drop open.

Ben's shock was so complete, so overwhelming, that it must have been obvious even to as casual an acquaintance as Armand Blauhaus.

"Mr. Cartwright," the visitor blurted, "are you all right?"

"Yes, certainly," Ben responded without thought. "Or . . . I don't know." He grimaced. "What . . . that is to say, who. . . ." His voice tailed away into an awkward silence.

"I've distressed you," Blauhaus said in an apologetic tone. "What did I do to . . . oh, of course. Sorry, Mr. Cartwright, so sorry if you misunderstand me. I am not here to collect a debt. No, no. Please forgive me if I gave that impression. Really, I mean if any of your family or employees were behind on payments, which none of them are of course, that is to say . . . Mr. Cartwright, I am becoming confused myself at this point. May we start over?"

"Please do, Mr. Blauhaus."

"I am not here in my capacity as a lender, you see, but as a purveyor of, um, superior quality gemstones."

"I beg your pardon?"

"As a jeweler, Mr. Cartwright. I come to see you as a jeweler. Hopefully, as your son's soon-to-be jeweler to be more precise about it."

"My . . . son's . . . jeweler," Ben repeated slowly, letting each individual word slide across his tongue as if he were tasting it. And not especially enjoying the flavor either if the truth be known. "May I ask . . . *which* son?"

Blauhaus smiled benignly and had a sip of tea before he responded. Ben was fairly sure that one sip required fourteen minutes to complete. Perhaps longer. The wait was agonizing. "Why, Joseph of course," Blauhaus said happily. He reached inside his coat and extracted a slim case of exquisitely soft leather. He fumbled for a moment with a gold catch—it looked like the real thing and not merely polished brass—and spread the case open. "I have here, Mr. Cartwright, a selection of engagement rings of the very finest quality. I chose them myself and I can assure you that I have brought with me only the very finest examples of the art. The diamonds . . . have you a loupe? would you care to borrow mine? . . . are all of white or blue-white hue, and the occlusions . . . well, you will simply have to judge those for yourself on a stone by stone basis. Naturally there are occlusions. No matter what anyone else may try to tell you, occlusions are a perfectly normal occurrence even in diamonds of this quality. You see that I am hiding nothing, not even the occlusions, while certain, um, others who may sell jewelry but who are not jewelers will pretend that such things do not exist. Those are the men . . . notice I do not say gentlemen . . . who would resist any attempt by the customer to view their wares under the magnification of a loupe. I prefer that my customers learn to use a loupe so they can judge the quality for themselves. As you can see, I have nothing to hide, nor do I fear close examination. Now if I may, Mr. Cartwright, I will give you a brief overview and, with your permission, make a few suggestions. Then, of course, it will be up to you and Joseph to choose a ring of suitable quality and, um, price. Which I believe you will find to be entirely fair and competitive. And, frankly, much much lower than what is asked for those inferior rings my esteemed peer Mr. Cuddahey has been trying to palm off on your son."

Ben blinked. The initial shock was still with him, surrounding his head like mounds of goosedown pillows and cushioning the meanings of Blauhaus's words even while allowing most of them through.

It was as if he could snatch a phrase here, a meaning there. He felt detached from them. Not uninterested, though. It was more that he was numbed by what Blauhaus was saying.

Oh, but the words and the meanings did sneak through. A bit here, a bit there.

Rings. Engagement. Diamond. Engagement. Joseph. Engagement. *Joseph.*

BANTAM DOUBLEDAY DELL
PRESENTS THE
WINNERS CLASSIC SWEEPSTAKES

Dear Bantam Doubleday Dell Reader,

We'd like to say "Thanks" for choosing our books. So we're giving you a chance to enter our Winners Classic Sweepstakes, where you can win a Grand Prize of $25,000.00, or one of over 1,000 other sensational prizes! All prizes are guaranteed to be awarded. Return the Official Entry Form at once! And when you're ready for another great reading experience, we hope you'll keep Bantam Doubleday Dell books at the top of your reading list!

OFFICIAL ENTRY FORM

Yes! Enter me in the Winners Classic Sweepstakes and guarantee my eligibility to be awarded any prize, including the $25,000.00 Grand Prize. Notify me at once if I am declared a winner.

NAME

ADDRESS   APT. #

CITY

STATE   ZIP

REGISTRATION NUMBER   **01995A**

Please mail to: LL-SBA
BANTAM DOUBLEDAY DELL DIRECT, INC.
WINNERS CLASSIC SWEEPSTAKES
PO Box 985, Hicksville, NY 11802-0985

OFFICIAL PRIZE LIST

GRAND PRIZE: *$25,000.00 CASH!*

FIRST PRIZE: FISHER HOME ENTERTAINMENT CENTER
Including complete integrated audio/video system with 130-watt amplifier, AM/FM stereo tuner, dual cassette deck, CD player, Surround Sound speakers and universal remote control unit.

SECOND PRIZE: TOSHIBA VCR *5 winners!*
Featuring full-function, high-quality 4-Head performance, with 8-event/365-day timer, wireless remote control, and more.

THIRD PRIZE: CONCORD 35MM CAMERA OUTFIT *35 winners!*
Featuring focus-free precision lens, built-in automatic film loading, advance and rewind.

FOURTH PRIZE: BOOK LIGHT *1,000 winners!*
A model of convenience, with a flexible neck that bends in any direction, and a steady clip that holds sure on any surface.

OFFICIAL RULES AND REGULATIONS

AN ORIGINAL BASED ON THE
LANDMARK TELEVISION SERIES!

BONANZA

THE PIONEER SPIRIT

Stephen Calder

Ben Cartwright came west to stake his claim to the American frontier and the American dream.

As a young naval officer , he learned his lessons well. He learned the value of justice, honor, and hard work; he developed the qualities of resourcefulness and courage to stand on his own. But the love of a woman would call Ben back home to Boston...then sorrow would send him and his new son Adam away again, bound for an open country where a young family could grow tall and strong and proud.

The legend of the Cartwright clan, which thrilled generations of Americans on the beloved series *Bonanza*, lives once again in this stirring, all-new saga of the Western frontier.